Amy felt her heart catch and her breath stall in her lungs.

Nick Culhane was nothing at all like she remembered him.

He seemed far more imposing now, and infinitely more disturbing, hard and honed, a mountain of muscled masculinity in worn denim and work boots. Maturity had carved character into a face that had already been impossibly handsome.

She didn't remember him being so big. Or his eyes so blue as his guarded gaze moved slowly over her face and slipped down her slender frame.

Never in her life had she met a man who knotted her nerves or stole the breath from her lungs simply by glancing at her.

And Nick Culhane—the man she'd once secretly worshipped, the man who had broken her sister's heart—was the *last* man on earth who should elicit such heated reactions....

Dear Reader,

What if…? These two little words serve as the springboard for each romance novel that bestselling author Joan Elliott Pickart writes. "I always go back to that age-old question. My ideas come straight from imagination," she says. And with more than thirty Silhouette novels to her credit, the depth of Joan's imagination seems bottomless! Joan started by taking a class to learn how to write a romance and "felt that this was where I belonged," she recalls. This month Joan delivers *Her Little Secret,* the next from THE BABY BET, where you'll discover what if…a sheriff and a lovely nursery owner decide to foil town matchmakers and "act" like lovers.…

And don't miss the other compelling "what ifs" in this month's Silhouette Special Edition lineup. What if a U.S. Marshal knee-deep in his father's murder investigation discovers his former love is expecting his child? Read *Seven Months and Counting…* by Myrna Temte, the next installment in the STOCKWELLS OF TEXAS series. What if an army ranger, who believes dangerous missions are no place for a woman, learns the only person who can help rescue his sister is a female? Lindsay McKenna brings you this exciting story in *Man with a Mission,* the next book in her MORGAN'S MERCENARIES: MAVERICK HEARTS series. What happens if a dutiful daughter falls in love with the one man her family forbids? Look for Christine Flynn's *Forbidden Love.* What if a single dad falls for a pampered beauty who is not at all accustomed to small-town happily-ever-after? Find out in Nora Roberts's *Considering Kate,* the next in THE STANISLASKIS. And what if the girl-next-door transforms herself to get a man's attention—but is noticed by someone else? Make sure to pick up Barbara McMahon's *Starting with a Kiss.*

What if… Two words with endless possibilities. If you've got your own "what if" scenario, start writing. Silhouette Special Edition would love to read about it.

Happy reading!

Karen Taylor Richman,
Senior Editor

Please address questions and book requests to:
Silhouette Reader Service
U.S.: 3010 Walden Ave., P.O. Box 1325, Buffalo, NY 14269
Canadian: P.O. Box 609, Fort Erie, Ont. L2A 5X3

Forbidden Love

CHRISTINE FLYNN

Silhouette

SPECIAL EDITION™

Published by Silhouette Books

America's Publisher of Contemporary Romance

SILHOUETTE BOOKS

ISBN 0-373-24378-2

FORBIDDEN LOVE

Visit Silhouette at www.eHarlequin.com

Printed in U.S.A.

Books by Christine Flynn

CHRISTINE FLYNN

admits to being interested in just about everything, which is why she considers herself fortunate to have turned her interest in writing into a career. She feels that a writer gets to explore it all and, to her, exploring relationships—especially the intense, bittersweet or even lighthearted relationships between men and women—is fascinating.

Lake Superior

MICHIGAN

• <u>CedarLake</u>

Eau Claire
•

WISCONSIN

Green Bay

MINNESOTA

Lake
Michigan

Madison
★

IOWA

ILLINOIS

All underlined places are fictitious.

Chapter One

"I don't believe I've ever seen you this restless, Amy. Are you sure everything is all right?"

Amy Chapman ran her fingers through her short dark hair, the motion as agitated as her pacing. With a quick, distracted smile, she focused on the list in her hand. "I'm positive, Grandma. There's just a lot to do before I can get you out of here. Now, I've called these contractors—"

"It's not like you to pace."

"Honest. I'm fine."

"Well, you don't seem fine," the elderly woman insisted. "I've never seen you fidget as much as you have since you've been home. You've always had energy, but this is different. You're acting...unsettled."

"I'm not 'unsettled,'" Amy replied, still pacing. "I just want to get this taken care of."

"You're tense, then." Her grandmother's thin, rose-red lips pinched. "Do you know what I think you need?"

"What's that?"

"A man."

Amy came to a dead stop at the foot of the raised nursing-home bed. Her grandmother sat propped against a crisp white pillow, her long white hair hanging in an enviably thick braid over the shoulder of her fuchsia bed jacket and her hazel eyes sharp behind her silver-rimmed bifocals.

"Well, you do," Bea Gardner pronounced, casually eyeing the uninspired cream camp shirt her youngest granddaughter had tucked into a pair of equally understated khaki slacks. "You're almost twenty-eight years old, and you haven't had a serious boyfriend since you stopped seeing Scott last year. I'm sure there are plenty of nice, eligible men over there in Eau Claire. Why aren't you going out with any of them?"

"Because no one has asked."

"I don't believe that for an instant. You're a beautiful girl, Amy. You're kind. You're smart."

"You're prejudiced."

"You're right. But I don't buy your reasoning. If it's true no one has asked you out, then why don't you find someone interesting and ask him? It's not like when I was young, and a girl had to wait around for the man to call her. From what I hear, men nowadays like it when a woman takes the initiative. It takes the pressure off them."

Amy's mouth curved in a smile that looked like affection but felt more like defeat. It was truly pathetic when a woman's eighty-two-year-old grandmother was gutsier than she was. She couldn't begin to imagine making the first move on a guy.

"You say 'find someone interesting' as if all I'd have to do is put my hand in a hat and pull out the man of my dreams. It's not that easy out there. The good men are all gone." She gave a casual shrug. "The hat's empty."

"That's nonsense. There are plenty of good men out there. It's just a matter of giving them a chance to prove themselves." The frown on Bea's gracefully aged face added another row of wrinkles to her forehead. "You're just never going to find the one who's right for you if you keep turning down the interesting ones and turning the rest into buddies."

"Grandma," Amy said patiently, "I'm here to get you back into your house. Not discuss my nonexistent love life." Prepared to move on to something more productive, she held up the list, only to lower it as her brow pinched. "Who did I turn down that was interesting? You don't mean Scott, do you?"

"My heavens, no," came the gently chiding reply. "I know your parents thought he was perfect for you. And he would have fit right in at your father's accounting firm. But frankly, dear," she said, dropping her tone in deference to her room's open door, "whenever I saw you together, I never had the feeling there was any passion there. A woman needs passion in her life," she informed her, much as she might speak of the need for a good mechanic. "She needs a man who makes her melt when he touches her and makes her feel that she'll simply not be the same without him in her life. That is *not* what I sensed between you and Scott. I'm talking about that new man in your apartment building. The geologist. Didn't you say he was attractive? And what about the new principal at your school?"

Amy glanced toward the doorway herself, though there wasn't anyone in the bright hallway who would have been able to overhear, much less care about what they were discussing. It just disconcerted her to know that her grandmother had been aware of something like passion—or the lack thereof—in her relationship with Scott Porter.

The woman was absolutely right, though. There never had been any spark or fire between her and the promising young accountant. Not even in the beginning of their two-year relationship. But then, there had never been any real passion in her life. Period.

She was not, however, going to get depressed about it now. Being home for the summer was enough to cope with at the moment.

"The geologist isn't interested in a relationship. Not the kind I'm interested in, anyway," she replied, knowing for a fact that she'd find no passion there. She preferred fidelity in a man. "He was going out with the nurse in Three B and the masseuse in One C until they found he was two-timing them. Rumor has it he's currently working on the Rosenburg twins on the first floor. As for our principal," she said, glancing again at the paper she held, "we play softball together, but he's just a friend. It's never a good idea to date someone you work with, anyway."

From the corner of her eye Amy saw Bea peer at her over the tops of her bifocals. Before her grandmother could pursue the subject, however, Amy changed it. She simply didn't feel like explaining that the problem probably wasn't with the men, but with her.

"I called all the contractors on this list," she repeated, referring to the sheet of aqua stationery covered with Bea's surprisingly bold script. "Triple A Renovators will be there this afternoon, but they won't give you separate bids for the wheelchair ramps and the room addition. With them, it's all or nothing. Cedar Lake Construction will have someone out to give us an estimate Thursday morning. And Four Pines Remodel and Repair can't take another job before September, and I'll be gone by then."

Bea made a faint tsking sound. "That's too bad about Four Pines. They do such good work." Straightening the sheet tucked at her waist, she watched Amy bend over one of the Danish Modern visitor's chairs by the plant-lined window and stuff the paper into her oversize canvas tote bag. "There's really no one you're interested in?"

Amy didn't consider herself a particularly virtuous person. Her faults were myriad and, compared to certain members of her family, her accomplishments few. If she could claim any redeeming trait at all, it would be patience. The virtue helped enormously when working with six-year-olds, which she did nine months out of the year, from September to June. But patience was an absolute necessity when it came to surviving her family.

"No, Grandma," she replied quietly. Of all her relations, she most admired the outspoken and energetic octogenarian watching her so closely now. Her mother's mother was her own woman. She did things her own way, whether or not convention approved, and she possessed the energy and outlook of a woman twenty years her junior. It had taken a broken hip to even slow the woman down. And then, she'd fallen while painting her kitchen cabinets fire-engine red. *To add a little life to the place,* she'd said.

If Amy had had the nerve, she would have loved to emulate her grandmother's sometimes outrageous sense of style. But she had grown up to realize that she was really just a practical, beige sort of person, and whatever sense of whimsy she found herself wanting to indulge, she shared only with her first-graders.

"There really isn't anyone I'm interested in," Amy finally concluded.

Recognizing a dead end when she saw one, the elderly woman picked up three bottles of nail polish from the tray table straddling her bed. "Pity," she murmured, and finally let the matter go.

"By the way, dear." Glass clicked lightly as she tried

to decide between shades of bright coral or a more subtle mauve. "I called Culhane Contracting for an estimate, too. Michael Culhane is sending his nephew over this morning so he can look at the house."

Amy's head snapped up. Her grandmother was studying one gnarled hand, her rose-tinted lips pursed in concentration.

"Culhane?"

"Mmm," Bea hummed, still undecided about the color. "I heard from Mae Cutter that Nick is working for his uncle's construction company now. He's finishing up a medical office for her grandson and his partner over on Maple Grove. He's doing nice work, too. From what I hear. Mae said her grandson is pleased, anyway."

Confusion swept Amy's expression as she watched her grandmother calmly hold the bottle of coral next to her skin, then do the same with the mauve. It made no sense that Nick Culhane would be working for a builder in such a small town, no matter who owned the company. The last she'd heard, he was an architect in New York. A very successful one, at that. It made even less sense that her grandmother would want anything to do with him.

"What's he doing in Cedar Lake?" She shook her head, her confusion compounding by the second. "And why are you even talking to him? Have you forgotten what he did to Paige?"

Bea's weathered hand remained splayed as she patiently glanced up at her youngest grandchild. "Contrary to what your mother sometimes thinks, Amy, there's nothing wrong with my memory. I remember exactly what he did to your sister. He walked out on her a month before their wedding. That was ten years ago. And it has nothing at all to do with getting an addition built onto my house. The more companies I get bids from, the more informed a decision I can make about who to hire. A woman should always have options.''

She glanced back at the bottles, choosing coral. "Stop scowling, dear. It causes wrinkles.'' Behind the bifocals, her eyes narrowed on the hall beyond the wide doorway. "I do believe I see Nick coming now.''

Amy dutifully straightened the scowl, but her usual easy smile was conspicuously absent as she watched her grandmother push aside her polish in preparation for her company. The recalcitrant woman certainly sounded lucid to her, but she couldn't help but think that her favorite relative's mental acuity had finally slipped. Bea Gardner tended to disagree with half of her family and barely tolerated the rest, but she was loyal to every last member when it came to defending them to the rest of the world. Amy had inherited that unquestioned loyalty in spades. She'd barely been seventeen when Nick Culhane had told Paige he couldn't marry her, but she could still remember how badly he'd hurt her older sister.

The sound of heavy footsteps grew closer, the rhythm steady and certain—until it went dead silent at the doorway.

"Nick,'' Bea said, by way of greeting.

"Mrs. Gardner,'' came the deep, rumbling reply.

"Well, do come in.'' Extending her hand, the gesture faintly regal, she motioned toward the foot of her bed. "You remember Amy, don't you?''

Amy wasn't in the habit of being rude. Refusing to develop the tendency now, she turned with the thought of offering a polite hello—and felt her heart catch as her breath stalled in her lungs.

He stood six feet behind her, a mountain of leanly muscled masculinity in chambray, worn denim and work boots. Maturity had carved character into a face that had already been impossibly handsome, deepening the creases bracketing his chiseled mouth, fanning the tiny lines from the corners of his eyes.

She didn't remember him being so big. Or his eyes so blue. His dark hair was meticulously cut, his face and forearms tanned from working long hours in the summer sun. He was hard and honed, the sort of man who dominated whatever space he occupied, and Amy felt an overwhelming urge to back up as his guarded glance slowly moved over her face and slipped down her slender frame.

"Yes. I do," he replied in that polite way people have when a memory is there, but vague. Clearly cautious, he turned his attention to the woman holding court from the bed. "Since you have company, maybe we should discuss our business later."

"Amy isn't company," Bea countered, sounding every bit as businesslike as he did. "She's family. And your business is with her. My granddaughter has kindly come from Eau Claire to rescue me from this...place...my daughter has stuck me in and is handling what I obviously can't. She'll take you out to the house so you can do whatever it is you need to do to figure your estimates.

"As I told you on the phone," she continued, ignoring both Amy's look of surprise and Nick's sudden and definite hesitation, "I need a new bedroom built downstairs. I won't be able to climb the stairs to my old one," she explained, sounding more annoyed with the inability than inconvenienced by it. "And I need a wheelchair ramp so Amy can get me in and out of the house. I can't leave here until the ramp is in, and I would really like to return to my home."

A wistful smile touched her once-full lips. "I've already missed seeing my lilacs bloom, and I know my roses need tending. Would your uncle's company be able to take on the work now, assuming we agree on a price, or would there be a wait?''

"I can't answer that until I know exactly what you have in mind for the addition."

Bea inclined her head at his hedge. "Well, then, there's nothing for me to do other than leave you in Amy's capable hands. She can explain what I need, and we'll go from there.

"You'll call me this afternoon?" she asked her grand-daughter.

"Of course." She could count on it.

"Good. Then, if you'll excuse me, I want to do my nails before bridge this afternoon." She picked up her polish again, her shrewd glance cutting to the man who'd taken a step back to let Amy pass. "Thank you for coming, Nick. I wasn't sure you would."

Amy could practically feel his big body stiffen, though all she saw for certain was the jump of a muscle in his jaw a moment before he spoke. To his credit, not that Amy was inclined to give him much, his deep voice betrayed no reaction at all to her grandma's doubt.

"My uncle owns the company, Mrs. Gardner. It's not up to me to turn down business. It's good to see you looking so well," he concluded, deftly refusing her a chance to unearth what he'd rather leave buried. "I'll get back to you with an estimate as soon as I can."

Taking another step back, he caught Amy's eye and arched one dark eyebrow. "Shall we?"

He looked remarkably unhurried as he stood waiting for her to precede him out the door. Or so it seemed until she noticed the little knot of muscle still twitching near his ear. Uneasy herself, rather wishing she hadn't given her grandmother carte blanche with her services, she picked up her bag and slipped the straps over her shoulder.

This was one little twist she hadn't imagined in the scenarios that had plagued her every time she'd thought about coming home the past couple of weeks. She'd known she would run into resistance from her mom about moving Grandma Bea back into her home. And she'd known Paige would side with their mom for reasons that had nothing to do with their mother's objections, but which would still leave Amy to deal with the task by herself. She'd just never dreamed she'd have to deal with the man who had broken her sister's heart.

Amy knew what it was to lose a friendship because love just wasn't there. But she couldn't imagine a worse breach of trust than for a woman to put all her faith and hope in a man, then have him leave her for another woman.

Amy knew for a fact that was what Nick had done. She'd even heard him admit there was someone else. The night he'd broken up with Paige, they'd been arguing beneath her bedroom window.

Telling her grandmother she'd talk with her later, she moved past him and into a bright hallway that smelled strongly of disinfectant and the lilies in the open day room. From a room behind them a frail voice kept up a constant litany of indistinguishable phrases. Ahead of them, a nurse steadied an elderly gentleman out for a stroll with his chrome-plated walker. The facility was the best available in Cedar Lake. Her mom had seen to that. Still, Amy couldn't blame her grandmother for wanting to get out of there.

"What's wrong with her?" Nick asked, his deep voice low as he fell into step beside her.

"I've been asking myself the same thing." She simply could not believe her grandmother had called him.

"I mean physically," he muttered.

Feeling a tug of chagrin, Amy protectively crossed her

arms as they headed for the double doors of the exit. "She broke her hip a few months ago. That's why she won't be able to use stairs. I know she wants an addition built onto the house for a bedroom," she continued, deliberately keeping her focus on her task, and the man with the walker. "But it might be faster to close in the back porch."

"It sounds like you're in a hurry to get out of Cedar Lake."

"I'm in a hurry to get my grandmother settled back in her home," she countered. "She needs to be in her own bed. She isn't resting well here and I'm worried about her."

And you're right, she thought, though she wasn't about to admit it to him. She did want to leave. Whenever she was in Cedar Lake, there was always part of her that wanted badly to get back to Eau Claire. There were things she truly loved about the charming east Wisconsin town where she'd grown up. Mostly she loved the quaint feel of it and the friendliness of people whose families remained, year after year. It was small enough that a person couldn't walk down Main Street without running into someone she knew. But it was big enough that not everyone knew everyone else's business.

The only reason she'd left was that she wanted to be out from under the collective thumb of her family. Except for her grandmother, they treated her as if she'd never quite grown up. As her grandmother had just pointed out, she was nearly twenty-eight years old. Would be, in fact, in less than a month. She had been on her own since she'd graduated from college at twenty-one. Yet all she had to do was come back home, and she felt all of twelve again.

"I'll take a look at the porch and see what I can do."

"Thank you."

Nick reached past her, pushing open the glass door by

its horizontal metal bar. As he did, she swept past him, leaving behind the scent of something light and airy and impossibly, inexplicably erotic.

The muscles in his gut tightened, the response adding yet another dimension to the other frustrations that had been clawing at him all day—every one of which had seemed to compound itself in the past five minutes.

Amy was two feet in front of him on the wide walkway. Catching her arm, he felt those frustrations merge as he pulled her to a stop.

"Hold on a minute."

The noonday sun caught shades of amber in her short sable hair as she jerked her head toward him. Her eyes were a rich, deep chocolate, her fine features delicate, and she had a tiny dimple in her left cheek. It was there when she smiled, anyway. He'd seen it when she'd smiled at her grandmother. But she wasn't smiling now. She was looking at him with the same caution he'd felt since Bea Gardner had called his uncle's company yesterday and asked him to bid on a job for her.

"Who else is going to be there?" he asked.

"Where?"

Beneath his hand he felt the tensing of smooth, supple muscle. Her warmth seeped into his palm, the softness of her skin registering somewhere deep in his consciousness.

"At your grandmother's house. I'm not up for any more surprises today." He had enough to deal with as it was. Between a delivery problem with materials, an associate in New York who wanted his drafts yesterday and butting heads this morning with his uncle over the need for the man to slow down, his patience was precariously close to nonexistent. "I want to know who's there. Any more of your family?"

She shook her head, feeling wary, trying not to sound it. "There's no one."

"Your sister isn't waiting out there?"

"I said there's no one." Amy eased from his grip, fighting the urge to cover the spot where the heat of his hand still lingered. "I'm staying alone at the house."

She thought he might look relieved by the assurance. If anything, the furrows in his brow only deepened as he stepped back. The muscle in his jaw wasn't jerking anymore, though. It had simply gone rigid.

He must have decided he had no choice but to believe her. His guard firmly in place, he turned toward the nearly empty parking lot. "Do you have a car here?"

"It's right over there." Reaching into her tote for her sunglasses and her keys, she nodded toward the crayon-yellow Volkswagen sitting alone by the tree-lined curb. Her mother thought the thing looked like a windup toy. Her students loved it.

"I'll follow you," he muttered.

Nick could have sworn he saw relief flash in her eyes an instant before she slipped on the dark glasses and told him that would be fine. She was clearly no crazier than he was with the idea of having to make small talk if they took the same vehicle. But he didn't want to think about his ex-fiancée's little sister. Amy was just doing what her grandmother had asked her to do. It seemed far more prudent to consider the motives of the elderly woman inside the long, low building they'd just left.

He hadn't seen Bea Gardner since the night before he'd left town after breaking up with her older granddaughter. That had been ten years ago. The decade had taken its toll on her, too, put more wear on a face that had probably once been quite beautiful, made her aging body that much more fragile. She wasn't a big woman. He doubted she'd ever been taller than Amy's five-three. But she'd always had a presence that more than made up for her diminutive size.

That presence had never been more impressive than when she'd come across him on the highway that long-ago evening and stopped to give him a ride. He'd had way too much to drink after he'd left Paige's house, but he'd had enough sense left to walk home rather than risk plowing the first new car he'd ever owned into a pole. Somewhere out on the highway between the Twin Pine Tavern and his uncle's house on the opposite side of town, Bea had come sailing by in the old boat of a Cadillac she'd driven since 1966.

She'd opened her window, told him he should be ashamed of himself and to get in before he wound up like the deer that crossed the highway to the lake and some sleepy trucker turned him into roadkill. Beyond that, what he remembered most was that she'd mercilessly prodded him with questions about why he'd broken up with her granddaughter—and that after he'd wound up spilling his guts to her, she had agreed that he'd had no choice but to do what he'd done, and to leave.

As uneasy as he'd felt facing the old woman again, his caution had doubled the instant he'd laid eyes on the slender young woman with the doe-soft brown eyes and the short dark hair. Amy had been the polar opposite of her bubbly blond older sister. She'd possessed a natural vitality, but it had been more innocent, more unassuming. He'd recognized her instantly, though. He just hadn't been prepared for how truly lovely she'd become.

Chapter Two

A rain shower, so typical to the area in summer, had moved through that morning. The quick, heavy cloudburst had left the air heavy with the scents of damp earth and blooming wildflowers. Amy normally would have taken pleasure in the way the wetness intensified the deep green of pines, the shimmering sage of aspen, the emerald of oak and maple. She loved the nuances of shade and color. But she barely noticed any of what surrounded her. As she pulled off the narrow road that looped around one of the area's secluded lakes and headed down the shaded lane that led to her grandmother's house, her only thoughts were of the man turning onto the lane behind her.

Nick was nothing at all like her memory of him. The man who'd endeared himself to her family had possessed a congenial manner, a quick smile and a kind of charm that put everyone around him at ease. He seemed far more imposing now, more dominant and infinitely more disturbing. Never in her life had she met a man like him whose tension knotted her own nerves, or who stole the breath from her lungs simply by touching her.

Remembering how she'd responded to him had her hands tightening on the wheel. Nick Culhane was the last man on earth who should elicit such reactions from her. She could still recall her sister sobbing in her room the night he'd broken up with her and the frantic dash over the next couple of days to undo plans that had been taking shape for months. While Paige had remained behind her locked door, their mom and Grandma Bea had canceled the church, the reception hall and the caterers. They'd called the florist, the photographer, the bakery and Marleen's Hair Affair, where they'd all had appointments for shampoos, blow-drys and manicures the morning of the big event.

Grandma Bea had been the only person gutsy enough to defend the enemy by pointing out that Nick had at least possessed the decency to call everything off the day *before* the invitations had gone into the mail. He and Paige were to have taken them to the post office together the next morning. But right after that, she'd said she was glad he was gone because he'd just have hurt Paige more if he'd stayed. Then she'd taken the billowing gown of satin and pearls from where Paige had hung it outside her bedroom door and given it to Amy to hang in the attic.

The fabulous creation had stayed there until her sister had sold it at a consignment shop a few years later, and when Paige had married Dr. Darren Hunt six years ago, the gown she'd worn, along with the ceremony and reception, had been simplicity itself. Even years after the fact, she'd obviously wanted no reminders of the elaborate affair she and Nick had once planned.

Amy pulled the car to a stop under the sweeping arms

of an ancient maple and glanced at the rearview mirror. As she watched the dark blue truck rumble to a stop behind her, she wondered if Paige knew Nick was back.

The slam of his door reverberated like a gunshot in the stillness surrounding her grandmother's venerable old house. Her own door echoed the sound a second later, birds scattering from the high pitch of the gabled cedar roof to settle in the trees and along the telephone line running in from the road.

Wishing she could bolt, too, she watched him walk toward her in the dappled sunlight. Pine needles and gravel crunched heavily beneath his boots as he looked from the pristine white house with its butterscotch-yellow trim to the rippling blue water of the deep glacial lake.

A wooden dock, its boards weathered to silver gray and edged with lichen, jutted alongside a boathouse painted with the same cheery trim as the main house. Except for the broad expanse of lawn carpeting the land to the bare earth near the water's edge, the property was surrounded by woods.

The set of Nick's guarded features never changed when his glance shifted to her.

"I can think of worse places to spend the summer."

It really was lovely there. Quiet, peaceful. The nearest neighbor was on the other side of the little lake, too far away to be seen, much less heard.

"It's probably the best part about being here," she conceded, hoisting her bag over her shoulder as she headed past the wide side porch to the back where the porch was enclosed. She had truly loved every moment she'd spent there as a child, swimming in the cool, clear water, sunning on the dock with her friends while they listened to the radio and giggled over bags of chips and *Seventeen* magazines.

"I don't know if you remember much about the house from before," she continued, determined to stick to business, "but Grandma wants her new bedroom to be the same size as her old one. The back porch is a little bigger, but I think it would work."

"I don't remember anything about this place. I was never here."

"You weren't?"

The genuine surprise in her eyes faded the instant she looked up at him. She'd thought for certain that Paige would have brought him out here when they'd been together. This house was like the cornerstone of their family. But the way he was watching her, studying her as if he might be trying to figure out what he recalled about her, short-circuited the thoughts.

Doubting he remembered much about her at all, she glanced from the compelling blue of his eyes and focused on climbing the back steps.

He was right behind her, the wooden stairs groaning at his greater weight.

"When did you move to Eau Claire?" he asked over the squeak of a loose board.

As soon as I could, she thought. "About seven years ago."

"I take it that the rest of your family has moved away, too."

Not sure why he would assume such a thing, she opened the screen door, holding it back for him. "Everyone is still right here in town."

"Your parents and Paige still live in Cedar Lake?"

"You sound surprised that they're still here."

"I am."

Truly puzzled, she glanced behind her as he grabbed the door. "Why?"

"Because it doesn't make any sense."

"That they'd still be here?"

His tone went as flat as the lake. "It doesn't make any sense that you came from two hours away to take care of this for your grandmother when your mom, dad and sister live within ten minutes of the place."

He stood with one arm stretched out as he held the door, his broad chest blocking her view of the overgrown garden, his carved features knitted in a frown. She was aware of his nearness, his size and his obvious incomprehension. Mostly, she was aware that she wasn't moving.

She stepped onto the enclosed porch, ignoring for now the chairs and chaises that needed to be wiped down and the potted plants she'd watered when she'd arrived yesterday but still needed to trim. Her mother simply hadn't had time to give them their usual care while Bea had been convalescing. After three months of hit-and-miss tending, Amy figured they were lucky to still be alive.

"My family is busy," she defended, on her way to the middle of the expansive, screened-in area. "Summer is Mom's busiest time of year for house sales. Dad has been spending a lot of time out of town on a big audit. And Paige has a husband, two little girls, a big house and her Junior League committees to keep up with. No one else has the time except me."

She'd thought for certain that mention of Paige and her family would give him pause. At the very least, the mention of her being married should raise an eyebrow, providing, of course, that he didn't already know.

All he did when she stopped to face him was give her a slow, disbelieving blink.

"So they go on with their lives while you put yours on hold."

"I wouldn't put it that way," she replied, not caring for the way the thought made her feel.

"I would."

She already felt disquieted by him. The feeling only increased with his flatly delivered statement. "My only plans this summer were to take a course I need to keep my teaching certificate current and to spend a month in Europe prowling museums. I can take the class in the fall and do the museum tour next year. I've already postponed it twice, anyway."

"I wouldn't have thought that Junior League was more important than classes and a vacation."

"Junior League does charity work," she informed him, determined to maintain her position. "Being involved in the community is important, too."

Nick's brow furrowed as he watched her glance slide from his. A person would have to possess the sensitivity of a stone not to notice how completely she'd minimized and dismissed her own plans, or how staunchly she stood up for the more self-focused members of her family. Especially Paige. His ex-fiancée had probably been the first to come up with a list of excuses about why she couldn't handle the responsibility Amy had so willingly taken on.

"Why do I have the feeling you're the only one who thinks your grandmother doesn't belong where she is?"

Because you're incredibly astute, she thought. "I don't know," she replied, preferring not to discuss family disagreements with him, or be impressed by his insight. "Why do you?"

"For one thing, you're the only one willing to be inconvenienced."

"I told you—"

"Yeah. I know. They're busy," he muttered. "You

don't need to defend your family to me, Amy. I was just trying to make conversation.''

He wasn't sure what annoyed him the most. Her coolness, or the fact that he was letting her get to him. That coolness didn't even suit her. There was too much generosity in her spirit, too much warmth in her soul. Or there had been, anyway. It took amazingly little effort for him to recall how she'd befriended nearly every small child and animal in her neighborhood, or how easily her shy smile could come once she'd gotten to know someone. Her warmth was still there, toward her grandmother, anyway, and her generous spirit still thrived, but she'd clearly choke before he'd get a smile out of her.

"Look," he muttered, knowing no way around the problem but to address it. "I know I'm not your family's favorite person, but what happened between me and Paige happened a long time ago. It sounds like she's moved on. So have I. There's no reason—"

"You don't need to defend yourself to me."

"I'm not defending myself," he shot back, not caring for how neatly she'd turned around what he'd said to her moments ago. "I'm just stating facts. And one of those facts is that it was your grandmother who asked me to come here, so I'd appreciate it if you'd drop the chill."

He looked about as flexible as a granite post with his eyes boring into hers and his hands jammed on his hips. Amy didn't doubt for a moment that he expected her to back down and, if not drop her guard, then at least be a little more hospitable.

As a woman who went out of her way to avoid confrontations, who made her students apologize and play nice whenever there was a difference of opinion, she normally would have found his expectation to be the more diplomatic course of action. Especially since he looked a little short on patience at the moment. But she didn't feel diplomatic. What she felt was unnerved. His glance had slipped to her mouth, lingering there long enough to heat the knot of nerves in her stomach. If she was feeling anything at all at the moment, it was a strong and distinct need for distance.

"I realize Grandma called you. And as long as we're stating facts," she echoed politely, "I'm not totally convinced that her doing that is rational behavior. It makes no sense that she would do something that could bring back bad memories for a member of her family. She can be a little unconventional at times, and she's certainly outspoken, but she's not inconsiderate.

"You hurt her granddaughter," she reminded him. "Which reminds me," she continued, loyalty to her sibling melding with a heavy dose of feminine self-defense, "did you ever marry the woman who stole you from my sister?"

She got the distance she was after. In the space of a heartbeat, Nick's expression closed like a windblown shutter.

"No. I didn't marry her. I have no intention of ever marrying anyone," he informed her, his voice low and certain. "And just for the record, no one can steal someone from another person. If a man doesn't care enough to stick around and make a relationship work, there were fundamental problems to begin with."

The tension in his big body was almost palpable as his glance shifted over her face, his eyes revealing nothing as his gaze penetrated hers. That gaze was disturbing, intimate, and whatever it was he saw in her face caused the telltale muscle in his jaw to jerk before he turned away.

With his back to her, he drew a breath that stretched the fabric of his shirt against his wide shoulders.

"Where does your grandmother want the ramp?"

Amy swallowed, her heart hammering.

"We thought putting it by the back steps would be best." There was no escaping his irritation. It seemed to follow her even as she stepped back. "It's closer to the driveway and the path to the lake."

"That won't work if you want this area converted." He pointed beyond her, turning his head enough for her to catch his strong profile. "What's that door on the side porch? The one we passed coming in."

There had been an edge to his manner before. Now, having dispensed with any conversation other than the absolutely necessary, that edge felt sharp enough to slice steel.

"It leads from the dining room," she replied.

"The ramp will have to be either there or by the front steps."

"I suppose the dining room would be more convenient."

He gave a nod, the confirmation to himself, not to her. "I'll need to look around out here for a minute and get some measurements. This is the size of room she wants? This space here?"

"Yes."

"Okay." He took a step away. "Thanks."

He didn't need to say another word for her to know her presence was no longer required. With his back still to her, he pulled a pencil and paper from his shirt pocket and unclipped a silver measuring tape from his belt. Even as she headed for the door that led into the kitchen, she could hear his heavy footfall moving away from her.

The door opened with a squeak. Nick practically sighed with relief when it closed with a quiet click. It was as clear as the collection of crystal obelisks lining his office credenza, design awards bestowed on his work over the past ten years, that Amy wanted as little as possible to do with him. That was fine with him. He wanted as little as possible to do with her, too. Seeing her again only brought back memories of a time that had forced him to face a few hard truths about himself. Life-altering truths that had affected everything from how he'd planned his future to what he thought of himself as a man. Though he'd learned to live with his flaws, he could hardly blame her for her disapproval of him.

He pulled out the tape, running it along the far edge of the wide space. He couldn't fault the way she felt, but that didn't mean he had to like her attitude. He didn't have to like much of anything about being there.

He especially didn't appreciate his physical responses to her.

The thoughts had come into his mind unbidden, unwanted. Just noticing the gentle curve of her mouth, the taunting fullness of her lower lip, had been enough to put a distinct ache low in his gut. But the thought of how it would feel to taste that fullness, to taste her, had him feeling as tight as his tape when it snapped back into its coil.

He made short work of measuring the other wall and headed outside to study the foundation. He really didn't want to be there. From Amy's response about this place being the best part about being in Cedar Lake, he strongly suspected she didn't want to be there, either. But she was clearly going to do what she had to do for her grandmother. And despite the fact that he was still wary of Bea Gardner's motives for giving him her business, he'd do what he had to do, too. His uncle Mike's construction company was deeply in debt. He couldn't afford not to bid on the job.

* * *

"Triple A Renovators wants me to sign all this before they'll even give me an estimate?" Amy's grandmother frowned at the three-page agreement Amy had just given her and promptly pushed it aside. "I don't think so. Did Cedar Lake Construction come this morning?"

"Their estimator called yesterday to reschedule. He's coming at two this afternoon." Paper rustled as she pulled from the sack the *People* magazine her grandma had requested and set it on her tray table. So far, she'd been to the grocery store, the library and the plant nursery. As soon as she stopped by the hardware store, she could take another stab at cleaning up the paint that had splattered all over her grandmother's kitchen. It had dried before anyone could clean it up after Bea's fall. "I haven't heard back from Culhane Contracting."

"I have. Nick's uncle called last evening."

Amy's motions slowed as she folded the sack and glanced toward the woman in the purple plaid bed jacket. Bea was already flipping through her magazine.

"Either he or Nick will be out in a couple of days to start on the ramp," she added.

Disquieted by the announcement, trying not to look it, Amy stuffed the sack into her tote to recycle. "You don't want to wait for the other bid?"

"The only estimate he gave me was for the ramp. And that's all I've agreed to for now. How are you doing with the paint? Is it coming off?" she asked, seeming perfectly oblivious to her granddaughter's consternation.

"Sort of," Amy murmured absently, tucking the sack a little deeper.

This really isn't a problem, she hastily assured herself. The fact that Nick's uncle had called Bea told her that Nick wanted as little to do with her and her family as possible. He'd obviously worked up the bid, given it to his uncle and bowed out. No doubt he'd do the same when it came to the job itself. She couldn't imagine him doing anything else. By the time he'd left the lake house, conversation had been reduced to only the polite and the necessary.

That had been roughly forty-eight hours ago. And in that forty-eight hours she'd tried everything short of self-hypnosis to put the encounter out of her mind. Yet, try as she might, she couldn't shake her unwanted but undeniable curiosity over why he'd sounded so adamant about his lack of interest in marriage, something that made no sense at all to her and shouldn't matter even if it had.

"Amy?"

Her brow was still furrowed when she glanced up from her tote.

"I asked what 'sort of' means."

"Oh, sorry," she murmured, distractedly running her fingers through her hair. "It means the remover I bought yesterday will work on the appliances, but I need something different for the floor and cabinets."

"I told you I can hire that work done, dear."

"There's no need for that. I want to do it. I need to do *something* while I'm here." Other than pace, she thought, feeling the urge to do just that. It had to be the weather. She always got restless when the heat and humidity rose.

"Unsettled" her grandmother had called it. Until a couple of days ago, Amy honestly hadn't felt anything she couldn't attribute to simply being in a place she didn't really want to be. She hadn't felt *unsettled* until she'd had to deal with Nick.

She glanced at her watch and promptly grimaced. "I'm late," she announced, refusing to tell her dear grandmother that she'd only added to the restlessness she'd been so concerned about. "I was going to go to the hardware store on the way to the house, but I don't have time now. The guy from Cedar Lake Construction is supposed to be there in ten minutes."

The man was late, too. "J.T. from CLC," as he identified himself, left a message on the answering machine her sister had bought her grandmother two Christmases ago saying he was still running behind and that he'd be there later that afternoon.

J.T. had underestimated his delay. He hadn't shown up by the time Amy had trimmed and fertilized all thirty-one of her grandmother's potted plants. Nor had he arrived by the time she'd given the forgotten African violets in the upstairs bathroom a decent burial, washed out their little ceramic containers and repotted them with the fresh plants she'd purchased at the nursery. When five o'clock came and went, she wondered if the man possessed the manners to even call again. Then she heard the doorbell ring as she was positioning the last plant on the upstairs windowsill at six-fifteen, and figured he'd decided to show up after all.

Shoving her hair out of her eyes, she hurried down the open staircase to the little foyer with its faded Aubusson rug and mahogany entry table. A quick glance in the mirror above the table drew an immediate frown. Plucking a leaf from the shoulder of her nondescript white cotton tank top, she shoved it into the pocket of her denim shorts and kept going. Her hair looked as if it had been combed with her fingers, which, in fact, it had. She had a streak of dirt on her shirt, and she had abandoned her sneakers hours ago. Knowing her mother would be appalled that she was answering the door looking like an urchin, certain "J.T." wasn't going to care, she pulled open the door—and felt her heart slide neatly to her throat.

Nick stood on the front porch, his hands jammed at the waist of his worn jeans, and a faint V of sweat darkening the gray T-shirt stretched over his wide shoulders. The blue of his eyes looked as deep as sapphires as his glance ran from the scoop of her top, down the length of her bare legs and jerked back up to her face.

"I just wanted to let you know I was here before I started working," he said without preamble, and turned away.

"Wait a minute."

He was on the last of three steps leading from the wide wraparound porch when the door banged closed behind her. She stopped on the top one as he reached the walkway and reluctantly turned around.

"Grandma said no one would start for a couple of days."

"Is my being here now a problem?"

She wasn't surprised by the challenge in his tanned features. What struck her was the fatigue. It etched more deeply the faint white lines around his eyes, took some of the edge from his tone.

"I just wasn't expecting anyone from your uncle's company right now." And I wasn't expecting it to be you at all.

"My uncle's already put in a full day," he replied, explaining his own presence when she would have so clearly preferred someone else's. "I had the time now, so I thought I'd get started."

"So late?"

"There're still a couple good hours of daylight left. My uncle said he'd have someone over in a couple of days," he acknowledged, "but we can't pull anyone off the other job we're working just now. I know your grandmother wants to come home soon. If I work until dark for the next few evenings, I should have the ramp finished in less than a week.''

He looked from the steep pitch of the stairs to run another glance the length of her slender body. The look didn't hold an ounce of interest or flattery. It was merely appraising, which was pretty much the same expression that had creased his features when he'd inspected the underpinnings of the side porch yesterday.

His attention caught on her raspberry-pink toenails before returning dispassionately to her face.

''By the way,'' he said, looking as if he might as well get all of his business with her taken care of while he had her there, ''when I ran the work order by the nursing home for your grandmother to sign a while ago, she said you were having trouble cleaning up some paint. She had me promise I'd show you the easiest way to clean it up. She also nitpicked the contract and talked me down ten percent on our bid. You can stop worrying about your grandmother's mind,'' he muttered flatly. ''The woman knows exactly what she's doing.''

He turned then, leaving her standing on the porch while he headed for the battered blue pickup he'd parked behind her bright yellow ''bug.'' None of the weariness she'd seen in his face was evident in his long-legged stride, or in his movements as he reached into the truck's bed and pulled out a pick, a shovel and a bundle of wooden stakes.

She lost sight of him as he headed for the side of the house and disappeared beyond the showy blooms of the huge gardenia bush trellised at the corner of the building. From the dull clank of metal, she assumed he'd dropped what he'd carried somewhere opposite the double French doors leading from the dining room. He didn't reappear. And she didn't move. She just stood there staring at the foliage, feeling chastised and more than a little guilty.

There was no doubt from the fatigue in his eyes and the condition of his clothes that he'd already put in a full day. Yet he was willing to work evenings so an elderly woman wouldn't have to spend any longer than necessary in a place she didn't want to be.

He'd also made the effort, grudging as it was, to let her know he'd seen nothing to indicate there was a problem with her grandmother's mental faculties. The fact that she'd insulted him when she'd expressed her worry about that particular concern only made his gesture that much more generous. He hadn't had to bother with the reassurance at all.

She couldn't believe how deeply his consideration touched her, or the ambivalence it caused her to feel. The thoughtfulness he'd just shown was the very sort of thing the man who'd been engaged to her sister had done in the past, the sort of consideration that had endeared him to her entire family. Yet he'd gone on to so callously betray Paige's trust.

Amy hated what he had done. She hated why he'd done it. But if she were to be perfectly honest with herself, what she hated most was that, in a way, he'd hurt them all. He'd made himself a part of them, made them care about him, then walked out of their lives as if their existence hadn't mattered to him at all.

The guilt she felt jerked in a different direction. Thinking of herself as an injured party was petty and selfish, and entirely irrelevant. Her dad had shelled out a small fortune in nonrefundable deposits for the wedding, so his anger had been understandable. Only the fact that Nick had sent him an unsolicited check a month later had stemmed the flow of his ire. And their mom had spent months excitedly planning with Paige, followed by weeks of consoling her heartbroken daughter. If anyone other than Paige had the right to feel injured, it would be them. Her own role had been completely insignificant.

They would be the first to point that out, too.

The hollow sensation in her stomach was too familiar for comfort. Determined to ignore the thoughts her family provoked, annoyed with herself for indulging them, she turned for the door just as Nick appeared by the gardenia bush on his way to the truck. Not caring to have him see her still standing there, she hurried inside.

She had run back upstairs to make sure she'd turned off the bathroom light and was passing through the dining room on the way to the kitchen when she caught sight of him through the panes of the glass doors. He was back on the porch, tape measure in hand.

She kept going, only to hear him tap on one of the small panes. Glancing past the long mahogany table with its white lace runner and huge ruby glass compote, she saw him hold up a quart-sized can.

"I might as well give this to you now," he said the moment she swung in one of the doors. He held the can of solvent toward her. "Be sure to let it sit at least an hour and use it with gloves. Then scrape it off with a putty knife. If that doesn't work, I'll get you something else to try."

He was doing what her grandmother had asked, telling her how to remove the paint. He also clearly intended to limit his assistance to supplying her with products and advice, not elbow grease, which was fine with her. Working with him would only add to the strain of his presence.

As long as she had advice available, however, she would take it.

"How do I make it sit on a vertical surface? It's on the front of the cabinets."

"She told me you were trying to get paint off linoleum."

"That's the only part I told her about," she admitted, looking down at the directions. All she actually saw were the buckle of his belt, the worn white threads on the zipper of his faded blue jeans and the creases in the fabric above his powerful thighs.

"I'll take a look at the cabinets," he muttered, resigned. "I need power, too."

Her glance jerked from his groin, incomprehension covering her flush.

"Electricity," he explained. "Is there an outlet I can use for a few minutes? I have to cut out a section of railing, and there are no outlets out here." He nodded to the power saw and a huge coil of what looked like orange rope. "I have an extension cord that'll reach just about anywhere."

There was an outlet behind the buffet, but it would be easier to access one straight through in the kitchen. She told him that as she turned away, aware of his glance moving down her back as she padded across the hardwood floor and into the big, old-fashioned kitchen.

For as long as she could remember, the cabinets lining the room had been pale yellow and the floor black-and-white tile. The walls had been the variable. Over the years, orange paper scattered with swirls of avocado green had given way to paper of mauve and blue. Five years ago, her grandmother had stripped the walls bare, painted them shiny, enamel white and hung brilliantly colored stained glass birds in the windows to throw swaths of azure, magenta and chartreuse into the room.

On days when the sun was brightest, being inside the room was like being inside a kaleidoscope. Bea's most recent alteration would have slashed color into the room even on the dreariest of days.

"What the...?"

Amy knew exactly what had brought Nick to a dead halt behind her. She'd had the same reaction when she'd first let herself in and seen the mess her grandmother's accident had created. Her heart actually felt as if it had stopped—just before she broke into a grin at her grandmother's daring.

The paint her grandmother had chosen for her cabinets was called Crimson Cherry—and when she had fallen from the ladder while painting the upper trim, nearly a gallon of the bright bold red had splattered over the counter, the floor, the front of two upper cabinets and all but three of the lower ones.

Amy had managed to clean the streaks and splatters off the white enamel of the old stove, a project that had taken her most of yesterday, but the shock of scarlet stood out in macabre relief against the yellow and black and white of everything else.

"It looks like a crime scene in here."

"I know," she replied. "That's what I thought when I first saw it."

"This is what she was doing when she fell?"

Amy nodded, watching his frown move from the worst of the spill on the floor to a rather artful spray of bright droplets on one of the cabinets under the sink. A thick splotch of solid red the size of a dinner plate graced the cabinet next to it.

"Why?" he asked.

"She said she wanted to add a little life to the place."

"I mean, why didn't she pay to have it done?"

"Because she wanted to do it herself."

The frown intensified. "A woman her age has no business doing something like this by herself. She's—"

"Capable of making her own decisions," Amy interrupted defensively. "She knows her own mind and once it's made up, no one can change it."

"You make her stubbornness sound like a virtue," he muttered. "The woman broke her hip doing this."

Amy turned, can in hand. "You sound just like my mother," she muttered back, and set the can on the yellow Formica counter. The sound, like the admission, was far sharper than she intended. Drawing a breath of air that smelled faintly of paint thinner and the gardenia-scented breeze coming through the open windows, she did her best to tamp down the annoyance eating at her.

"It doesn't matter now what she did," she quietly amended. It wasn't his fault this particular subject so sorely tested the only real virtue she had. "All that matters is getting this cleaned up and getting her back home. There's an outlet over there," she said, motioning to her right. "That's probably the most convenient."

She wanted him to get on with his task so she could get back to hers. Nick had no problem with that. Getting his job done and getting out of there was infinitely wiser than standing there wondering at how quickly she'd buried the frustration that had been so evident seconds ago. She'd done it too quickly not to have had considerable practice.

Spotting the outlet, he turned to leave.

With some reluctance, he turned right back and motioned to the splatters. "Mind if I ask how long ago this happened?"

"About three months. Why?"

"I just wondered why no one cleaned it up before now."

The late-afternoon sun slanted through the window over the sink, catching the brilliant colors of the stained glass birds hanging across the upper pane. A slash of ruby touched fire to the dark sweep of her bangs.

A memory stirred at the sight of that light in her hair, but all that surfaced was the thought that her hair had felt incredibly soft and that it had once smelled like...lemons.

"Mom wanted to bring someone in to clean it up," she said, jerking him from the flash of buried memory. "But her idea of cleaning up was to repaint the cabinets yellow like they were. Grandma said she didn't want yellow anymore. She wanted red, and that it made no sense to pay for them to be painted a color she didn't want. So no one did anything."

"I see," he muttered, getting a better understanding of the frustration he'd just witnessed. Her mom hadn't gotten her way, so she'd simply refused to help. "And your sister?"

"She agreed with Mom. She thinks yellow is a kitchen color and red isn't."

"I mean, why didn't she step in and help?"

"Because she's—"

"Busy," he concluded, sounding as if he should have already known what she would say.

So that left you, he thought, forcing his attention from the faintly exasperated look she gave him. Standing there in her little tank top and shorts, the long lines of her body firm and lithe, her feet bare, she didn't look much older than the seventeen she'd been when he'd last seen her. Only, when he'd met her when she was seventeen, her hair had been long and streaked from the sun, her skin had looked like golden satin—and it had felt as soft as silk.

He'd known how soft her skin was even before he'd felt it under his hand in the nursing-home parking lot.

The memories drew a scowl. They were unwanted. Pointless. Dangerous.

Ruthlessly shoving them aside, he crouched down, knees cracking, to inspect a lower cabinet. "This would have been easier if it hadn't been left to dry," he muttered, pushing his thumbnail into the plate-sized blotch. "To do these right, the doors need to be taken off, stripped and sanded."

Looking straight ahead, all he could see was the long length of her shapely legs. Feeling his gut tighten, he jerked his glance upward.

He fully expected to see dismay or displeasure. What he saw in the delicate contours of her face was contemplation.

"Should I strip them all? Even the ones that aren't messed up?"

"If you want them to match, yeah. You should."

"Okay," she said.

Just like that. No questions. No hesitation. Just "Okay."

Amazing, he thought, rising.

"You can use the same stuff I gave you for the floor. But take the doors into the sunroom or outside. The ventilation is better. Are there any sawhorses around here?"

"I have no idea." Amy glanced in the direction of the storage shed on the far side of the house. She hadn't a clue what was out there.

"The job will be easier if you use them."

She gave him a nod, then saw the muscle in his jaw jerk as he waited, giving her a chance to ask any questions she might have. He was clearly only doing what her grandmother had asked of him—showing her how to best clean up the paint. So she told him she'd be sure to look for sawhorses, and watched his glance settle where her arms crossed over the odd little knot of nerves jumping in her stomach.

He said nothing else. He just gave her a look she couldn't read at all and, having complied with her grandmother's request, he headed to the porch for the extension cord. Within minutes, he'd shattered the early-evening stillness with his power saw as he cut a five-foot-wide chunk out of the beautiful porch railing opposite the dining room's double doors.

He worked until dusk, pounding stakes, running strings, loosening two circles of soil with a pick. Then he left without saying a word.

He also left a pair of his sawhorses for her on the back porch.

Chapter Three

Amy climbed down from the ladder, stripped off her gloves and hoped fervently that she'd be able to put her grandmother's kitchen back together now that she'd dismantled it. She'd taken all the doors off the cabinets on the sink side of the room and stacked the dishes and glasses that had been in them on the delft-blue table in the breakfast nook. The stained glass pieces that had hung in the window were over there, too. Newspaper covered the counters to keep the thick goop she'd spread on the cabinet's center supports from dripping onto the Formica.

She was winging it here. Other than to help a friend paint her baby's nursery, the only painting projects she'd ever tackled involved finger paints or watercolors with her first graders. It wasn't the painting she was concerned about, anyway. It was the stripping and sanding part she knew nothing about. The directions on the can of solvent seemed explicit enough, though taking off the doors had presented a challenge, until she'd found the proper screw-driver.

She was just grateful to be busy. As long as she was busy, she wasn't worrying about whether or not her mother was still annoyed with her, or wondering how long she could put off talking to the man who'd arrived nearly two hours ago and started to work without bothering to tell her he was there. She needed to thank him for the sawhorses. She just wasn't overly anxious to approach him.

Aside from that, since he hadn't made any effort to talk to her, it was apparent that he wanted only to do his job.

He wasn't wasting time doing it, either. While she'd climbed around on the counter, taking down the stained glass and painting on the solvent, he had dug two holes the size of beach balls twenty feet out from the side porch and centered a short length of four-by-four in each hole. He was now filling the holes with concrete he'd mixed with a hoe in a wheelbarrow.

As she looked out the window now, she could see him wiping his forehead with his forearm. Unaware of her, he turned, his back to her as he shoveled more concrete around the support. He made the task look effortless, but beneath the gray T-shirt straining against his shoulders, strong muscles flexed and shifted with his every move.

It took little imagination for her to picture how beauti-fully developed those corded muscles were. The cotton and denim he wore molded to him, betraying a body formed as perfectly as the Greek sculptures she'd once studied with such dedication. She'd even created those compelling lines herself in art classes with handfuls of clay, shaping, perfecting, struggling to get every line and curve right. The human body had fascinated her. Its movement. Its expres-sions.

Nick had fascinated her, too, and by the time she had

entered college he had become her own standard of perfection. As she'd worked the clay, she had imagined the
feel of those muscles beneath her hands, the strength in
them, the smoothness of his skin. She had imagined the
corrugated plane of his belly, the leanness of his hips, and
how it would feel to be held against his very solid chest.

Watching his biceps bunch as he lifted more cement,
she wondered the same thing now.

The breath she released sounded faintly like a sigh.

The one she drew caught, her eyes widening as she realized she was remembering how she'd once fantasized
about him. Conscious of the fact that she was doing it
again, she jumped back from the sink.

The ceiling fan rotated slowly overhead. Turning it up
a notch against the lingering heat of the day, she headed
for the refrigerator and pulled out a can of diet cola. With
the cold can pressed to the skin above the U of her pink
T-shirt, she swallowed a flash of disbelief and guilt and
tried to decide between grilled chicken breast or a hamburger for dinner. It was nearly eight o'clock. If she didn't
fix herself something decent to eat soon, she'd wind up
doing what she'd done last night and settle for an apple
and Oreos.

The disconcerted sensation that had jerked her from the
window eased with the diversion. What replaced it was an
equally discomfiting sense of obligation. She still needed
to talk to Nick. To thank him.

Since putting it off would only give her more time to
dread it, she grabbed another can of cola and closed the
fridge with her hip. He might not be interested in talking
to her, and she still thought him terrible for what he'd done
to her sister all those years ago, but she couldn't ignore
the need to return his thoughtfulness. Not just for leaving

the sawhorses. But for what he was doing now—pushing himself so an elderly lady could return to her home.

The metallic clank of colliding metal greeted her as she walked onto the porch outside the dining-room doors. Beyond the gap in the porch railing, she saw Nick turn from where he'd just tossed the shovel and a hoe into the wheelbarrow. A dusting of fine gray powder coated his work boots, his worn jeans sported a frayed hole above one knee, and a streak of something dark bisected the Manhattan Athletic Club logo on his faded gray T-shirt.

She was wondering if he'd belonged to the prestigious-sounding club when he'd lived in New York when his eyes, blue as lasers, locked on hers.

Caution immediately clouded his face.

"You look thirsty." Aware of the faint flutter of nerves in her stomach, she walked to the edge of the porch, her sneakers silent on the wide yellow boards. She held out a can of cola. "I noticed that your water bottle is empty," she said, nodding toward the clear plastic container on the strip of lawn between them and the driveway. "I hope you don't mind diet. It's all I have."

Warily eyeing the can she held, he walked over to where she stood in the center of the gap.

She was thinking about telling him she hadn't poisoned it when he reached up.

"Diet's fine. Thanks," he murmured, taking what she offered.

"Are you about finished for the day?"

"Just about. I just need to wash out the wheelbarrow and clean up the tools." He popped the top on the can, the sound sharp against the evening stillness. The sun skimmed the treetops, slanting long shadows in what was left of the hour before dark. "The footings didn't take as long to put in as I thought they would. If I'd brought lumber with me, I could have started framing the ramp tonight.''

From the self-deprecating frown that creased his brow as he raised the can to his mouth, it was apparent that he wished he had realized how quickly the work would go. The hour he could have put into the project now would have put him that much closer to getting the job finished.

Not wanting to hold him up now, she figured it best to do what she needed to do so he could leave. ''I just wanted to thank you,'' she said, watching him tip back the can and swallow. ''For leaving the sawhorses,'' she explained. ''That was very kind of you. But especially for what you're doing for Grandma. It can't be easy working all day then coming out to do this.''

He'd drained half the can before he lowered it. Contemplating its pull ring, he muttered, ''It's not a problem.''

''I appreciate it, anyway.''

''Then, you're welcome.''

''Did you have dinner before you came here?''

The question was out before she realized she was going to ask it, much less have time to consider where it would lead.

Nick looked caught off guard by it, too.

''Uh…no,'' he murmured, glancing at his watch as if he might have been putting off knowing exactly what time it was. ''I didn't want to waste the daylight.''

Amy's conscience tugged hard.

''I was just getting ready to grill a hamburger,'' she said, aware of exactly why he hadn't wanted to waste it. He wanted to help an old woman go home. The very least she could do was repay his kindness. On behalf of her grandmother, of course. ''If you don't mind staying, I'll make one for you, too. I can have dinner ready by the time you get your things cleaned up.''

For a moment, Nick said nothing. He just stood with the can of cola dangling at his side while he considered the wariness in Amy's eyes, along with the delicate curve of her jaw, her throat. She did nothing to call particular attention to herself. Her makeup, if she was even wearing any, was minimal. Her clothes were loose and practical. Yet her tousled hair fairly begged a man to sink his fingers into it, her lush ripe mouth taunted him with its fullness and her willowy little body was as tempting as sin itself.

If you don't mind staying, she'd said. He would have laughed at the irony of the suggestion had he been in the mood to find anything even slightly amusing about being there to begin with.

In the past couple of hours, he'd done what would have taken some men twice as long to accomplish just so he could get away from her. It seemed as if every time he'd looked up, he'd caught sight of her as she'd worked by the open kitchen window above the sink. And each time he'd seen her, he'd found himself having to try that much harder to shove her out of his thoughts.

The first time he'd noticed her, she had been reaching to take down the little stained glass birds that had hung along the top of the window. Her waist-length top had ridden up, exposing the strip of flesh between the waistband of her ragged cutoffs and the band of her bra. He hadn't known which he'd found more tantalizing: the glimpse of ice-blue lace or the smooth expanse of her flat stomach.

He still hadn't decided, even though the images were burned into his brain.

The last time he'd noticed her, she'd been standing on the counter painting something—solvent, probably—on a cabinet. Mostly what he'd seen then was the sweet curve of her backside and the long length of her legs.

Certain he'd have to be unconscious not to be aware of her, and mindful of his less-than-illustrious history with her family, he told himself the wisest thing to do would be to leave. But he was a pragmatic man. And a logical one. His job there would be infinitely easier if he and Amy could somehow call a truce. Since she was offering the opportunity, it seemed only reasonable to meet her half-way.

Aside from that, he was starving.

"Do you still burn them?" he asked, his tone mild.

"Excuse me?"

"Hamburgers. The last time you made them when I was around, they were charred on both sides and gray in the middle. We wound up having cold cuts."

She blinked at the unexpected hint of teasing in his eyes. But before she could ask what he was talking about, she remembered, too.

The exact sequence of events was fuzzy, but she remembered him being at her parents' house with Paige for a family barbecue. Amy had been left in charge of the grill, and she'd knocked over a cruet of salad oil that had been set on its sideboard. The resulting ball of flame had turned the meat into little lumps of coal.

"I can't believe you remembered that."

"I remember a lot of things about you," he replied, his glance holding hers. "And yeah," he murmured, "a hamburger would be great."

The carved lines of his face were inscrutable in the moments before he swiped up the empty cement bags and carried them to the truck parked in the drive. He sounded as if remembering her was merely a matter of fact, as unremarkable to him as recalling his own name. She just had no idea why he would recall anything about her beyond the fact that she'd simply been around.

Unless, she thought as she headed into the kitchen to search drawers for matches, it was because he'd been aware of how awkward she'd felt around him, or because he'd been present during some of her more embarrassing moments. At least, they'd been embarrassing to a shy girl of seventeen with a desperate need to please her family.

She'd certainly been embarrassed the day she'd incinerated the family meal. Yet Nick hadn't let on if he had noticed how badly she'd wished she could twitch her nose and disappear. As gallant as the hero in any young girl's fantasies, he'd come to her aid, quietly removing the smoldering evidence to the trash while everyone else had come down on her for not paying attention to what she'd been doing. Then he'd told her with a wink that he hadn't been in the mood for hamburgers anyway, that any one of them could have done the same thing, and whisked Paige off with him to the deli around the corner for packages of turkey and ham.

She had felt pitifully grateful to him for his kindness, and had thought him quite wonderful for defusing her little disaster. But she'd already thought him pretty wonderful, anyway. The problem was that she'd grown to feel more than simple gratitude. She had begun to feel things she had no business feeling toward a man who was going to be her brother-in-law. Things that had made her heart hurt when she'd realized he wouldn't be part of their family. Things that had actually made her feel relieved when he'd gone, because her feelings toward him had started making her feel uncomfortable with her sister. She and Paige had next to nothing in common and Paige had always done everything so much better than Amy felt she ever could, but Amy had never in her life felt envious or jealous of her until she'd fallen so hard for Nick herself.

No one had known she'd had such a crush on him. And

a crush was all it could have been at seventeen. No one but her grandmother. When her confused feelings had driven her to confide in the dear woman, Bea had gently assured her that it wasn't at all unusual for a young girl to become infatuated with an unattainable older man. It was simply part of growing up.

Amy absently adjusted the flame on the grill. The flash of guilt and attraction she'd experienced earlier as she'd watched Nick from the window was back. Only now, the disturbing feelings were a little harder to tamp down, a little harder to deny.

She pointedly turned to the house, putting her heart into the effort anyway. She had been young and impressionable then, but she was adult enough now to know that it was only memories making her feel those old conflicts. That, and being back in Cedar Lake, back in a place where she would perpetually feel the insecurities of being seventeen.

"Mind if I go inside and wash up? I could use some soap."

Nick's deep voice vibrated over her nerves like the roll of distant thunder. Her stomach jumped. Pressing her hand to it, she turned to see him a few feet behind her on the concrete patio.

He'd washed out the wheelbarrow with the hose at the side of the house. Skimming a glance past the water-darkened spots on his jeans, she dropped her hand to her side. "Go ahead," she murmured, wondering if he'd ever suspected how she'd felt about him. She would have died of mortification if he had. "Take the door to the left inside the kitchen. It's the first door on your right in the hall."

He glanced from the gas jets sending flame over the metal coals. "Is there anything I can do to help?"

"I'll call if there's a fire."

She saw the corner of his mouth kick up in what almost

passed for a smile, then watched him take the six back stairs two at a time and disappear into the house. Moments later, she followed, making herself concentrate only on the task of feeding him. The man was probably famished. Considering what she'd seen some of the older boys at school pack away, she had the feeling one little hamburger wasn't going to cut it.

It took her mere minutes to throw the patties on the gas grill, pile sliced tomato, onions and cheese on a plate and gather condiments and buns and set them on the table on the back lawn. She was on her way back in after flipping the meat when she met Nick coming into the kitchen.

He'd washed his face. Splashed water on it, anyway. The neck of his shirt was damp and his thick hair was darkened to almost black from the water he'd used when he combed it. She didn't know if it was because he'd combed his hair straight back or because it was darker, but his chiseled features seemed more elegant, somehow, the blue of his eyes more intense.

Preferring to ignore the catch in her pulse, she set a small sack of chips on top of a container of deli salad she'd taken from the fridge.

"Go on out," she said, balancing the salad and chips in one hand as she reached for the napkins, utensils and plates. A bunch of grapes she'd rinsed sat in a bowl by the sink. "It's just about ready," she told him, thinking she'd have to make one more trip.

"What do you want me to take?"

"Nothing. I've got it," she insisted, and decided to stack the plates on top of the bowl.

Seeing what she was trying to do, ignoring her disclaimer, he took the bowl himself.

"Is this everything?" he asked.

She hesitated. "I could heat some baked beans if you

want. There's canned goods in the pantry. Or I have some yogurt. Except for cereal, this is all I have. I didn't buy much at the store.''

Confusion flashed in his eyes. Seconds later, comprehension replaced it. ''I'm not talking about what you're fixing for dinner, Amy. Whatever you have here is fine. I mean to take outside. There's no reason for you to carry all this by yourself.''

''Oh,'' she murmured, aware of the brush of his hand against hers as he took the chips and salad. ''Thank you.''

''You're welcome,'' he murmured in return, and moved ahead of her so he could hold the door.

The sun had just dropped below the horizon, the pale light of evening turning the pine trees a dusky shade of blue. The calm water of the lake reflected nothing but shadows, crickets called to each other and from the rocks along the water's edge the deep croak of frogs filtered through the balmy air.

Amy was acutely aware of the twilight stillness as she took what Nick carried for her and placed it on the old redwood picnic table that sat halfway between the house and the water. It was a time of day she had once found welcoming and restful. Since she'd been in Cedar Lake this time, it had simply seemed lonely.

She attributed the unfamiliar feeling to the isolation of the place, and the fact that she was there by herself. She was accustomed to feeling isolated when it came to her family, but this was different. She'd never been at the lake house alone before, and it felt odd without her grandmother around. As Nick lowered himself to the long bench opposite her seat, she had to admit it felt even more strange to be alone there with him.

Her glance caught his across the table. The way he was

watching her, he didn't look all that certain about being there, either.

Refusing to let her gesture turn uncomfortable for them both, she handed him the relish plate. "Help yourself," she said, and reached for the salad she really didn't want.

He immediately took her up on her suggestion, piling tomato slices on his cheeseburger. "I always thought it would seem like one long vacation living in a place like this. On the water, I mean. I used to really envy the kids who could hang around a lake during the summer."

"You make it sound as if you never had access to one. There are dozens of lakes around here."

"That doesn't mean I had the time," he informed her, adding lettuce. "I spent every summer from the time I was ten years old working construction with my uncle. We'd go out to Blue Springs for a Sunday picnic once in a while," he said, speaking of one of the public lakes in the area, "but there was never time to spend a whole day just hanging out." Adding the top bun to the three-inch-high sandwich, he nodded toward the water. "It's nice here."

His tone was conversational, his manner less guarded than it had seemed just a short while ago. She figured that had to do with the fact that she was feeding him. It would be rude of him to be sullen.

"You worked construction when you were ten?"

"From then through college," he confirmed, taking the container of salad she handed him.

"That's awfully young." It was also unconscionable, she thought. A ten-year-old was merely a child.

An image of him as a young boy wavered in the back of her mind as she watched him spoon pasta salad onto his plate. She could easily imagine the fresh, eager faces of her male students and all that budding manhood trapped in their energetic little bodies. But there was too much of an edge to the man sitting across from her for her to imagine him that innocent.

He handed the salad back.

"I was hardly an abused child, if that's what you're thinking." From the troubled look on her face, Nick had the distinct feeling that it was. The woman was as transparent as window glass. She always had been. "I had to beg Uncle Mike to take me with him at first. If I remember right, I promised I'd wash his truck for him if he'd let me go."

"Why?"

"Because I didn't want to stay with my aunt and cousins while my mom was at work. It's not that I didn't like my relatives," he qualified, in case she got the wrong idea there, too. "It was just that they were all female. There was more appeal to being with the guys and wearing a hard hat than being around a bunch of girls."

Realizing she was still holding the salad, she set it aside and absently reached for the tomatoes herself. She had no problem imagining a young boy preferring the company of men over girls. She just couldn't imagine a responsible adult allowing a child to deliberately be where it wasn't safe. "But wasn't that dangerous? A child being at a construction site, I mean?"

"It sounds more dangerous than it was." Nick took a bite of burger, wondering as he did if she realized how much of her guard had slipped. By the time he swallowed, he'd decided she hadn't simply forgotten to be wary. He actually detected real concern. "Mike had a partner back then," he explained, wanting her to know there was no way his uncle would have put him in jeopardy. "And the company was bigger. He and Roy, his partner," he clarified, "supervised the jobs, rather than actually working on them the way Mike does now."

The way he's had to do since his partner retired last year, Nick mentally muttered, hating how hard his uncle was working just when he should be slowing down himself. But Mike couldn't slow down. He'd borrowed to buy out his partner's interest in the business and he'd also lost money on contracts because it was taking him longer to complete them with less help.

Feeling his stomach knot with the thoughts, Nick glanced across the table and met the quiet interest in Amy's guileless eyes. Drawn by that interest, distracted by it, he felt the quick surge of frustration fade.

"He would let me watch some of the craftsmen as long as he was nearby," he told her. "The rest of the time, he stuck me out of the way with a stack of wood and a hammer. Or I'd sit in the truck after he explained what they were working on that day and try to figure out where they were on the blueprints. He didn't really put me to work until I was a little older."

"And you really liked it," she quietly concluded.

"I couldn't learn enough fast enough. Building something from nothing fascinated me. That's when I first decided to become an architect," he admitted, eyeing his hamburger again. "Except I wanted to live in a city and build skyscrapers."

He offered his last comment casually, as if his ambition were a mere aside in life, and turned his attention to his meal. It didn't seem to Amy that it bothered him to be working once again for his uncle. If anything, he seemed completely accepting of it. Yet, as curious as she found that, considering the brilliant future her parents and Paige had once thought he had ahead of him, what struck her most was what he'd said about his family.

She knew nothing about them. Though he and Paige had gone out together for nearly a year in college, he had been

around the Chapman house only for a few months—mostly
on weekends because he'd taken the job in New York by
then—before he'd disappeared from their lives. If mention
had been made of his family, it had never been around her.

She told herself it was only to keep the silence from
growing awkward that she asked about them now.

"I didn't realize you have so many relatives here."

"I don't have anymore. Just Uncle Mike, Aunt Kate and
one cousin. The rest have moved away."

"Your mom, too?"

It occurred to Nick that she had yet to touch her meal,
something that struck him as odd, since she'd had him do
all the talking. Reaching across the table, he nudged her
plate closer to her and told her that his mom had taken a
transfer to Florida a few years ago when the insurance
company she worked for opened offices there. Because
Amy asked if he and his cousins had been close, he then
told her that all six of them were like sisters to him. At
least, as he imagined sisters would be, since he had no
siblings of his own. He and his mom had lived only a
couple of blocks from them, and his aunt and uncle's cha-
otic house had been like a second home.

He had no idea why he told her that. It wasn't like him
to talk about the things that had mattered to him the most
when he'd been growing up. Until he stopped, he hadn't
even realized how easily he'd been talking. But the quiet
didn't feel uncomfortable. At least, it didn't until Amy
casually lit the citron candle on the table to ward off the
bugs and the dark now that the sun had set and asked about
the one person in his family he hadn't bothered to mention.

"What about your father?" she asked, her skin glowing
golden in the candlelight.

His glance slid from hers. "What about him?"

Amy tipped her head, watching as he distractedly traced

the logo on his empty cola can. He looked almost as non-chalant as he sounded. It was the way he'd so quickly looked away that gave her pause. Until that moment, she hadn't realized how relaxed he'd become with her.

And she with him.

"You haven't said anything about him." She offered the observation quietly, thinking it obvious that he had great affection for his extended family. It was just that he and his uncle seemed to have been the only two men in it.

"There's nothing to say." The light of the flame glinted like a spark off the silver metal as he nudged the aluminum container aside. "He left when I was nine."

"So Mike is more like a father to you than an uncle."

At the quickness of her quiet conclusion, he met her eyes. "You could say that. Yeah," he admitted, since it didn't feel right to be vague about the role the man had played in his life. "He is."

His glance skimmed her face, drifted to her mouth. Realizing how closely he was studying her, he forced his attention away. He didn't want to wonder why she was interested in any of this. He didn't want to be curious about her at all. But more than anything else, he didn't want to sit there with that soft light playing over her delicate features and think about how appealing he found the melodic sound of her voice and how comfortable he felt at her table.

"Speaking of Uncle Mike," he muttered, wanting to cut off the thoughts that had crept in anyway, "I really have to get going. I need to talk to him before he goes to bed." He also had another job to tackle tonight. He only hoped that, unlike last night, he wouldn't fall asleep at his drafting table.

"But before I go," he said, pulling a pen from his

pocket, "I need you to tell me more about the room addition your grandmother wants. Your idea to close in the porch is good, so we'll start with that."

Pushing aside their plates, he slid a clean napkin toward her. "Show me what you have in mind." Half a dozen bold slashes and he'd roughed out the shape of the porch and indicated the entrance to the kitchen. "Mark where you think she'd want windows and doors. And give me an idea of the space she'll need for a closet."

He leaned closer, repositioning the candle between them, and handed her the pen.

She took it, aware of the odd flutter of her nerves at his nearness, and tried to concentrate only on doing what her grandmother had asked of her as she explained what she thought the older woman would want. She also tried very hard not to feel flattered by the glints of approval she caught in his eyes when she offered a couple of suggestions her grandma hadn't mentioned, or to feel pleased when he thanked her for dinner and told her her cooking skills had definitely improved. After all, she was no longer the naive girl she'd once been, and he was no longer the white knight she'd believed him to be.

He was the man who had hurt her sister.

Chapter Four

"I'm in the laundry room, Amy. Come on in."

"I can't." Hearing her sister's muffled voice, Amy tugged on the latch and squinted up through Paige's back screen door. "You've got the child lock on."

"I can get it!" came a little voice over the scrape of a chair being dragged across a shining white pine floor. Grinning through the silver haze of wire mesh at her aunt, the dainty little three-year-old with crystal blue eyes and a headful of blond curls gave a final shove and climbed up on the custom-upholstered seat. "Are you gonna take us to Gramma Bea's house to play in the boat, Aunt Amy?"

"Not today, sweetheart," she murmured, watching her youngest niece push up the high latch with a wooden spoon. "I have work to do. And it looks like it's going to rain."

"Can we come tomorrow?"

"I'll talk to your mom about it. Be careful, Sarah. I don't want you to fall."

"Sarah Marie, what are you doing?"

The latch opened an instant before the little girl whipped around, all angelic innocence and golden curls. "Aunt Amy can't get in."

"So much for child locks," Paige muttered, catching her youngest daughter beneath the arms of her pink coveralls and lifting her to the floor. "Go find your sister. Lunch is ready.

"Amy," the striking blonde continued, sounding relieved as she pulled the chair out of the way and pushed open the door, "I'm so glad you're here. I was planning to use my jade runners and an arrangement of iris and stones on the table for the dinner party we're having next week, but Darren just called and said the Johnstons are in town and that he invited them to come. Now I have to use something else."

"Why?"

"Because that's what I used the last time they came to dinner," she replied, looking seriously troubled at the thought of repeating the same table setting. "I have a sage runner I haven't used before and I saw some wonderful amethyst lotus bowls in town that would be perfect filled with hydrangeas. I can be in and out of the store in no time if you'll stay with the girls. I know I have days to get them, but I'll need three and I'm afraid they might not have them if I wait."

The screen door closed behind Amy with a refined whoosh as she stepped into the bright and airy gourmet kitchen. To her left, the white pedestal table in the huge breakfast nook was covered with pale green and cream dried flowers that her sister was arranging into a spray. Through the archway on the other side of the expansive white granite-topped cooking island, Amy could see the girls' Barbie mansion and little school-type desks in the solarium.

Paige had settled well into her life as the wife of a successful orthodontist and mother of two adorable little girls. Flourished in it, actually. Like their mom, she was ruthlessly organized, enormously capable and invariably had several major projects going at once. Yet even on her busiest days, she somehow managed to have her home, herself and her children looking as if they'd just stepped from an ad in *House Beautiful.* Except for the project on the table, which somehow managed to look artful even in its disarray, there wasn't a dish or pot out of place in the kitchen. Paige herself looked impeccable in a short coral shift, her gleaming blond hair swinging in a perfect wedge at her shoulders.

Amy surreptitiously smoothed the pale yellow T-shirt she'd tucked into a pair of khaki cargo shorts. To the dismay of her mother and the bafflement of her sister, she simply hadn't been able to get enthused about clothes and makeup and table settings the way they had when she'd been growing up. All that had really mattered to her was that she looked presentable and that the people around her were happy.

That was pretty much all that mattered to her now, too. And she was content with that. Except when she was around her mom and her sister. Whenever she was around them, she tended to feel either invisible, inept or as if she'd just stepped in from a gale. She also couldn't help but notice how much more accomplished they were, and how she'd never mastered their delegating techniques, the latter of which meant she was usually running behind schedule. As she was now.

Feeling rushed and windblown, trying to ignore both, she watched Paige sweep by.

"No problem," she said, replying to the request that she watch her nieces for a while. Unconsciously smoothing her hair anyway, she smiled at the older version of Sarah racing toward her. Brittany was fourteen months older than her little sister and just as blond, though her hair was long and straight. She also fancied herself quite grown-up, except for when it came to hugs with her aunt Amy. Throwing her arms wide, she swooped in and latched on to her aunt's knees.

"How's my favorite four-year-old niece?"

"I'm your only four-year-old niece," the little girl replied with a giggle.

"And I'm favorite three," Sarah piped in, claiming a hug for herself.

"That you are." Wrapped in the scents of baby shampoo and something that smelled suspiciously like their mom's perfume, she saw her sister walk toward her with her purse. "Didn't I hear your mom say your lunch is ready?"

"On the table in the solarium," Paige murmured absently. "They can have a cookie when they're finished."

"How about two?" Amy whispered to the girls, nodding.

The girls seemed to think that was a fine idea. Ignoring the droll look their mom shot their aunt, they disentangled themselves in the space of seconds and were off like little bullets, hot pink tennis shoes squeaking on polished pine.

The forbearance in Paige's expression lasted only long enough for her to dig out her keys. She never minded that Amy liked to spoil her girls. "I won't be long. Are you on your way to see Grandma?"

"I just came from the nursing home. Now I'm on my

way to the hardware store for more solvent. The cleanup at the house is a little more complicated than I'd thought it would be.''

"Well, since you're insisting on doing it, I'm sure you can handle it," she mused, not looking especially interested in hearing what those complications were. "I'm still not sure about this idea of hers to add a bedroom. I really wish you wouldn't keep encouraging her.''

"Actually," Amy said, watching her sister glance around the room as if she were trying to think of what else she might need as long as she was out, "that's why I came by. Grandma hired Nick Culhane, Paige. She hired his uncle's company, anyway. Culhane Contracting. Nick is working for him.''

Amy suspected Paige was only half-listening to her, partly because Paige tended to tune her out whenever the topic was one that didn't interest her—which cleaning up paint definitely did not—and partly because she was already preoccupied. Several seconds passed before the name of her ex-fiancé finally registered, and her statuesque sibling swung around.

Paige blinked, her expression stunned. "She hired Nick?''

"A couple of days ago.''

Incomprehension melded with incredulity. "Why on earth would she do something like that?''

"Because she wants an addition built.''

"That's not what I mean. I mean, I know that. But he's not a builder. He's an architect," she blurted, then lowered her voice so she wouldn't be heard over the video playing in the solarium. "He doesn't build things," she insisted. "He designs them. And why would she have anything to do with him, anyway? Has she forgotten what he did to me?'' She paused, pressing her hand to her chest, and she shook her head. "I can't believe this," she muttered. "Did you tell Mom?"

She turned away, clearly at a loss. Then she turned right back, accusation narrowing her eyes. "I know why she did it," she pronounced, not giving Amy a chance to do anything more than open her mouth. "She did it to get back at me for agreeing with Mom that she needs to be in a nursing home.

"Honestly, Amy," she insisted, her tone both pleading and insistent, "there's no way I could go to her house every day to take care of her. I have the girls and Darren and my committees...not to mention keeping up this house and helping at the girls' preschool. Mom can't do it, either. Not with her business. I have no idea as it is who's going to take care of her after you've gone home."

The wings of her eyebrows lowered, the scope of her irritations broadening. "Did you even stop to think about that? You will have moved her back into her house and left us to take care of everything. I simply can't understand why you didn't think this through."

A hollow sensation had formed below Amy's ribs. Crossing her arms over it, she drew a deliberately deep breath. "I did think it through," she quietly informed her sister, hating the taunt as much as she did the edge in the atmosphere. "We can hire a nurse and a housekeeper."

Paige shot her a look of utter disbelief. "Hire strangers to take care of Grandma?"

"Who do you think is taking care of her now?"

"I'm not having this discussion," Paige announced, changing the subject the way she always did when something wasn't moving in her favor. "We're talking about Nick." Threading her well-manicured hand through her hair, she took a deep breath of her own. "I had no idea he was back here."

"I didn't, either." Amy offered the concession with a certain relief. She didn't want to argue with her sister about Bea. She understood that Paige didn't have any extra time. She understood that Paige was probably feeling guilty about not making time, too. But her grandmother had asked for her help and she couldn't have refused if she'd wanted to.

Conciliation entered her tone. "There's no reason to make a big deal out of this. Grandma and I are the only ones who have to deal with him. And it's not like he'll be out there that long. I only mentioned it to you because I didn't want you to bring the kids out to the lake house and unexpectedly find him there."

With her purse and keys forgotten on the island, Paige distractedly tucked one side of her hair behind her ear. "Thank you," she murmured. "I appreciate that." She paused, considering. "You say he's working for his uncle?"

"Mike."

"I remember him. I met him. And his aunt."

Kate, Amy started to say, but kept silent because it seemed wiser somehow.

"I just don't understand why he'd be back here," Paige admitted, her tone confiding. "His work was brilliant. He had offers from the top firms in the country. The position he did take came with memberships in the best clubs and a subsidy for this great apartment overlooking Central Park. A corner of the park, anyway," she qualified. "We'd just started to furnish it," she said, then cut herself off, losing enthusiasm for that part of the memory.

"The point," she stressed, her wedding ring flashing as she waved off what didn't seem relevant, "is that he'd wanted to be an architect from the time he was a little kid. He was going to build skyscrapers. Not room additions.

He studied all over Canada and Europe before he came back to Wisconsin State,'' she said, referring to the university where they'd met, ''and he couldn't imagine anything that could get him to move back to Cedar Lake. I can't remember how many times he told me he just wasn't a small-town person.''

Amy's voice was quiet. ''It seems he's changed his mind.''

''I have no idea how. The man I knew, knew exactly what he wanted when it came to what he'd do for a living. What he wanted to do with his entire life,'' she stressed, making it sound as if the man had planned everything right down to when he'd open his children's college funds. ''He was so obsessed with his master's research when we met that I had to ask him out three times before he could find a night free for me.''

''You asked him out?''

''That was my first mistake,'' Paige muttered, not looking nearly as impressed with her bold confidence as Amy was. ''My second was trusting the creep.'' She gave a mirthless little laugh. ''It's been ten years. I don't feel that awful hurt anymore, but I can sure remember the humiliation.''

Not knowing what to say that would help, Amy remained silent.

''Well?'' Paige prompted, searching her sister's face.

''Well, what?''

''Have you talked to him?''

A tiny mirror belonging to one of the girls' dolls lay on the island. Amy picked it up and ran her finger over the pink and purple flowers on the back.

''A couple of times.''

''Did he say why he was here?''

''No.'' All he'd told her was what it had been like for

him when he was in Cedar Lake when he was a child, how his uncle had taken him under his wing when his own father had walked out on him, how he'd inspired him. Until Paige had mentioned it moments ago, Amy hadn't known that he had shared her own desire to leave the little town, or how extensively he'd traveled. But she'd known of his dream to build skyscrapers.

It was hardly as if he'd shared some earth-shattering secret, yet as they'd sat surrounded by the night last evening and she'd listened to the deep, smoky tones of his voice, their conversation had felt intimate, personal. The knowledge he'd shared had felt strangely special to her. And even though she'd tried to deny it, she'd wanted to know more.

Paige hesitated, her expression suddenly pensive. "How did he look?"

Big, Amy thought. And handsome. And hot. "Would it help if I said he's fat and bald?"

Her sister sent her an appreciative glance. "It would be sweet of you. But I wouldn't believe it." Her voice dropped. "Although there was a time when I thought warts and a hunchback would do him justice."

"Aunt Amy? Can I have more milk, please?"

Brittany was walking toward her, her arm outstretched and her hand grasping a purple plastic tumbler.

"Sure, honey," Amy said with a smile, enormously grateful for the interruption. She didn't know what to make of the ambivalence she felt at her sister's comments, or the contradictions in her own reactions toward the man they were discussing. At the moment, she was concerned mostly with preserving the status quo, and protecting her sister's feelings. That was why she hadn't mentioned how thoughtful Nick was being, especially since Paige could quite rightfully point out that it had hardly been thoughtful of him to dump her for another woman.

Had he done to her what he'd done to Paige, the last thing on earth she would want would be to hear her sister defending him.

Certain her loyalties were in place, she moved across the room to the fridge. She couldn't blame Paige for being curious about Nick. Or for being disturbed to learn that he was around again. And it was natural that she'd have questions about him.

Amy just didn't want to be the one to answer them.

It was nearly six o'clock before Amy returned to the lake house, hours behind her original schedule. Not that she had to have one. As Paige had pointed out when she'd returned from the store three hours later than she'd intended because the department store had been having a sale and she tended to shop when she was upset, Amy had all summer to get their grandma's kitchen put back together. Amy, feeling as distracted as Paige had looked, had agreed. It was just that she liked to pretend she had a grasp on her life, and a schedule, even if it wasn't followed, at least told her where she should have been.

The schedule she'd taped next to the mirror in the old-fashioned eyelet-and-lace bedroom she used at her grandmother's house was actually more of a list. It included the book a week she'd assigned herself to read over the next couple of months: three to improve her mind, three to maintain a positive outlook and two that were pure mind candy. She'd also brought the French and Italian tapes she'd listened to for the past couple of years in preparation for the trip she'd had to cancel, so she wouldn't forget what she'd learned, and four shoe boxes full of photographs, which she fully intended to arrange chronologically in albums before she returned to Eau Claire.

She had the steps of the project in the kitchen on the list, too, though there, she was actually going backward. As soon as she finished changing into her work clothes, which now consisted of the cutoffs she'd ruined with a couple of streaks of dissolved red paint and a white tank top with streaks to match, she had to haul back up to the porch the dozen doors she'd taken outside.

The rain shower she'd heard forecast after she'd left this morning appeared to be on its way. The sky had turned a decidedly threatening shade of slate.

She was halfway down the staircase when she heard Nick's truck pull into the drive. Heading through the back hall, she told herself that his presence really didn't matter to her one way or the other—which was the same thing she'd told herself after he'd gone last night, and after she'd left Paige's house a while ago thinking about how distracted her sister was acting by the news of his return.

There was no reason it should matter, she coached herself, crossing the kitchen to the back porch. He would do his job, she would do hers, he'd disappear from their lives again and all would return to normal. There was no cause for concern. Except for the fact that he lived there now. And Paige had clearly been shaken to learn he was back.

Not wanting to think why those thoughts made her so uneasy, she hurried down the back steps and across the yard. She didn't want to think about her sister and Nick. She didn't want to think about Nick, period. After all, it wasn't as if he'd shown any more interest in her than he ever had. In his mind, she was sure she was still Paige's little sister.

She felt the first warm drops on her bare arms as she reached the sawhorses and the dozen doors she'd propped against them on the lawn. The drops turned to a drizzle just as her fingers curled around two of the two-by-three-foot rectangles of paint-splattered wood.

"Amy. Here. Cover them with this."

She turned on the thick grass to see Nick jog to stop and hold out a tarp.

"Grab an end," he instructed, taking one himself as he walked to the other side of the sawhorses. "You don't need to move these. Just anchor the tarp ends under the doors in case the winds kicks up. They'll be fine."

The huge green tarp billowed like a flailing sail in a matter of seconds, covering what she'd wanted to protect.

"If you've got this," he said, rising like a monolith from where he'd anchored his ends, "I need to go cover the wood and equipment in the truck. I was just getting ready to unload it."

Amy rose, too, aware of the rain falling faster. Circles of darker blue bloomed on his chambray shirt where each drop fell, but the thought that they were going to get drenched had no sooner occurred to her than he left her to jog back across the lawn. His movements were powerful, his stride easy. But Amy's only thought as she stared at his broad back was that the man didn't play fair. How could she not think of him when he'd so obviously just thought of her first?

Prodded by her conscience, she hurried right behind, following him onto the rutted driveway to where he'd parked his truck near the gap in the side-porch rail. Rain ticked on the leaves of the trees. Birds dived for cover.

Thinking cover wasn't a bad idea, she snagged one end of another tarp he pulled from the pickup's bed and stepped back to help him do what he'd just done for her.

Nick knew she was there before he saw her slender hand reach toward the heavy canvas. He hadn't heard her come up behind him. Between the sound of the rain and the birds squawking as they scattered, it would have been impossible to hear her running on the grass. He simply sensed her presence, felt it humming along his nerves with a kind of energy that heightened his awareness, put him on alert.

"That's good," he told her, flipping another piece of plastic over the longer boards protruding past the tailgate. Grabbing her by the wrist when she started to tuck that piece under, he glanced up at the darkened sky and tugged her toward the porch. "Leave it. This won't last that long."

There were no steps where he'd cut the gap in the rail, and the porch itself stood over three feet off the ground. Jumping up first, he caught her wrist again and pulled her through the gap, catching her at the side of her hip to steady her in front of him when her feet were both on the wide yellow planks.

"Thanks," she murmured, grazing a glance from his chin to the middle of his chest.

One hand still curved at her side. The other held her wrist, her small bones feeling incredibly delicate. Beneath his fingers, her pulse leapt.

"No problem." He was already aware of her. Standing close enough to catch the scent of her shampoo, he felt that awareness kick into overdrive.

He strongly suspected that she was aware of him, too.

Common sense told him it didn't matter, to not invite problems, to pull back. Something more primitive caused his fingers to flex against the soft denim covering her firm little hip.

The two-second battle ended when common sense tied with Amy's intervention. His fingers slid from the soft denim as she stepped away and swiped water from her arm.

She turned toward the gap. "Like you said, the good news is that these summer cloudbursts don't last long."

"As opposed to the bad news...which is...?"

Amy shrugged, her eyes finally meeting his.

"Does there have to be any?"

For a moment, Amy didn't think he was going to answer. He just looked at her, his glance narrowing as it roamed her face, touched on her hair and slipped over the droplets of water clinging to her shoulders and bare arms. It seemed to her that he appeared even more tired than he had yesterday. The smile lines fanning from the corners of his eyes seemed to be carved a little deeper. His expression looked more weary. But a smile suddenly moved into his eyes, unexpected and totally disarming, and some of that weariness actually seemed to fade.

"I don't know many women who could get caught in a cloudburst and not find something negative about it."

"It's just water."

"True." He didn't know too many women who would adopt that attitude, either. "But you're pretty wet."

It was the smile in his eyes, the teasing quality in it, that caused Amy's hand to shoot to her head. Her hair was damp enough that her bangs stayed swept to the side when she pushed them away instead of falling back to brush her eyebrows, and the skin exposed by her damp tank top was slick with rain. Suddenly aware of how awful she must look in her painting clothes, she started to fluff up her hair when Nick caught her wrist.

"You're fine," he told her, drawing her hand down. "I've seen you wetter than this."

"You have?"

The muscle in his jaw jumped as he let her go. "Yeah. Outside your parents' house. A long time ago. So," he murmured, turning to face the soft, steady rain, "do you want to make a bet on how long this will last?"

She blinked at his profile. She was conscious as much of the faint tension that had slipped into his manner as she was of the quick and deliberate way he'd changed the subject. She had no idea when he would have seen her wet, unless he'd been around when she'd come back from swimming in the neighbor's pool. She had no idea either what made that memory seem less than pleasant. Unlike his recollections of the hamburgers, this one didn't make him smile.

Figuring he was associating something disagreeable with the memory, wondering if perhaps he and Paige had been arguing that day, she turned her attention back to the misty gray of the distant landscape.

"I give it fifteen minutes," she said.

"I'll give it ten. There's a patch of blue out there." He pointed over the tops of the trees to indicate a slice of azure between two sheets of billowy gray. Casting a sideways glance at her crossed arms, his brow drew down. "You're cold."

The air was cooling with the rain, but it had dropped only a few degrees from where it had hovered in the mid-seventies. It was the moisture on her bare arms and legs making her shiver. That, and the way his glance skimmed the swell of her breasts before jerking back to the scenery.

"I'll get a towel."

She followed the porch around to the front door because the dining-room door was locked, and had dried herself off by the time she walked through the dining-room doors and handed him a towel, too. Thinking she'd wait until he was finished with it, she watched him swipe it over the back of his neck and over his forearms.

"I had my whole class on the playground once when

this happened," she said, far more comfortable talking with him than she was with silence. "I had twenty-six students playing Red Rover when the sky opened up. They were absolutely drenched."

"What did you do?"

"Hustled them into the gym and raided the P.E. towels."

A smile entered his voice as he handed her the rectangle of royal-blue terry cloth. "What grade do you teach?"

"First," she said, not sure why he was walking away.

"I had a feeling you worked with the younger kids instead of the older ones."

"You did?"

"Sure." He gave a shrug, then lowered himself to sit with his back to the wall by the double doors. Motioning her to a spot beside him, he planted one booted foot on the wide porch planks and hooked his wrist over his raised knee.

"You were always great with the little ones," he told her, watching her hesitate a moment before she walked over and dropped the towel by the door. She slid down the wall two feet away from him and hugged her knees. "I remember the kids in your neighborhood following you around, and you showing them how to play soccer in front of your house. You were always baby-sitting a bunch of them. There was this one little kid you used to cart around on your hip. I think she lived next door to you. In the house with the orange shutters."

That would be the Meiers' house, Amy thought. Her mother had always hated the fact that their neighbors insisted on keeping that color. According to her, no house should ever bear trim the color of fruit. "Sheri," she said, identifying the child. "What about her?"

"I just remember you with her. You'd walk around with

her on your hip like she was your own." The thought made him pause. "As good as you were with kids, I guess I'd be surprised if you hadn't chosen to work with them. You're a natural."

Amy kept her focus on the rain-blurred wall of camellia bushes visible through the slats of the porch rail. He'd done it again—told her he remembered her. There was something terribly seductive about that, terribly flattering.

She knew she shouldn't let herself be flattered by him, even though deep inside she craved that approval. It wasn't just seductive. It was dangerous.

"Everyone seemed to feel that way. That I should work with children," she clarified, feeling flattered anyway.

From the corner of her eye she saw the dark slashes of his eyebrows lower. He said nothing for a moment, though. He simply considered her long enough that his silence drew her glance to his.

"What about you?" he asked. "How did you feel about it?"

She offered a smile. "You said yourself it seemed natural."

"That's not what I asked," he reminded her mildly. "I asked how *you* feel about what you do."

"I love working with children." That much she could say with absolute certainty. "I have a great job, and I work with great people. I'm even looking forward to school starting in the fall."

"That's because you're stuck here for the summer."

That was true. Partly, anyway. "I said I like what I do," she insisted, because it really was the truth.

Nick, however, was like a rat terrier with a bone. "But?" he prompted, clearly refusing to settle for what would have satisfied anyone else.

The rain pounded steadily on the porch roof, the sound

blending with the beat of it on the ground, the leaves of the bushes and trees. He was watching her as if he didn't doubt for a moment that she was omitting something essential. Feeling exposed, not at all sure she liked it, she turned her attention to a little waterfall tumbling over the eaves.

"So what did you really want to do?"

She gave a little laugh, slowly shaking her head at his tenacity and his insight. The man had a definite knack for hearing far more than she actually said. "Before or after I admitted that a career needed to produce an income to be practical?"

"Before."

"Before," she repeated, encouraged by the smile in his eyes. "You know those statues you see in shopping malls or plazas of a man reading a newspaper or a woman walking a dog?"

"Sure. I commissioned a few myself for projects. They're usually bronzes."

"Exactly. That's what I wanted to do. I wanted to live in a converted warehouse and wear bright colors and create life-sized bronzes of ordinary people doing ordinary things."

"So why didn't you?"

"Because I needed a way to support myself," she replied, liking the way he seemed to find nothing at all extraordinary about the goal. "I had an art instructor in college who wanted me to apprentice with a friend of his in California, but the whole idea just wasn't practical."

She could still remember her mom insisting that being a sculptress was not a proper career, and her father wanting to know if she'd ever heard the term, *starving artist*. Her mom's argument had lacked any logic that Amy could identify, mostly because she could see nothing "improper'' about it, but her father was less concerned with what others would think. He had expounded on the benefits of job security, health insurance, a steady paycheck—and the fact that they were footing the bill for her education and that they weren't going to pay for anything so frivolous. She just didn't care to dwell on the discussions that had so effectively extinguished the spark of her dream—as admittedly impractical as it had been.

She hugged her knees more tightly.

"I'm still fascinated by sculpture, though." The admission came easily, prompted as it was by his unquestioning acceptance of her interest. He understood the attraction of creating something from nothing. He'd told her so himself.

"Is that why you want to go to Europe? To prowl the museums?"

His question had her turning toward him, curiosity washing away the caution she should have felt at confiding in him. She hadn't mentioned the purpose of her trip to a single soul. No one would understand that it was like a pilgrimage to her. It even sounded crazy to herself when she thought of it that way. She knew her family and friends would understand her wanting to see the Louvre and Bargello. Millions of tourists flocked through those famous museums every year. But they would never comprehend why she would want to waste her time sitting for hours studying *Winged Victory* or *David* when she could be experiencing the sights, the sidewalk cafés and the shopping.

"Yes," she quietly admitted. "That's exactly why."

Nick didn't even blink. He just absently flicked at a piece of flaking paint on the porch between them and said, "That's really the only way to do it. You can study all the books and pictures you want, but nothing can take the place of studying the real thing."

She flicked at a piece of paint, too. No amount of explanation would have made her family understand. Yet Nick had understood with no explanation at all.

"So why do you keep canceling your trip if it's something you really want to do?"

With a shrug, she tried to fit the brittle fleck of paint she'd dislodged back into place. She'd forgotten she'd told him that. "It just hasn't worked out. Last year, Paige needed me to baby-sit so she could go to a couple of dental conventions with Darren. The year before that, Mom needed me to fill in at the realty while her receptionist was on vacation."

It wouldn't have surprised her if he told her he hoped she'd have better luck next year. Or if he assured her that she'd get there someday. Since he understood why the trip mattered to her, it stood to reason he'd know she would appreciate the implied support. But he didn't seem inclined to share his thoughts as he kept his focus on what she was doing.

She'd just given up on the fleck when he reached over and slipped his fingers under hers.

"Do you still work with clay?" he asked, picking up her hand and turning it palm-up in his.

She swallowed, aware of a flutter in her stomach as his thumb moved over the base of her fingers. "Only with my students."

He brushed the tips of her fingers, looking at her hand as if he were simply studying a tool, then frowned at a scrape on one knuckle. She'd worn gloves when she'd worked with the solvent, but her nails were bare of polish and chipped from any of the dozen tasks she'd tackled in the past few days.

Her hands didn't look at all feminine to her at the moment. And she didn't doubt for an instant that her mother would have either cringed or sighed at the sight of them and sweetly suggested they go get her a manicure. But held in his hand, her own looked small, soft and impossibly delicate.

His own hands were big, and tanned from hours of working in the sun. She would have thought he'd have calluses from all that physical work, too, and maybe a few scars from the heavy tools and boards he handled. But his wide palms were relatively smooth, and the only scrapes she noticed were still new enough to be pink.

"So you settled for passing your passion on to them?"

"My passion," she repeated, sounding as if the word were totally foreign to her.

"That's what it is, isn't it? Anything that's stayed with you as long as this has is more than just an interest."

Her grandmother had talked of passion. She'd spoken of it as easily as Nick did now, as if it were something everyone needed or pursued or possessed in some form or other.

"I don't think of it that way." Passion, she mentally repeated. The word sounded so...fiery...to her. So...emotional. It was a word to describe something a person desired to the very depths of her soul.

As a child, she'd known that fierceness, but she'd eventually learned to temper her sense of expectation. As an adult, she never dared let herself want anything that badly.

"How do you think of it, then?"

"I don't think of it at all. Not about sculpting, anyway. And you don't have to make it sound as if I allowed myself to pursue second best by teaching," she countered, catching his quick frown. *So you settled,* he'd said. That seemed so much safer to think about than want or need or desire when he was sitting so close. She pulled her hand from his, curling her fingers to hold in his heat. "I made a practical decision. It takes extraordinary talent to make it as a sculptor. And I didn't have it.''

The carved lines of his frown sharpened to a scowl. ''Art professors don't suggest apprenticeships if a student doesn't have talent. Who told you you didn't have it?'' he quietly demanded. ''Your parents?''

''Of course not.'' Her parents weren't cruel. ''Not in so many words,'' she amended, because it was impossible to look him straight in the eye and evade his question. The suggestion that she'd starve had certainly indicated her parents' lack of confidence in her abilities. ''They were only thinking of my future when they pointed out that it would take years to gain the expertise I'd need. Since I needed more training and couldn't get it and a teaching degree at the same time, I decided not to bother with it at all.''

''What about doing it for the pleasure of it?''

''Because there wasn't any pleasure in it anymore,'' she said before she could think about what she was admitting. ''All I could see were my mistakes.''

She gave a chagrined little laugh as she shook her head. She felt exposed and a little embarrassed by her failing. And a little puzzled by how easily she'd shared it. ''I have no idea why I'm telling you this. I'm not sure why we're talking about it at all. It's not like any of it matters anymore.''

''Maybe you're talking about it because it does matter to you,'' he suggested, his tone utterly matter-of-fact. ''It's easy to lose enthusiasm for something when you're not getting any support. Real desire gets past that, though.''

He took her hand again, cradling it in his the way he had before. Looking as if he might be imagining how she would hold and shape her clay, he again traced her fingers with his. ''Maybe the real reason you quit was because

there was something more that you needed. Some...
thing," he emphasized, "that kept you from pushing past
your parents' resistance. Or maybe," he proposed, as little
licks of heat raced from her arm to her belly, "the timing
was just all wrong."

She couldn't begin to imagine what she might have
needed, or how she could possibly have plowed past her
parents' admittedly logical conclusions. Not with him
playing with her hand. He touched her as if the contact
were the most natural thing in the world. What disturbed
her was that it felt natural to her, too.

"There's another possibility," she pointed out, her
voice quiet and blessedly steady

"What's that?"

"Maybe it just wasn't meant to be."

His motions stilled as he met her eyes. The soft beat of
the rain surrounded them, seeming to close them inside
their little space on the sheltering porch. Or maybe, she
thought, her breath stalling when his glance drifted to her
mouth, the sound seemed to close everything else out.

She should move. The admonishment registered vaguely
in the back of her mind, along with the admission that she
should have pulled away long before now. But moving
wasn't possible. Held by a need that had been there far
longer than she cared to consider, it was all she could do
to breathe.

"There are definitely some things beyond a person's
control, Amy." He spoke her name quietly, his deep voice
flowing over her as he lifted his hand and tucked the short
strands of her hair behind her ear. "But a career doesn't
have to be one of them."

Her heart bumped her ribs at his gentle touch. "What
about yours?" He had no business questioning her decisions. He had no business jerking around with her heart

rate, either. But as long as he was, she felt entitled to know why he hadn't fought for his own aspirations. "What happened that you quit? You said being an architect was important to you."

"It's still important. And I didn't quit." Not at all concerned that she'd thought he had, he trailed his fingers along the curve of her jaw. "I just took a leave from the firm to work with Uncle Mike until his company is out of debt." Soft, he thought. He'd never felt anything as soft as her skin. "Aunt Kate wants him to retire." Totally distracted, he let his thumb slip just below the mesmerizing fullness of her lower lip. "I'm working on a small project for the firm in my spare time."

Her breath fanned his fingers as she whispered a quiet "Oh."

He hadn't known how badly he'd wanted to touch her until he'd found himself reaching for her hand. Had she hesitated at all at the contact, had she withdrawn or done anything to indicate that he was making her uncomfortable, he would have let her go and settled for conversation to satisfy his inescapable curiosity about her. He hadn't been able to get her out of his head. The girl she'd been. The woman she'd become. But she'd allowed his touch. Her breath had caught at it.

Just as it had the other day.

Just as it had seconds ago.

She wasn't immune to him. The knowledge enticed him, pulling him closer as he curved his fingers around the back of her neck.

Amy felt his mouth touch hers. His lips were firm and cool, and for the space of a few uneven heartbeats she remained utterly still. Something warm was gathering in the pit of her stomach. The sensation spread outward, radiating through her limbs like liquid honey as the pressure of his lips slowly increased.

That lulling, languorous feeling turned to a spear of pure heat when she opened to him, and his tongue slipped inside her mouth.

A faint moan sounded in her throat. With that sigh of need, her fingers curled around his biceps. But she'd no sooner leaned closer than his hands cupped her elbows and he slowly pulled her to her knees.

Gripping his shoulders to balance herself, lost in the intimate kiss, she felt his hands slide up her back and his fingers slip into her hair. Holding her head in his hands, he drew her deeper, plundering, exploring, urging her to explore, too.

She couldn't believe what she was doing. She was on her knees, leaning over him, kissing him as thoroughly as he was kissing her. She couldn't believe what she was feeling, either. Forgotten longings raced to the surface, released by his touch, urged on by the hunger she felt tensing the muscles in his big body as he shaped the curve of her hip, her waist, her ribs. His breath filled her lungs, flowing inside her, becoming part of her, and when he nudged her chin up to trail his lips down her neck and his fingers brushed the taut buds of her breasts before his mouth closed over hers once more, she knew she'd never in her life been kissed the way Nick was kissing her now.

Lightning. Nick felt as if he'd been struck by it. Sharp, hot and devastating, heat raced through him. He hadn't expected that raw sense of hunger. He hadn't expected need to escalate so rapidly. But he'd tasted her sweetness, breathed in her scent and by the time he'd swallowed her small, kittenish moan, all he'd wanted was to strip her naked and roll her beneath him.

That he was thinking about doing just that was the very

reason he gritted his teeth against the hunger clawing low in his gut and skimmed his hands to her waist when what he really wanted to do was slide them under her shirt. That was also why he didn't draw her back when she slowly lifted her head.

Her breathing was ragged, her mouth damp. There was something incredibly erotic about seeing his moisture on her mouth and knowing it was his touch that had so thoroughly altered her breathing. But she'd done a number on him, too. With his heart hammering in his chest, he wasn't feeling all that steady, either.

He also wasn't feeling too good about himself at the moment.

His fingers flexed at her waist. "I don't suppose I should have done that."

She edged back, her hand sliding from his shoulder. "No," she whispered, her eyes dark, her breath trembling. "I don't suppose I should have, either."

He pulled his hand from her waist, letting it rest on her knee when she sank back. For long moments he sat unmoving, his eyes searching hers. She looked shaken, uneasy, though she was doing her best to hide it.

Running her fingers through her hair, she finally edged away, drew herself to her feet and moved to the gap in the railing to face the rain.

A few long moments later, wishing he'd left well enough alone, he slowly rose.

Curiosity had driven him. An old curiosity that had been fed by old memories and his constant awareness of the fact that she was no longer seventeen. But he hadn't been prepared for the guileless way she'd responded to him, or the aching need that guaranteed a long and restless night.

It was as clear as the caution clouding her eyes when

he came up beside her that her response to him had thrown her, too.

"The blue is gone," he said.

"What?"

"The sky." Nodding toward the ceiling of solid gray, he pushed his hands into his pockets to keep from reaching for her again. He should have kept them there to begin with. There was no chance of a relationship between the two of them. And as undeniably appealing as the thought was, sex with her was out of the question. Any man with an ounce of integrity—or a sense of self-preservation—didn't mess around with his ex-fiancée's little sister then move on, which was exactly what he would do when he finished his commitment there. Getting involved would only cause problems for them both. "This doesn't look like it's going to let up soon after all.

"Listen, Amy," he said, watching her cross her arms to look toward the trees herself. "I'm going to go. I'm not going to get any work done here and I have things I can do at my uncle's."

She lifted her chin, hugging herself a little tighter. She didn't look cold to him now. Her stance looked purely protective. "The project you're doing for your firm in your spare time?"

"That, too," he said. "I was thinking mostly of finishing the layout for your grandmother. I got a good idea of what she needs after we talked last night. Now it's just a matter of plugging the measurements into the computer and doing a little tweaking. It's a pretty simple project."

Compared to what he usually did, she thought. Without the distraction of his touch, she was beginning to appreciate the implications of what he'd told her a while ago, and to understand why he looked so tired. He wasn't working for his uncle as an employee. He was helping the man get ahead so he could retire. When he wasn't exhausting himself with that, he was doing his own work on the side.

"I have an appointment with your grandmother at noon tomorrow," he continued, sliding his hand into the front pocket of his jeans for his keys. "Do you want to be there when I show her what we came up with?"

"If you think it would help," she replied.

"It will. Mike's company can use this job. I'll take any help I can to get it."

Mike, she reminded herself. He was doing this for his uncle. Just as she was doing what she felt she had to do for her grandmother. "Then I'll be there."

"Good. I'll see you then."

He wasn't going to touch her again. He was going to turn and walk away and pretend that nothing at all had happened between them. It was best, really, she told herself, because getting involved with him made no sense at all. Even if her family didn't regard him as one step removed from pond scum, the man had serious commitment issues when it came to women.

"Great," she murmured, and watched him hesitate long enough for the muscle in his jaw to tighten before he jumped off the porch and ducked his dark head against the softly falling rain.

It was a moment before she moved, though. Just before he'd turned, she could have sworn she glimpsed the same hint of regret she'd seen in his eyes when they'd spoken of how some things simply weren't meant to be.

Chapter Five

Amy was running late when she hurried through the doors of the Cedar Lake Nursing Home at twelve-fifteen the next day. She would have been on time if she hadn't stopped to get gas, but the woman in the car behind her had turned out to be JoBeth Chandler, who'd had the locker next to her all through high school. There had been so much to catch up on that they'd barely started talking before Amy realized she was late, but she'd promised JoBeth, who was now JoBeth Watson since she'd married Bud Watson, whom she'd gone with since fourth grade, that she'd meet her a week from Saturday evening for a girls' night out. According to JoBeth there was gossip to share and, being generous with that sort of thing, she'd call Tina Ashworth and Judy Jamison, also friends from high school, so they could all get together and share it.

Amy was all for catching up with her friends. She was looking forward to the evening, too. Gossip, however, she could live without. Heaven only knew how their little grapevine would buzz if they ever discovered that she'd sat on her grandmother's porch yesterday, getting up close and very personal with her sister's ex-fiancé.

Just the thought of Nick put an odd little knot in her stomach. She couldn't tell if it was anxiety or anticipation, but the fact that she'd suffered a complete lack of resistance to the man was something she'd been grappling with all morning. For a number of reasons, not the least of which were loyalty to her sister and the man's admitted allergy to commitment, she should be putting up walls with him. Not baring parts of herself she never exposed to anyone else.

The fact that she'd been putty in his hands wasn't doing much for her state of mind at the moment, either. All he'd had to do was kiss her and she'd pretty much been all over him. She'd been preoccupied all morning with that disturbing phenomenon. Which was why, as she approached the door of her grandmother's room, it only now occurred to her that she hadn't noticed Nick's truck in the parking lot.

Nick wasn't even there.

But her mother was.

From the doorway of her grandma's room, Amy saw the back of Susan Chapman's perfectly cut blond wedge and almost turned on her heel. Nick wasn't there, but he would be any minute, and the last place she wanted to be was in the same room with him and her mother. The fact that her grandmother caught her eye the moment she saw her hesitate and frowned as if to say, "Don't you dare" immediately canceled any thought of escape.

Automatically straightening her shoulders so her mom wouldn't remind her not to slouch, she stepped into the room. With any amount of luck, her mother would be gone before Nick arrived. Unless, she thought, giving Bea an uneasy smile before she glanced toward where her mom was fussing with the plants on the windowsill, he'd already been there, and her mother had sent him packing.

"…what the rush is all about," her mom was saying as she snapped a yellowed leaf from a potted pathos. "If adding on is still what you really want to do, we can talk about it in the fall when I have time to make the arrangements. In the meantime," she continued, decapitating another stem, "you've put Amy in the position of having to deal with someone who has about as much character as an alley cat."

"Hi, Mom."

Caught middiatribe, her mother glanced over her shoulder. She had appointments today. Amy could tell because she was wearing one of her power suits, a tailored ivory with taupe lapels that made her look efficient and capable and played up her delicate coloring beautifully. Crumpling a handful of withered blooms and yellowed leaves, she pinched her rose tinted mouth just before she sighed.

"I can't believe you've gone along with this, Amy," she accused by way of greeting. The spent vegetation landed atop the crumpled tissues in the wastebasket. Clearly distressed, she turned back to her task. "I know you don't want to be disrespectful of your grandmother," she assured her. "I don't mean to be disrespectful, either," she explained to the woman in the bright turquoise bed jacket, "but this simply isn't acceptable. We welcomed that man into our family. We treated him like a son. Then he practically left Paige standing at the altar while he ran off after some…some…other woman," she concluded, because it wasn't proper to call people names.

The high coil of Bea's braided bun gleamed like platinum in the overhead lights. "He did give her a month's notice," she calmly reminded her daughter.

"Notice?" Amy's mother swung around, exasperation written plainly in her perfectly made up features. Despite the frown digging furrows into her forehead, she looked amazingly youthful for fifty-three. "You make it sound as if he'd merely laid her off a job. He embarrassed her, Mother. He made her the object of speculation and pity among our friends. Worse than that, he broke her heart. I held that child while she cried until she couldn't cry anymore. She lay in my arms and sobbed like a baby, and that broke *my* heart."

She pressed her hand to her chest, her memories of that painful time abundantly clear.

"And the expense," she went on, wanting to remind her mother of all the older woman seemed to have forgotten. "You know as well as I do that we spent a small fortune on that wedding. We couldn't get back even half of the deposits, and I hate to even *think* of how much we paid for that gown."

"I remember how difficult it was, Susan." Bea's voice was placating, her elegantly weathered features totally sympathetic. "But, in all fairness, he did send Paige a check that covered everything."

"There was nothing 'fair' about any of this. And that check didn't cover the turmoil in the house for the month Paul stormed around fuming about getting stuck with all the bills. I've never seen him so upset. The way he carried on, I was afraid he was going to have a stroke, his blood pressure got so high."

"We all remember Paul's storming, dear. I think his blood pressure was highest when he'd get going about what he'd do if he ever got his hands on Nick. I believe his wish was to have him neutered."

"That was one of them," Susan muttered.

"But the boy made what amends he could."

Before her mom could voice her disapproval over her mother's defense of the man, Amy edged up to the foot of the bed. "Has he been here?"

"Your father?" her mom said, turning an uncomprehending frown on her.

"Nick."

"No," Bea told her. "He called a bit ago and said he would be late. He had to take one of their workers to the emergency room for stitches."

"That's another thing," Susan declared. Since she wasn't getting anywhere with her mother, she turned to her daughter. "We have hardly any information at all about Culhane Contracting."

"Nick's uncle owns it."

"That much I do know," her mother replied. "It was Fallon-Culhane Contracting until last year. And their reputation was fine. I have clients who'd used them. But I have no idea how good the company is now that the other partner is gone and Nick has moved in.

"Honestly, Amy," she continued, her agitation showing as she abandoned the plants to straighten a perfectly straight blanket at the bottom of the bed, "I couldn't believe it when Paige told me what was going on here. You going along with Grandma's idea to add on to her house is causing trouble enough. But agreeing to work with Nick just isn't like you at all. You're usually so sensible."

There had been a time when Amy would have cringed at her mother's last words. She couldn't count the times growing up that she'd been admonished to be reasonable, be practical, be *sensible,* which invariably meant that whatever she was doing or whatever idea she had just voiced was either too outrageous or impractical to warrant further discussion.

Like the time she'd wanted to join the Cub Scouts when she was eight because she thought the stuff the boys got to do was neater than what the girls got stuck with. Or when she was ten years old and wanted to cover her bedroom wall with a wallpaper mural of the San Francisco skyline at night. There had been something magical to her about all those lovely lights. But her mother's immediate response had been to "be sensible, Amy. Little girls don't have things like that on their walls. How about a nice pink rosebud print? Or something with butterflies?"

"I am being sensible." She truly was. The trait was now too ingrained for her to question it. "Grandma is going to get her addition built with or without our help. It will be easier on her if I take care of the details she can't handle right now."

"Amy," her mother said in that flat way that made her feel all of twelve years old, "you've completely missed the point. The company she has chosen may not be the best available for the job. On top of that, the man working that job has not exactly endeared himself to this family. Then there's the fact that without your help, she wouldn't be moving forward right now at all. We need to consider what's truly best for your grandmother."

Behind her silver-rimmed glasses, Bea's eyes flashed with impatience.

"Susan," she began, her tone echoing the chiding one her daughter had used with her own offspring. "I know you have my best interests at heart, but I happen to know the best thing for me is to leave here. I'm going home. And I promise, neither you nor Paige will be inconvenienced by my decision."

Color suffused Susan's cheeks. "This isn't only about

what's convenient," she defended. "You were getting around fine when you fell, and look what happened to you. How will you manage on a walker?"

"I'll be safe," Bea assured her, calmly dismissing the rationalization she'd heard a dozen times by now. "I've told you before, when Amy leaves I'll hire whatever help I need. I've lived in that house for sixty years. I have every intention of dying there."

"You're not dying, Mother."

"I didn't say I was doing it right now." Chiding turned to annoyance. "I have every intention of living for at least another decade. Two, if you don't stop treating me like a child. Now," she continued, letting her threat sink in, "as for who's doing the construction work, I doubt it would matter which company I decided to use. Once you accepted the idea that I'm going on with this project, you would have found something wrong with any contractor I hired."

Susan's mouth dropped open as she prepared to deny the assertion.

Bea didn't give her the chance. "You know you tend to take over, Susan," she informed her daughter, her voice low as she pointed out what the entire family accepted as fact. "You'd want to pick the company yourself. Which would be fine with me because I hate messing with these sorts of details. But I know how busy you are right now, and I didn't want to wait until fall or whenever it was you'd have time to do it.

"I don't want to argue with you about using Nick, either," she quietly informed her. "There isn't anyone in this family more aware of what he did than I am. And I'm certain he's well aware of our family's reservations about him. That's one of the reasons I'm inclined to hire him.

Under the circumstances, I'm sure he'll be very careful in both his personal and professional dealings with us.''

Her amazingly casual glance cut past Amy's shoulder. "Won't you, Nick?"

Amy felt her heart hitch an instant before she turned to see the man under discussion filling the doorway. Nick had either cleaned up after he'd left the construction site or he'd spent the morning doing something other than swinging a hammer. The khaki shirt covering his broad shoulders was neatly pressed and rolled to his elbows. His jeans, though worn, were clean, and sometime between kissing her senseless yesterday and the trip to the emergency room that had made him late, he'd stopped somewhere for a haircut.

He looked very big, very handsome, and he sounded as cautious as he looked. "Yes, Mrs. Gardner. Very careful."

The muscles in his jaw tightened as his glance left the elderly woman carefully watching him, skimmed past where Amy crossed her arms over the knot jumping in her stomach and settled on the woman who'd gone as stiff as a plank.

"Mrs. Chapman," he said, acknowledging his ex-fiancée's mother with a hesitant nod. "I didn't realize we'd all be meeting for this."

"We're not." Susan, her voice understandably cool, mirrored her daughter's stance. Only, the way Amy's arms were crossed made it look as if she were protecting herself. The way Susan snugged her arms beneath her breasts made it clear she was simply shutting him out. "I'm not part of this."

Nick carried a long paper tube. As he tightened his fingers around it, his glance shifted from the middle-aged woman who clearly wished he'd turn to dust and blow away and settled uncertainly on the woman studying him from the bed.

Amy could only imagine how awkward he must feel. She felt horribly awkward herself just being there as her mother turned toward the window. What wasn't being said was glaringly obvious. There were no polite amenities. No inquiries about family or mannerly comments about how well the other looked or how good it was to see him or her after all these years. It wasn't good. It was uncomfortable and distressing and Amy honestly couldn't blame her mom for literally turning her back on him.

Her parents had both been crazy about Nick. As her mom had said only moments ago, they'd treated him like a son, welcoming him into their family, their home, only to have him hurt and fail their daughter. And as Amy had considered herself only a couple of days ago, by doing that, he'd betrayed their trust in him, too.

"I think it might be best if I come back later."

Bea displayed no compassion toward him whatsoever. "I'd prefer to do this now," she countered, smoothing the sheet at the waist of her bright bed jacket. "Push that tray table over here for me and show me what you have."

It occurred to Amy that if her grandmother had wanted to put him in a position where he'd have to squirm, she had just rather neatly accomplished it. From the way Bea was watching him, it seemed she knew it, too—and that she was waiting to see what he would do. He could either escape the hostility permeating the room and risk displeasing a client. Or he could stick out the discomfort and protect a possible additional job for his uncle's company.

Amy could have sworn she felt the tension radiating from his body as loyalty to his uncle won, and he passed behind her. His features ruthlessly composed, he stopped at the side of the bed and adjusted the tray table in front of a strangely satisfied-looking Bea.

She was fairly certain Nick could think of about a thousand other places he'd rather be right then. Yet he didn't seem at all rushed as he opened the end of the tube and pulled out the drawings he'd prepared. There was almost an air of resignation about him, as if his sense of obligation and affection wouldn't allow his own desires to get in the way of doing what he knew he had to do.

As if he were reading her mind, he flicked her a glance, then looked toward her mom as he spread his plans in front of Bea.

"I brought two designs," he said, anchoring the stacked sheets with a water pitcher on one side and the television's remote control on the other to keep the edges from curling. "One for an addition off the east side of the house, which you would access off the main downstairs hall. And one that encloses the back porch and creates another porch beyond it similar to what you have now."

Tipping back her head to see through the lower portion of her glasses, Bea carefully studied the sheet in front of her. Without looking up, she asked, "Do you agree with Amy that closing in the porch is the better way to go?"

"If time is a consideration, yes, I do. The county doesn't require a permit to enclose a porch, but you will need one for new construction. This time of year, it could take months to get one."

"Have you seen this, Amy?" Bea inquired.

"Not yet."

"Then you might want to look at it, too. I imagine this was your idea. These windows here," she said, tapping one brightly polished nail on the area that represented a new hallway. "I like that. It would let in a lot of the light."

Amy moved to the side of the bed opposite Nick. He'd

taken the side that put his back to her mother. Deliberately, she was sure.

"Actually," she murmured, avoiding his glance as she looked at what her grandmother indicated, "multiple windows were Nick's idea. I'd only suggested one because I thought a hallway along there would be too dark."

"She was right." Nick touched the closed end of his gold pen to the paper. His initials winked from the clip. "You need this hallway to keep from having to go through your new bedroom to get from the kitchen to the back door. Without the windows, the only light would be artificial and the space would be claustrophobic. This way, you have light, a view of the trees and the hall feels open. With this wall and door here," he continued, tapping at a line across from the windows, "you have privacy in this whole area."

"My new bedroom."

"Correct."

Turning her head, Amy pointed to an angled line. "What's this?"

"That's a second door from the bedroom. We talked about needing access to the bathroom in the back hall."

"I thought you were going to put it between these two windows."

"You said she'd probably want to put her dresser there, remember?"

"Oh. Right." They'd actually come up with and discarded several options before the candle had sputtered out. "I like that you added a new porch."

"You said it needed to be there."

She looked up then, puzzled because she didn't remember such a discussion at all. "I did?"

"Yeah," he murmured. "You did." His blue eyes held hers, his expression as guarded as she felt. It stayed that way as his glance dropped to her lips, lingering there long enough to make her pulse skip at the memory of his mouth moving over hers, before calmly meeting her eyes once more. "You said you couldn't imagine the house without the back porch. That's why I added one."

He was remembering, too. She was sure of it. Once more his glance grazed her upturned face, only to jerk to his plans. The memory of how she'd opened to him was obviously more than he wanted to deal with just then. Or, more likely, considering how he'd viewed what he'd done as a mistake, it was a memory he didn't want to deal with at all.

"Of course, anything here can be changed," he assured his client, his businesslike tone betraying nothing. "The present porch can certainly be enclosed without adding a new one."

Pointedly ignoring how the knot in her stomach doubled, Amy watched her grandmother's curious glance shift from one side of the bed to the other.

"I can't imagine it without the back porch, either," Bea agreed mildly. "It would need to be screened-in, of course. Like the porch is now." She sat straighter, leaning forward to see past the big man blocking her view of her daughter. "Are you sure you don't want to look at this, Susan?"

The woman beside the plant-lined window said nothing. Had anyone else presented remodeling plans to her mother, Amy knew her mom would have been right there, making sure her mother was getting exactly what she wanted. But she was angry with Nick, upset by his presence. And she was angry with her mother, too.

A twinge of sympathy tugged at Amy. Her mom and her grandmother had always seemed like polar opposites to her. Much as she was the opposite of her mother, herself. But it had only been since her grandmother had broken her hip that she'd known her mother to really argue with Bea. Bea had always seemed so invincible, like a force that would simply always exist. But the fall had made them all realize just how vulnerable Grandma was, and that she wouldn't be around forever.

Amy couldn't help but wonder if the reason her mom had turned so testy was because she was scared.

Susan crossed to the bed, her heels tapping reluctantly on the shiny beige floor. "Where's this hall you're talking about?" she dutifully asked, doing what she could to placate the woman who was undoubtedly adding more gray hair to the collection she was already growing.

Letting her mom take her place, Amy stepped back. She had the feeling from the curious glances her grandmother bounced between her and Nick that she had picked up on both the cooperation and the heavy sense of caution existing between the two of them. Her mother, however, seemed blessedly oblivious to any tension other than her own.

Amy could only imagine how disappointed and upset she would be if she knew the reason her daughter was so tense herself was that she'd found herself drawn to the one man she was expected to disdain. The fact that he wasn't interested in her was irrelevant. Just knowing she was attracted to him made her feel like a traitor.

"Don't you think so, Amy?" her mother asked.

Amy's head snapped up. "I'm sorry. What did you say?"

"I said that it wouldn't hurt to look at another design or two. This is workable, but there might be a configuration that Grandma will like better."

"I'd be happy to work out something else, Mrs. Chapman."

At Nick's remark, Amy saw her mother's lips pinch. "I

was thinking that perhaps she'd want to see what someone else had in mind.''

Bea refused to let silence magnify her daughter's slight.

"I like this one," she pronounced. "How long would it take to build it?"

Nick was too controlled to look uncomfortable, but there was a definite hint of vigilance in the way he glanced from Susan to Bea. "I wouldn't be able to start on it until next week. Then it'll take me three, maybe four weeks to get it finished."

"And the cost?"

Paper rustled as he pulled a small sheet from between the two larger ones. "This breakdown includes hardwood for the hallway, but not the flooring for the bedroom. I mentioned to Amy that it's sometimes more difficult to get around with a wheelchair or a walker on carpeting, so you may want to look at some other options before you make a final decision about that."

Paper rustled as Bea took the sheet of neat figures from him. After considering his calculations for all of ten seconds, she handed it back. "This is fine. Just bring me whatever it is I need to sign. Can you give Amy flooring samples?"

"Certainly."

"Good. Then, Amy," she said, arching an eyebrow in her direction, "you can bring me the samples, and we'll figure out where to go from there. But I'll want some sort of carpet in there, too. An area rug. Something blue. Not some pale washed-out shade. Something with some character to it."

"I can do that." Nick was going to be around for a while. The thought made her heart sink even as it gave a betraying little leap. "I'll have the samples by the time you come home. It'll only be a few more days before the ramp is finished.''

"You'll have to bring the samples here. If it's only going to be a few weeks before my new room is ready, I think I'll just stay put. I wasn't looking forward to having my bed in the living room, anyway.''

Amy saw her mother blink in confusion. "I thought you were in a hurry to get home?''

"Me, too," Amy added, mirroring her mother's surprise.

Apparently sensing that now was as good a time as any to cut and run, Nick reached for his drawings. "Do you have any questions I can answer for you, Mrs. Gardner?''

"Not at the moment." Their business concluded, she helped expedite his departure by moving aside the water pitcher for him. "I'm sure you have other work to do, so I won't keep you. Is your worker going to be all right?''

"Yes, ma'am. It was just a small wire cut. I'll pick him up on the way back." Rolling the wide sheets, he slipped them into the tube. "Thanks again.''

He eyed the door, his muscles bunching with the thought that relief was only twenty feet away. The desire to bolt was strong, but before he took a single step his eyes sought Amy's.

She stood a couple of feet from her mother, who stood a couple of feet from hers. If there was any resemblance between the three of them, it totally escaped him at the moment. With the other two women watching his every move, he was aware only of how tightly Amy's arms were crossed and how her lovely brown eyes faltered from his.

Certain that what he'd done yesterday was responsible for much of her discomfort with him at the moment, he slid his glance to the woman in the trim ivory suit, who reminded him very much of Paige.

Since Susan Chapman was looking at him with all the warmth of a Popsicle, he gave her a nod so he wouldn't appear rude and headed for the door.

The murmur of hushed female voices followed him into the wide, welcoming hall. Over the rattle of a lunch cart, he heard Amy ask her grandmother again if she was sure she wanted to wait so long to go home. Right on top of that came the exasperated tones of Susan Chapman's voice. She wanted know how on earth they expected him to convert a porch to a bedroom in only three or four weeks, when it was taking him all of this week just to build a ramp.

"I told Mom the reason it was taking you so long to build the ramp is because you're only able to work on it in your spare time. I also told her that I'm sure you'll get the porch converted in the time you said you will," Amy said, keeping her report completely matter-of-fact. "She said she didn't see how."

"The job will be finished on time." Nick muttered the defensive promise from where he crouched ten feet out from the side porch. "What else was said?"

"Nothing that changed anything. Mom still isn't happy with Grandma."

"It's me she's not happy with."

Toying with the paint rag in her hands, Amy watched the little lines in Nick's forehead deepen in concentration as he lined up a length of wood. She'd been working on the back porch with the kitchen door open when she'd heard him knock on the French doors a few moments ago. When she'd answered, he'd asked her what had happened after he'd left the nursing home and promptly returned to the task the rain had caused him to abandon yesterday.

Judging from the rigid set of his jaw, his encounter with her mother had been on his mind all day.

"Can you blame her for not being happy with you?" she asked mildly.

"I never said I blamed anyone." The wood clattered against another board he'd measured as he tossed it aside and rose, knees cracking, to retrieve the metal brackets he'd set on the porch. "I just wondered if she'd talked your grandmother out of using the company. I don't want to do the paperwork tonight if she's just going to tell me she changed her mind. Mrs. Gardner seems pretty stubborn, but your mom's a pretty formidable woman herself."

Her mother would be pleased to know he thought so. "She didn't change Grandma's mind," she quietly assured him. "She stopped trying after I told her how you'd gone out of your way to do this because you knew Grandma was anxious to come home. Grandma told her that, too," she said, remembering how impressed the elderly woman had been when Amy had mentioned his thoughtfulness to her. Impressed, but, strangely, not at all surprised. "I think Mom has realized that Grandma is determined to come home, and that she's going to stick with anyone willing to help her get here."

"No matter who it is," he muttered tightly.

Amy stiffened. On her way back from the nursing home that afternoon, she had decided that the only way to get through the next few weeks would be to remain as impartial as she possibly could, to simply divorce herself from the personalities and problems involved and just handle what she was handed without letting anyone get to her. In theory, the approach sounded eminently practical. Reasonable. Sensible.

In practice, it was going to take…practice.

"I'd apologize for the way she acted, Nick, but I can

understand why she feels the way she does. You should cut her some slack.''

It was because she could understand her mother's position that she couldn't be totally sympathetic to Nick's defensiveness just then. But she couldn't blame him for feeling the way he did, either—which made her feel as if she was being yanked in two different directions, neither one of which particularly appealed to her at the moment.

Telling herself that the last thing she wanted to do was argue with him, she turned on her heel. Arguing would mean going into why her mom felt the way she did, which would mean bringing up Paige and all the emotional issues he was so well aware of anyway, and she didn't want to think about what he'd once shared with her sister.

The level he was working with hit the ground a moment before she heard the impatient thud of his boots on the porch. She was at the threshold of the dining-room door when his hand closed around her arm.

''Hey.'' Nick deliberately softened his voice, forcing the edge from it as best he could. She didn't deserve his irritation. Especially when he considered what she had done for him. When she'd answered her mother's comment about why it was taking him so long to get the ramp finished, she'd done more than simply respond to a question. She'd defended him. To her mother. The knowledge surprised him, touched him. And that made it that much harder for him to remember that he'd meant to keep his hands to himself.

''I'm not saying she isn't justified. It was a bad situation with Paige, and I caused it. I know it was my fault,'' he said flatly. ''But that doesn't mean I have to like how she treated me today.''

His blunt admission disarmed her—the acceptance in it,

the total lack of blame. So did the proprietary feel of his hold.

"I don't imagine it was the most pleasant experience you've ever had."

"I'll get over it." His thumb brushed the small curve of her bicep. "How about you?" he asked, his frustration fading a little more from his tone. "I know your mom is upset with you for helping your grandmother, too. It couldn't have made her any happier when you stuck up for me." Genuine interest flickered in the depths of his eyes. "Are you doing all right?"

The question surprised her as much as the concern she heard behind it. "She wasn't exactly thrilled with me," she admitted, caught off guard by that concern. She was usually the one making sure everyone was all right. It wasn't often that anyone thought to ask how she was handling whatever was going on. "I think she was a little shocked."

Understatement seemed to be the better part of valor at the moment. There was no reason to tell him that what her mom had actually said was that she thought it terrible enough that Grandma tended to defend Nick. But she found it totally incomprehensible that Amy would do such a thing herself.

With a tired little sigh, she let her glance drop from the carved lines of his face to the soft khaki covering his broad chest. She knew from balancing herself against his shoulders how very solid he was. But she didn't know how it felt to be held against him. The way he'd pulled her up in front of him when he'd kissed her hadn't allowed her the luxury of being held in his arms, of feeling the strong, steady beat of his heart against her own.

Drawn by the thought, feeling cheated by it, she touched her fingers to his pocket. "I just keep telling myself that what she's really upset about is the situation. Grandma has never had any problems before, and I think the idea of her getting old and frail frightens her."

"I can't picture that woman frail."

A smile touched her mouth. "Me, either."

Beneath the soft fabric she felt hard muscle move with every breath he drew. Along the inside of her arm she felt the slow caress of his thumb.

"You didn't answer my question," he quietly reminded her. "Are you all right?"

She glanced up, past the strong line of his neck, the five-o'clock shadow darkening the lean angle of his jaw, and met his hooded eyes. He wasn't talking only about how she was dealing with her family. She realized that the moment she saw him watching her mouth and felt the quick bump of his heart beneath her hand. He was referring to what had happened between them yesterday. The kiss that shouldn't have happened but had, and which had made her feel even more conflicted when he'd walked into her grandmother's room.

"I'm fine," she said, finding it easier to lie to his chest than his face. "Really."

For a moment, she thought he might force her hand and tell her he didn't believe her. He had the uncanny knack of perceiving far more than she thought she let on. He also had a way of pushing her until she found herself remembering long-ago desires that weren't at all sensible and soul-deep needs she'd never dared acknowledge. But after remaining silent long enough to make her think he'd considered what happened the last time he'd pushed for more, he opted to play it safe.

"Listen," he murmured, his thumb still moving against her arm, "I appreciate that you explained why this part of the job isn't going as fast as it could. But it might be a good idea if you didn't defend me around your mom again. I don't want her angry with you because of me. I don't imagine you do, either.''

The memory of his hands on her skin was enough to heat it. Just the thought of the hunger she'd felt in him was enough to arouse it in her. But it wasn't memory warming her just then. It was the heat of his palm seeping into her, the gentle way he caressed her. And despite the way his words only confirmed the distance they needed to keep between them, they also managed to keep her right where she was.

The thought that she didn't want to pull away suddenly made her conscious of the unquestioning way they were touching each other. Unnerved by it, amazed by how right it felt, she dropped her hand and stepped back.

He made no attempt to stop her.

"Of course not," she murmured, watching him curl his fingers at his side.

"I didn't think so." He stepped back himself. "I'd better get to work."

"Me, too."

"Still stripping cabinets?"

With a nod, she lifted the rag. "I have five more to go, then I can start sanding."

"Let me know when you get there, and I'll loan you something that'll make the job easier."

He gave her a smile then. Not much of one. But it was enough to let her know he didn't want to upset the truce the two of them had somehow managed. So she smiled back, just enough to let him know she didn't want to upset it, either, and told him she most definitely would.

Chapter Six

"That man said I had to ask you for more lemonade, Aunt Amy."

"That man did, huh?"

Brittany gave a decisive nod. "Yep."

That man was Nick. He'd arrived ten minutes ago to finish the ramp. Five minutes after that, Amy had hollered across the yard and asked if he would keep an eye on the two little girls at the picnic table just long enough for her to find the tire pump. With the water so close, she didn't want to leave them unsupervised.

He hadn't hesitated. He'd just called back, "No problem," and promptly hauled the new hand rail he was sanding away from the porch so he could watch the children while he worked.

"Why do you need more?" Amy now asked her niece, wondering if he suspected that the children were Paige's. "I just took the pitcher over there."

From where Brittany stood in the doorway of her great-grandma Bea's storage shed, she gave a shrug, then pulled up the strap of her lavender bathing suit. "It spilled."

Terrific, Amy mentally muttered. "Okay, honey," she said with a forgiving smile. "You wanted more air in the beach ball. Let me take care of that first."

With a mumbled, "'Kay," her oldest niece turned on the heel of her pink flowered sandals. Two steps later, she whirled right back around, her long blond ponytail flying. "I forgot. That man wants a washcloth. And a bandage and that stuff that kills germs."

Amy turned from the shelves of gardening supplies and old yard toys. Lemonade could wait. A request for first aid supplies sounded a tad more urgent. Abandoning her search, she stepped from the small dim space into the side yard. "What happened?"

"Sarah fell. She was hitting the birdie and Pete took it and he chased her and she tripped."

Pete was their dog. When Amy had told Paige she'd watch the girls for her while she did the last-minute running around for her dinner party that evening, she hadn't considered that her sister would bring the dog, too. But Paige had dropped off the energetic golden retriever with the girls at ten o'clock that morning, along with their backpacks stuffed with the books and games they'd pretty much ignored in favor of the old buckets and shovels and badminton set that had been at the house forever.

Apparently, Pete had thought Sarah was playing badminton with him.

"Is she okay?" Amy couldn't hear crying. Normally, all the younger child had to do was imagine that she was hurt, and she could carry on as if someone should be calling 9-1-1. The silence put urgency in Amy's step.

"Sure," Britt chirped. "The man got the birdie back."

Brittany clearly didn't appreciate the nature of her aunt's concern, but the urgency faded from Amy's footsteps the moment she rounded the corner of the house. Looking across the broad expanse of lush lawn, Amy could see that Sarah wasn't unconscious or sitting in a stupor, which to her were the only possible explanations for her silence. In fact, she looked fine. The man, as Britt had called Nick, had the child perched on the bench at the picnic table, and she was leaning over to peer at her knee.

A warm breeze rustled the trees and tugged at Sarah's flaxen curls. Like her sister, she was in a bathing suit. Only, hers was yellow with big white flowers. Nick was hunched in front of her, his old Manhattan Athletic Club T-shirt stretched across his broad back, and his powerful thighs encased in pale blue denim.

The little girl looked as small and delicate as a Dresden doll next to his imposingly masculine frame.

"I got an owie," the child said, her big blue eyes turning more teary when Amy stopped beside him.

"We have skid marks on a knee and a couple of scraped palms." Nick looked over, his glance running the length of Amy's legs before it jumped past her beige cargo shorts and pale yellow shirt. Giving her a distracted smile, he turned back to Sarah. "Nothing we can't survive. Right, sport?"

Not ready to be better, Sarah twisted her little mouth. "It hurts."

"Of course it does," he assured with the proper amount of sympathy. "But I bet Aunt Amy has something that can take care of that." Taking her little hands in his, Nick turned them over. Except for grass stains on the heels of her palms and a tiny scrape near one thumb, they looked fine as he held them up. "Here, Aunt Amy. Do your thing."

"My thing?"

"She needs a kiss to make it better. I figure that's your department." He glanced back to the little girl. "That is her department, isn't it?"

It was debatable as to whether or not Sarah understood the question, but her bright curls bounced as she nodded her head.

"She thinks so, too," he said to Amy, looking utterly serious.

Paige was right, Amy thought as she leaned forward to place a kiss in each little palm. The man could use a few warts. He had absolutely no business being so appealing.

"There," she murmured, trying to ignore the fact that she was inches from his head—and that he smelled of spearmint gum, aftershave and hard work. "Now let me see your knee."

Dutifully, Sarah stuck out her leg and promptly hissed in air. "Ow. Ow. Ow."

"It's okay," Amy murmured, easing the skinny appendage back down. "We'll get you inside and get this cleaned up. That'll stop the stinging. Come inside, too, Britt. I don't want you out here alone."

"Can I make the lemonade?"

"Not just yet," she replied with the ease of a woman accustomed to dealing with the multiple demands of small children. "We need to clean up that mess first." She nodded toward where a yellow insect hovered over the sticky spill at the far end of the long redwood table. She backed up, scooping Sarah into her arms and nudging Brittany with her as she did. "We're attracting wasps."

"Tell you what." Still on one knee by the bench, Nick angled toward her. "You take care of that one," he said, nodding to the child she held, "and I'll take care of this." He glanced toward the sprinkler the girls had run through earlier, then smiled easily at the little girl with the long blond ponytail eyeing him from beside her aunt.

"Can you drag that hose over here for me?" he asked Brittany.

Amy's oldest niece looked uncertainly up at her aunt. She'd done as Nick had requested of her before because her sister had been hurt and Amy had obviously trusted him when she'd left her and her sister in his temporary care. But the man was a stranger, and the child was understandably reticent about taking further instructions from him now.

Aware of the problem, Amy gave her a soft smile. "This is Mr. Culhane, Britt. He's...ah..."

"It's Nick," he corrected. "And I'm working for your great-grandma," he explained, saving Amy having to define how she regarded him. To say he was a friend would cause a swift and certain backlash for her with her family. To identify him as their mother's ex-fiancé would be to give the children information they didn't need to know. "I've known your aunt Amy since she was a kid."

Brittany's eyes brightened. "Like me?"

"Not quite that long," he admitted, remaining at eye level with her. "But I have second cousins about your age. Two of them, in fact. How old are you?" His eyes narrowed as he tipped his dark head. "Four?"

The little girl grinned.

"I'm three," Sarah piped in from her perch three feet above him.

"We know," Amy muttered, playfully tousling the girl's pale blond curls.

Beside Nick, Pete sat vibrating, his long tail whipping against the lawn like a giant windshield wiper and his long pink tongue lolling from his broad mouth. He wanted attention, too.

Rising to tower over all of them, Nick reached to absently stroke the wavy golden fur on the dog's neck. "Can you bring me the hose?" he asked Brittany once more.

Apparently deciding she could, the winsome child spun around and skipped across the lawn.

"These are Paige's kids," he said, the instant Britt was out of earshot.

Amy gave him a nod, understanding now why he'd sent the older child off. A four-year-old would pick up things in conversation that would be lost on one a year younger. For a moment, though, he said nothing else. He just glanced toward the house, his brow lowered as he checked out the porch and the windows farther along the back of the proud old structure.

"The way they were calling you Aunt Amy gave it away," he finally told her. "That, and the fact that they both look just like her." A muscle in his jaw jerked. "She isn't here, is she?"

"No. No," Amy quickly repeated, suddenly aware of why he looked so cautious. After his last reception at the nursing home, he undoubtedly preferred to be prepared for any encounters with members of the Chapman family, if not spared the experience entirely. "She's at the hair dresser and running errands before a party she's having tonight. I'll take the girls home in a couple of hours," she continued, assuring him that Paige wouldn't be coming by at all. "I'm going out to dinner tonight, so I'll drop them off on my way."

His broad shoulders visibly relaxed as his caution gave way to quick curiosity. "You're going out?"

"With old girlfriends. I'm really looking forward to it, too," she told him, hoisting Sarah in her arms to keep her from slipping. "It started out just being three of us," she expanded with a smile. "But the last I heard, it was up to eight."

"Eight women on a girls' night out? Sounds deadly."

"You only say that because you avoided large groups of females when you were young."

"My knee hurts, Aunt Amy."

"Should I turn the water on?" Brittany called, walking backward as she hauled the hose over by the sprinkler head.

Pulling her attention from the smile lighting the slivers of silver in Nick's incredibly blue eyes, telling herself she needed to stop noticing such things about him, Amy assured Sarah that they were going inside right now. Giving her another hoist, she saw Nick walk over to take the sprinkler from Britt.

The end of the child's ponytail swung at her waist as she tipped back her head. "When we're done, can you take us out in the boat?" Brittany asked him. "Aunt Amy won't do it when it's just us here."

"We've bothered Nick enough," Amy called back, stepping over a badminton racket. "But since he's here, I'll take you out in a while."

"Sorry," Nick said to the little girl hanging back with him. "I have work to do. Tell you what, though. After we wash down the table, you can help me while your aunt takes care of your little sister."

As she carried Sarah into the bathroom to clean up her scrapes, Amy had no idea how Nick planned for Britt to "help." But she wasn't at all concerned about leaving the child with him. He clearly understood children. Knew how to care for them. And though his ease with them didn't particularly surprise her because she knew how fond he was of his cousins and their families, having seen him with her nieces, she had to admit he had her truly mystified.

There had been nothing at all about him or his manner to make her think he'd wondered what the children would have been like had they been his and her sister's. He hadn't appeared bothered in the least by their parentage. But having seen how good he was with them, Amy couldn't help but wonder why he didn't have a family of his own. Why he didn't even seem to want one.

She could still remember the way he'd responded the day she'd asked if he had married the woman who'd stolen him from Paige. He'd made it abundantly clear that he didn't believe a person could steal someone from someone else, that he believed problems had to exist in a relationship for someone else to interfere. She had no problem with that. At the very least, she supposed that one of the partners needed or wanted something he or she wasn't finding in the other. But it was what he'd said after that that had truly puzzled her. She'd never heard a man sound so utterly certain as when he'd said he had no intention of marrying anyone. Ever.

Obviously there had been a time when the idea of marriage had appealed to him. So what had happened, she wondered now, to make him change his mind? Had the woman he'd been involved with when he'd left her sister done what he'd done to Paige and broken his heart? Had she hurt him so badly that he simply couldn't move on? Had some other woman betrayed him somewhere along the line?

She was certain there were those who would regard such a circumstance as poetic justice. Specific members of her family immediately came to mind. Ordinarily, she would have been inclined to think so, too. But there had never been anything ordinary with regard to how she'd thought or felt about Nick Culhane.

Banishing the unbidden thought, she deliberately forced

her attention to the child anxiously squirming to get down from the counter so she could put on a life jacket. The prospect of going out in the boat had definitely taken precedence for Sarah. Grateful for the distraction herself, Amy followed the miraculously "healed" child out of the house, told her to get her sister from where Brittany was pounding nails in a board Nick had given her, and instructed the girls to walk, not run, to the path above the dock while she got the life jackets out of the boathouse. As long as she was occupied with the tasks of rowing and keeping an eye on the children in the boat, she wouldn't have time to think about the man who'd first started messing with her heart and her mind when she was only seventeen.

He should have been finished an hour ago. He would have been finished, too, Nick told himself, if he hadn't been looking up every other minute to make sure Amy was okay out there on the lake with the girls. She hadn't specifically asked him to watch out for them, but he understood why she was hesitant to go out on the lake with the kids without someone else being aware that they were out there. She was just being responsible. Prudent. Like anyone charged with young children should be.

Still, he'd watched. While he'd sanded the side rails of the ramp before he'd attached them, he'd watched her fasten the giggling girls into their bright orange life jackets and slip on a neon green one herself. They'd then all walked out onto the wooden dock, disappeared into the boathouse and emerged a few minutes later in the little blue row dinghy emblazoned with QE II on the stern.

It was apparent that she knew what she was doing. With an ease that betrayed the strength in her slender body, Amy rowed them out a quarter of the way across the mile-wide lake, leaving Pete waiting patiently for them at the end of the dock. The big blond canine held his post as vigilantly as a sentry the entire time Amy and the girls fed the fish— which was what Nick assumed they were doing, since every once in a while one of them would toss something into the water and ripples would appear on the glassy surface when the local denizens of the deep popped up to retrieve it.

Pete was still on guard as she rowed back now with the girls sitting as still as little statues on the bench seat in front of her. The kids clearly loved being out there. He could practically see the gleam of their little white teeth.

Wiping his forehead with the back of his forearm, he moved to where he'd braced a rail at the side of the ramp. The base and nonskid surface were already in place. With Amy on her way in, he returned his attention to his task, not bothering to question the protectiveness that had kept him sidetracked. When it came to Amy, he wasn't letting himself look too closely at anything he felt toward her.

It was easier. Safer.

"Don't call him, Sarah! Sarah! No!"

The warm breeze carried Amy's urgent warning up from the water, along with an ominous splash that sounded to Nick like his cousin-in-law Bert doing a cannonball into Bert's backyard pool. A high-pitched screech, the kind only little girls are capable of producing, pierced through it all.

His hammer hit the ground. Moments later, he slowed the sprint that had carried him to the end of the house in two seconds flat and watched the dog doing what retrievers love to do.

Pete was going for a swim.

Nick's only concern as he willed his heart rate to recover from the adrenaline surge was that the dog didn't paddle out to the boat and capsize it trying to get in.

Amy was about fifty feet from shore with the girls when she pulled her attention from the dog long enough to see Nick walk across the yard and onto the weathered old dock. With his hands in the pockets of his jeans, the breeze blowing his dark hair over his forehead, he stopped at the end of the little pier to watch Pete, happy as a clam, swim circles around the boat. Brittany waved at him and giggled. Sarah simply sat with her lower lip sticking out because her aunt had yelled at her.

"Problems?" he asked, biting back a grin as he reached for the bow of the boat when it bumped the dock.

The wooden oars clattered against the deck as Amy slid them under the narrow benches. "Nothing that hasn't happened before. All it takes is for someone to motion to Pete, and he's off like a shot. He loves the water."

Hunkered down, his thighs straining against his jeans, Nick tied the rope to a rusty cleat, eyeing the dog as he swam past. Head up, eyes bright, Pete paddled to the rocks and loped onto the bank. He'd barely reached dry land when he gave a great shake, water flying, and promptly trotted toward them.

"I can tell," Nick murmured, and reached to help Brittany, his little apprentice, out of the boat.

Shoving her fingers through her wind-tangled hair, Amy held out her other hand to Sarah, who was still in full pout. "We need to leave in about half an hour," she calmly told the child, "and I didn't want to take Pete in the car when he's wet. That's why I didn't want you to call him. Okay?"

Looking like an orange pumpkin in her thickly padded gear, the three-year-old muttered a barely audible "'Kay."

"Okay," Amy echoed, wanting her to know all was forgiven. "You girls are going to have to dry him off. Then we'll change your clothes."

Water lapped against the mossy pilings as she handed the somber little girl with the shining ringlets up to Nick, who went to work on the toggles of her life jacket. Brittany had already shed hers and was running up the dock, screeching, because Pete had just given another mighty shake and sprayed her.

"Get the old towels off the back porch," Amy called after her.

Amy wasn't sure Britt had heard her. With her attention divided between the children, the dog chasing Britt because making her screech was apparently fun, and the man coaxing a smile out of Sarah, Amy forgot the towels, for the moment, anyway. Her focus had just settled on the man who looked entirely too natural taking care of a child, and entirely too male when he sent the little girl after her sister and turned to hold out his hand to her.

She took it, and told herself it was only the rocking of the boat that made her feel a little off balance when she became aware of its strength and its warmth when his fingers closed around hers.

It was only to *keep* her balance that she reached for his arm with her free hand when he pulled her up, and she found herself standing close enough to see the steady beat of his pulse in the hollow of his throat.

"Thank you," she murmured, sliding her hand from his hard bicep. Her glance slipped down, stalling when it reached the firm line of his mouth. Staring at his mouth only reminded her of how it had felt on hers, so she let her glance fall to the faded lettering on his shirt. But staring at his chest wasn't any less disturbing. Faced with that broad expanse of hard muscle, she thought only that she still didn't know what it felt like to be held against it.

Before she could deny the longing the thought brought, he dropped her hand and turned away. He hadn't touched her since the day they'd encountered her mother at the nursing home. In the week since, it seemed to her that he'd even gone out of his way to avoid contact.

He swiped up the two little life jackets from the dock as she popped the plastic fasteners on hers. "Where do you want these?"

"They go in Darren and Paige's boat." Slipping off her Day-Glo green life jacket, she nodded toward the boathouse with its multipaned and rain-stained windows and the antique captain's bell beside the door. Her sister and brother-in-law kept a ski boat there. "But you don't have to do that. What did you need?" she murmured, taking the jackets to put away herself.

"I don't need anything."

She had her hand on the boathouse door. Glancing over her shoulder, she searched the inscrutable angles and planes of his face. "Then why did you come down here?"

"I thought you might need a rescue."

Baffled, she turned around completely, lifting her hand to shield her eyes from the sun as she studied him. "A rescue?"

"I thought the dog might dump all of you if he tried to get in the boat." One shoulder rose in a deceptively casual shrug. "It made more sense to be down here if that happened than up at the house."

He took a step closer, his head blocking the sun slanting across the lake. "What?" he asked, when all she did was drop her hand and continue to stare.

He stood three feet away, his head haloed by the late-afternoon light, his blue eyes intent on her face. She honestly had no idea how she was supposed to feel about this man. She wasn't even sure she knew how she did feel, whether she was supposed to feel it or not. There was so much about him that drew her. His inherent kindness. His generosity.

He'd come down just because he thought she might need him.

The realization had her shaking her head even as she pushed her fingers through her hair once more. What he had done was so very much like the man she'd once known. The man he was proving to still be. But there was a side to him that he refused to share with anyone, and even if she didn't have the inevitable tug of guilt reminding her of a few other reasons she shouldn't be thinking of him so much, she had two children and a dog demanding her attention.

"Aunt Amy!" Brittany hollered from the middle of the yard. "Pete smells!"

"Yuckie!" Sarah shouted.

"Oh, good grief," Amy muttered.

"Go on." Nick took the bulky jackets and nudged her toward the house. "I'll take care of these. What about the boat? Do you want it back inside?"

He nodded at the little blue dingy bobbing behind them. She told him not to bother, that it usually just stayed tied up at the dock, and headed toward where the girls were dancing around Pete holding their noses because they didn't like the smell of wet dog.

She knew it was important to be consistent with children. She knew she should follow through with her instructions and have them stay right there with her while they all dried off their hairy, soggy friend. But she really didn't want to be late getting them home or meeting her friends, so she scooped up the two old towels Brittany had retrieved and sent the girls to the screened-in porch to change back into the shorts and tops they'd left there. She'd take care of Pete herself. As soon as she could catch him.

The dog had spotted a little mallard drake and his mate that lived in the rushes beyond the rocks and, being a bird dog at heart, decided to terrorize the local wildlife. Before she could open her mouth to call him back, he hit the water with a splash that sent the ducks squawking back toward cover.

"I changed my mind," Nick drawled, stepping from the dock. "It's not that peaceful here after all."

At his droll comment, Nick saw her shoot him a look that would have passed for a glare, had she been capable of such an expression. As it was, her mouth twitched, and her eyes were smiling as the dog emerged from the water again, shook, stopped, shook again and loped toward her with what he could have sworn was a grin on its face.

"Would you do me a favor?" she called, heading to the left when the dog feinted in the other direction. "Head him off so I can catch him?"

Pete clearly thought they were playing—which would have been fine with Nick if the girls had still been out there with them. They might have distracted him from the way the slender muscles in Amy's legs flexed as she moved, the way the breeze tossed her feathered hair, the intent look in her laughing eyes when she lunged for the overgrown puppy. Mostly, they might have kept him from focusing on how what he and Amy were doing as they moved to intercept the drenched canine was the very thing they had been doing the day he'd realized he was about to make a huge mistake.

He tried to banish the thought. He'd already been working hard to take some of the load off his uncle, but the past week he'd nearly driven himself to the point of exhaustion simply so he wouldn't lie in bed at night wrestling with the memories that had resurrected themselves over the past couple of weeks.

Exhaustion guaranteed oblivion. Yet this particular memory had survived his best efforts to escape it. It just hadn't been as clear as it became in the moments they dodged and feinted, laughing as the dog cut an arc and slipped past their grasp.

Amy was still laughing when the dog tried the maneuver again and, ready for him this time, they caught him together—just as they had another dripping beast once before.

With her head inches from his, their arms around Pete's big quivering body, Nick breathed in the smell of wet dog, her shampoo and something that smelled like coconut. Her sunscreen, maybe. Or cream rinse. The mingled scents tightened his gut now just as they had that day so long ago. And just as he had then, he felt the tug of something distinctly carnal burn low in his gut.

He eased back as far as he could without letting the dog bolt. As he did, the sun caught the glints of topaz in her hair, lighting it just as it had then. The air had been just as balmy that day, the sun just as bright. She'd had a tan then, too, he remembered. A much deeper one than the sun-kissed glow she had now. But he remembered that only because he could distinctly recall seeing the white line of skin when her shirt and the strap of her bra had pulled from her shoulder. The neck of the T-shirt she wore now was cut too high to slip, but the fabric looked as if it could be just as transparent if it got any wetter.

He swallowed, far too aware of how soft her skin felt when he slipped his hand under hers on the dog's collar and held him while she went to work with a big green towel.

"What was the name of that Saint Bernard your family had?" he asked, feeling edgier than he had all day when she leaned closer to work on the panting dog's head.

"Bruno?" Her smile was as soft as summer rain, welcome, gentle. "You remember him?"

"Yeah," he muttered, looking for a diversion.

He got what he was looking for when she said she'd adored that animal, and asked if he'd had a dog when he was growing up. He told her he hadn't, but started talking about the strays that had found their way into his aunt and uncle's home over the years—for no other reason than to keep his mind from wandering.

It wandered anyway.

Back to the very hour he'd realized he had no business marrying Paige Chapman.

Amy had been washing the hulking Saint Bernard. Trying to wash it, anyway. She'd soaked it down, and it had gotten away from her just as he'd arrived to pick up Paige. The great lumbering animal had shot through the open side gate with a speed that totally defied its bulk and taken off across the driveway and the lawn. Amy had been ten feet behind, her long hair flying and her long legs bare beneath the hem of a white T-shirt that was three sizes too big and hit her where her shorts ended midthigh.

At the time, he hadn't noticed how wet her shirt was. He'd just seen her barreling after the dog and had realized she couldn't stop the animal before he ran into the street. So he'd taken after Bruno himself and headed him into the neighbor's front yard, where he and Amy had ended up in a heap with a hundred and thirty pounds of sopping wet fur, panting and laughing because the dog kept trying to lick their faces.

She'd been seventeen at the time, pretty in a fresh, innocent sort of way, and he'd already found his thoughts drifting in her direction. He hadn't worried about how his thoughts had strayed. It hadn't seemed necessary. The things he'd thought about had seemed harmless enough: how pretty her smile was, how much gentleness there was in her laughter, how she never hesitated to lend a hand when someone needed it. He'd never known her to meet a request for help with anything less than complete willingness, a trait that would have attracted him in anyone.

Just the night before, he'd seen her hurrying around the kitchen without any prodding at all, while Paige had rolled her eyes at every request her mother had made for her help to get the meal on the table. It had been the same way the week before. And the one before that. Paige had always done whatever her mom had asked her to do, which hadn't been much, but she never seemed to do it willingly. Not the way Amy did. And unlike Amy, she hadn't seemed at all aware of other people's needs.

To him, Amy had seemed almost like a hostess in her own family, always watching out to see what she could get for someone to make them more comfortable. Since he'd already been working in Manhattan by then, he'd been around only on weekends, but whenever he was at the Chapman home, he couldn't help but notice the differences between the sisters—and how the family rarely hesitated to take advantage of Amy's willing nature. That was why, on more than one occasion, he'd found himself stepping in to help her, simply because it had seemed as if she'd needed someone on her side.

But it had been the incident with the dog—and the image of her in that T-shirt—that had destroyed the notion that all he felt toward her was innocent affection. When she'd finally pulled herself from under the soaked dog, his glance had dropped from the smiling curve of her beautiful mouth to the perfect shape of her high, firm breasts. In her wet white shirt, the lacy outline of her bra had been clearly visible. So had the taut shape and shadow of her nipples.

He remembered thinking how perfectly she would fit in his hands, how soft her mouth looked when her smile faded, and the unmistakably sensual jolt he'd felt before he'd jerked his glance away, leaving her to get up on her own as he'd grabbed the dog's collar and told her she might want to give her shirt a tug. She'd glanced down at herself, promptly turned pink as she did as he'd suggested and hustled the dog off for its shampoo. But the image of her had lingered, and his thoughts had moved into decidedly forbidden territory.

He'd been engaged to one woman and was suddenly, constantly, thinking about another.

He'd also been brutally honest with himself about Paige. She had been pretty, outgoing, fun to be with, and when they'd started dating at the university he had been at a point in his life where he thought he was ready to settle down and get started on a big, boisterous family like Uncle Mike and Aunt Kate's. But seeing Paige around her family had revealed her to be something different from the woman he'd thought she was. And the girl who plagued his thoughts had been not only his fiancée's sister, she'd been jail bait.

"There." Amy pronounced the word with a certain degree of satisfaction and shoved her fingers through her hair as she stood. "If he stays out here for a while he should be dry by the time the girls and I leave. As long as he stays out of the water."

Nick cleared his throat, his focus on the towel as he rose and handed it to her. There was no way she could have known how she'd affected him that day. He'd done absolutely nothing to make her suspect the track his thoughts had taken. "I'll keep him up by me."

"Would you?"

"Sure," he muttered, and made himself keep his glance above her neck when he returned her oddly tentative smile.

She looked preoccupied to him as she quickly turned, a towel in each hand, and hurried across the lawn to the back steps. That preoccupation didn't surprise him. He knew she had things to do before she could leave, and the girls to take care of. He could hear their high-pitched little voices calling to her from the porch even then, but he had no idea what they were saying. With Amy walking away from him, his attention was on the gentle curve of her hips, the memory of how eagerly she'd responded when he'd kissed her, and the thought of how badly he wanted her under him now.

Except for the kiss, the thoughts were pretty much the same as those he'd fought all those years ago.

He felt as tight as a watch spring as he called Pete and the two of them headed for the task he'd almost finished. It was times like this that physical labor had definite advantages over working at a drafting table. There was something enormously satisfying about pounding nails when the talons of frustration dug so deep.

He'd hated the way he'd felt toward Amy. Yet, no matter how he'd berated himself, no matter how he'd tried to tell himself he could handle what he felt because he and Paige would be moving away, he hadn't been able to escape the fact that Paige wasn't who he wanted. He'd been about to do what his lousy excuse for a father had done, and there was no way on God's green earth he was going into a marriage knowing it would never work.

The solid thwack of the hammer against metal and wood rang out in the relative quiet. Frustration was what he felt now, but that hadn't been all he'd dealt with back then. He'd had to face his guilt. And anger. Anger with himself. With the circumstances. He'd also felt an overwhelming sense of responsibility to not screw up anyone else's life just because he'd screwed up his own. And that meant he'd had to tell Paige the wedding was off.

She was the one he'd felt most guilty about. There had been no time to give her little hints that there was trouble in paradise and slowly back off and back out. The best he'd been able to do was stay away the weekend before he'd broken up with her and come right to the point when he had shown up.

They'd been twelve hours away from taking their wedding invitations to the post office the night he'd told her he couldn't marry her. He was sure he'd been as gentle as he could. And he was sure he'd told her he didn't blame her if she hated him for the rest of her life, but in the long run, she'd see that he was really doing her a favor.

He couldn't recall too many details beyond that. He just remembered her tears and her anger. And that she'd somehow figured out that he was interested in someone else. Maybe it was because he had stayed in New York the weekend before, and he'd undoubtedly sounded a little distant on the phone when they had talked that week. He wasn't sure. He just knew that her feminine radar had zeroed in on whatever it was that gave guys away when there was something they were trying to hide, and he remembered thinking at the time that it was better to let her believe he'd been cheating on her with someone at work than to explain what had actually happened. For a number of reasons—including how she would feel toward Amy—the last thing he wanted to do was tell her he was fantasizing about her little sister.

Here he was, ten years later, fantasizing about her again.

He reached for the railing, pulling hard on it to make sure it was sturdy, and moved around the ramp to position the rail on the other side. The dog was barking at something off in the distance, but he barely noticed. He was too busy thinking that the fates must be having a field day jerking him around the way they were. Then he looked up when Pete darted past and decided the fates weren't just toying with him, they were being truly perverse.

A silver Mercedes SUV pulled into the drive.

Behind the wheel was his very blond, very attractive ex-fiancée.

Chapter Seven

Amy had forgotten about the incident with Bruno. At least, she had until she'd found herself facing Nick with Pete sandwiched between them a few minutes ago. With the memory taunting her while she helped the girls with their clothes, she had to admit it wasn't one that she really wanted to recall. Not when she was trying so hard to keep any feelings she had toward him in perspective.

The memory was there, anyway. It was one of those that had faded down to little more than a few disquieting images for her, but it was apparent Nick had some recollection of it, too, since he'd asked the name of the dog. The only thing that had saved her from feeling uneasy with him all over again was knowing that his memories had to be far more benign than hers.

He couldn't possibly know that what she'd remembered most was how rigid his expression had gone when he'd looked from her face to the front of her shirt. Or how something hot and liquid had stirred deep inside her at the look in his eyes in the moments before he'd glanced away and pointed out that he could see right through the fabric.

She couldn't recall exactly what he'd said. She just remembered feeling more embarrassed than she ever had in her life. She'd eventually realized that Nick had only mentioned her shirt to save her further embarrassment should she encounter anyone else. She knew, too, that the incident had meant nothing to him, because that weekend he continued to treat her as he always had. But after the worst of her distress had died, the memory of how he'd looked at her had come back to haunt her. And every time she'd thought of how his eyes had darkened before he'd looked away, her flesh would grow warm and she would find herself wishing she could know the feel of his mouth and his hands on her body.

She really didn't know what it was she would feel. She'd been kissed by only two boys at that point in her life. One who'd bruised her lip with his braces and one who'd lost interest when he discovered she wasn't interested in getting naked. With them, she'd never even come close to feeling anything like the sensations that had pooled inside her at the mere thought of Nick's touch.

The feeling had been powerful, confusing, and it had filled her with a need for him that left her aching, empty and riddled with guilt because she'd known feeling that way toward Nick was wrong. Wrong because even if he hadn't thought of her as a child, even if she could somehow have interested him, he was engaged to marry her sister.

So she'd buried the feeling. Learned to repress it. Much the way she'd repressed the urge to run in the house years earlier, because little ladies didn't run in her mother's house. Or the way she'd restrained herself from whistling, because little ladies didn't do that, either. It had taken a while. Months after he'd gone, actually. But eventually that awful longing simply went away.

Until Nick had kissed her.

The thought brought a frown, but she banished it right along with the thought of the feelings he had stirred inside her those few moments on her grandmother's porch. As she scooted the girls out the door ahead of her so they could pick up their toys, she reminded herself that she still had no business thinking about his hands on her body. And the thought that he was the reason she'd never felt that deep aching pull with any other man was too disturbing to explore.

She was halfway down the back stairs when she heard Pete bark. For a moment she thought he might be barking at Nick, trying to get his attention to play with him again. The Hunt family hound was shameless in his demands for attention when he discovered a soft touch. Then she heard a car pulling into the drive.

She wasn't expecting anyone, but in Cedar Lake people didn't always call before they stopped by. Just yesterday, Ida Jackson, who played bridge with her grandmother and had to be as old as Moses, had been out riding her bicycle and decided to stop and check the progress in her friend's kitchen.

Amy suspected that what she'd really stopped by to check out was Nick. Ida and Bea had been friends forever and Bea had told her he was putting in her ramp. Nick hadn't been there yesterday, though. A problem with one of his other jobs had demanded his attention. So Ida had contented herself with looking over the ramp and the cabinets Amy had now stripped and sanded with the rotary sander Nick had loaned her and shown her how to use.

Then Ida had ridden off, with the flower on her straw hat bobbing in the breeze.

Since what Amy heard now was the slam of a vehicle door and not a bicycle bell, it was a safe bet that whoever was there wasn't the geriatric card shark being nosy again. She just hoped whoever it was didn't mind that she was in a hurry.

Swiping up the half-deflated beach ball as she walked past it, she headed to where she could see the driveway—and came to a dead stop when she saw who had just arrived.

From the middle of the yard she watched Nick watch Paige walk around her shiny new silver Mercedes. Her sister stopped by the front fender, clearly oblivious to anyone but the man standing as still as stone.

An insistent little hand tugged on the hem of Amy's shorts. "Aren't you taking us home?"

She glanced down to see Britt clutching one badminton racket. "I guess not," she murmured, her smile feeling plastic. "It looks like your mom decided to come get you." Either that, she thought, or your mom's curiosity about her ex-fiancé finally got the better of her. "Go help your sister find the other racket and the birdie, then we'll get the rest of your things together."

The child ran off, calling to her sister that Mommy was there, while Amy slowly walked over to pick up a pink hair ribbon that had slipped from the child's ponytail. Curiosity was a perfectly natural thing for her sister to feel. Any woman would feel it, she told herself, not sure why she felt so compelled to justify Paige's presence. And curiosity was a powerful thing.

So was pride.

Amy didn't doubt for a moment that a heavy dose of the latter was also prompting her sister. Paige had just come from the salon. Her shining hair looked fabulous. Though Amy was too far away to really see her face, she knew her makeup would be flawless. And the black knit tank tucked into her white slacks fit her willowy frame to perfection. She looked classy, chic and, to Amy, utterly stunning.

Between the way she looked, the diamonds flashing on her impressive wedding ring and the pricey little vehicle she was driving, Paige was letting Nick see what he'd passed up, and making it apparent that she'd done quite well for herself without him.

Had the woman not been her sister and if the man had been anyone else, Amy would have silently cheered the not-so-subtle statement of survival. Any woman who had been dumped the way Paige had deserved the chance to let the louse see that she'd not only survived, she had flourished. But this particular louse was Nick, and Amy couldn't believe how conflicted she felt watching them size each other up over the narrow gap of grass and gravel.

She could hear the hesitant murmur of their voices as Brittany ran up to give her the ragged old birdie. But she couldn't bear to even think of eavesdropping as she turned with a knot in her stomach that felt disgracefully like envy and helped the girls gather their toys.

His past had definitely come back to haunt him.

The thought registered vaguely as Nick watched the striking blonde eye him across the drive. His aunt Kate owed him big time, he figured, since it was she who'd asked him to come back and help out his uncle before the man worked himself into an early grave.

"So," Paige said, her crystal-blue eyes thoroughly checking him out, "you're back."

Nick did a little visual reconnaissance of his own. She

looked good, he thought. Beautiful, in fact. In a cool, ice-princess sort of way. But then, he could hardly blame her for the chill. The last time he'd seen her, she'd given him back his ring.

Thrown it at him, actually.

"I've been back before," he told her, because he hadn't tried to stay away. Since their families didn't move in the same circles, chances had been slim that he'd run into her.

"To visit your family," she concluded.

He lifted his shoulder in a shrug that looked far more casual than it felt. "I grew up here. This is home."

She knew that. Just as she knew he had as much right to be there as she did. But she wanted to know why he was back now. He'd be willing to bet his Porsche that she wasn't going to ask, though. She didn't want him to know she was that curious.

"I hear that my grandmother hired you," she said, fishing for information that way instead. She tipped her head, the smooth wedge of her hair shimmering with streaks of silver and gold. "I have to admit, I was more than a little surprised."

"That she would hire me? Or that I'd be doing this kind of work?"

"Frankly?" Her glance darted from the faded logo on his T-shirt to the serviceable but unimpressive Culhane Contracting truck he was driving. "Both."

He had to smile at her honesty. "Yeah, well, she surprised me, too," he admitted, not feeling inclined to rise to her bait. Or to confide the reason he was working with his uncle. Preferring to change the conversation's direction entirely, he focused on her. "You're looking good, Paige," he told her, because it was true. "You've got a couple of great little girls over there, too." He honestly hoped she was doing as well as appearances would lead him to believe. He'd once cared a great deal about her. To want anything less than contentment for her wouldn't have occurred to him. "Your husband is a lucky man."

A bit of her antagonism grudgingly slipped. Flattered by his compliments, and looking a little surprised by how easily he'd offered them, she replied with a quiet "Thank you."

"Are you happy?"

"Very," she assured him. Still studying him, her curiosity became more obvious. "What about you?"

"Which? Am I happy, or did I get married?"

"You make it sound as if they're mutually exclusive."

For some people, they were. "Yes, I'm happy. And no, Paige. I never got married."

"Never?"

"Never," he repeated at her obvious surprise. "Some of us just aren't cut out for it."

She didn't seem to know what to say to that. He couldn't help notice, though, that she looked more than a little vindicated by the fact that no one else had been able to get him to the altar, either. But what he noticed most was that, polished and pretty as she was, he felt no attraction at all toward the woman he'd very nearly married. He was far more interested in the breeze-blown young woman reluctantly walking toward them with her arms folded over a nearly deflated beach ball.

Amy's nieces ran ahead of her, eyes bright and chattering a mile a minute.

"Pete got wet," little Sarah informed her mother. "He was a bad dog 'n' he got me in trouble."

"Can we stay longer, Mommy?" Brittany asked. "Please?"

Amy stopped several feet back. Fighting the urge to smooth her hopelessly boring brown hair, she wanted desperately to believe she wasn't trying to hide her unclassy shorts and T-shirt behind a beach ball. "I was going to bring the girls home in about half an hour," she said to her sister, avoiding Nick's eyes by watching Sarah hug Paige's leg. "I don't quite have their things ready. But it won't take long to get them together."

Paige shot her a smile, one that looked understandably tense and faintly preoccupied. "You won't need to do that," she assured her, taking a quick peek at her watch. "Actually, I need you to do me a favor."

Nick turned back to his project. He was gentleman enough to hide his relief at being let off the conversational hook, but Amy caught the glance he flicked toward her and hugged the beach ball a little tighter. She had no idea what was going on with her sister. Paige was usually pretty easy to read, but all Amy sensed in her was the same ambivalence she was feeling herself at the moment.

"What's that?" she asked.

"I need you to keep the girls for me tonight. The sitter canceled. Can you believe it?" Clearly concerned with the kink in her plans, she headed around the car and opened the back passenger door. "I have sixteen people coming for dinner in a little over an hour. I still have to dress and set out the hors d'oeuvres. I don't know what I'd do if I couldn't count on you," she said in a tone that assumed cooperation. Realizing that Amy hadn't followed her, she glanced over the open door and frowned. "You can do it, can't you?"

"We get to have a sleepover?" Britt asked, her blue eyes alight with anticipation. "With Aunt Amy?"

Hesitation didn't appear to be the response her sister expected.

"I suppose I can," Amy finally said, trying for her little

nieces' sake not to sound as halfhearted as she felt. "I mean, sure." She forced a smile. "I'd be glad to."

From where Nick worked a few feet away, she heard his metal tape measure rewind and snap into a coil. Looking toward him at the sharp sound, she saw his glance dart to where Paige reached into the back seat before settling hard on her.

His eyebrows bolted into a single, puzzled slash. "What about the friends you're meeting? I thought you were going out?"

"I am. Was," she corrected.

"So?"

"So now I'm not."

"I mean," he returned patiently, "why aren't you going?"

She had no idea why he was frowning at her. "Because she needs my help," she told him, thinking it obvious. He was standing right there. He'd heard what Paige had said. She needed someone to keep the girls, and leaving them with her was the most practical solution to the immediate problem.

If the disapproval etched in Nick's features was any indication, he didn't appear to agree. "What about your friends?" he asked, his tone low and just shy of demanding.

"It's a big enough group. They'll barely know I'm not there."

She saw disbelief merged with displeasure, but she couldn't imagine what he had been about to say—or why he should care one way or the other how she spent the evening. His strange disapproval had shifted to the woman standing by the fender again. Paige held two little suitcases, one pink, one lavender, and she was openly watching them both.

Instead of saying anything else, he just shook his head at Amy and turned his attention to the task of driving the remaining nails into place. The heavy thud of the hammer hitting wood sounded as exasperated as he'd looked before he had turned away.

The knowledge that he was somehow upset with her tightened the knot in her stomach. The rather significant look her sister gave her doubled the size of it.

"Come on." Walking past her with the pastel suitcases, Paige dipped her head toward the back of the house. "Let's take these inside."

"I thought you were in a hurry."

"I am." Hustling her along, Paige handed her a suitcase, which Amy passed on to Brittany, who was more than happy to lug it to the porch. Not to be left out, Sarah took the other case from her mom and battled it to the porch behind her sister. "I want to know what's going on with you and Nick."

"There's nothing going on." There really wasn't. Nothing definable, anyway. And there was certainly nothing going on on his part.

"Then how is he so familiar with your plans?"

They stopped at the corner of the house, their tones hushed despite the fact that they would need a megaphone to be heard over the staccato beats of the hammer.

"We talk," Amy said simply, refusing to feel guilty about something she could hardly avoid. "We've had to discuss what Grandma wants done here. And since he's been around so much, other things have come up. It doesn't mean anything."

Paige wasn't buying. "That was not the look of a disinterested man over there, Amy. That was possessiveness."

That was ridiculous. "It looked more like annoyance to me," Amy muttered.

"Then maybe I should put it this way," her sister said, a little too mildly. "What gives him the right to be annoyed with you?"

Amy had no answer for that. Mostly because she couldn't figure out herself what his problem was.

Paige looked wounded. "I can't believe you'd do something like this to me."

"Do what?"

"Fall for the man who left me for another woman."

"I'm not falling for anyone." Not deliberately. "And I'm not doing anything to you," she insisted, her guilt back and battling feelings of disloyalty to her sister. To Nick. To needs that had lain dormant far too long. "You're happily married, remember? You adore Darren. Nothing about Nick should even matter to you."

Behind the less-redeeming feelings she was berating herself for at the moment, Amy felt true concern. Her sister had a wonderful marriage. A wonderful life. Amy would give up everything short of her soul to be as loved as Paige was by her husband and her children.

Her sister must have recognized that concern. The starch went out of her affronted stance, and her beautiful face softened.

"It's obvious you've never had your heart ripped out and handed back on a platter," Paige muttered. "But you're right. I do adore Darren." She pulled a breath, blew it out. "Even if he is a little bald."

He was a lot bald, but certain points were best ignored. "He's a great guy."

"I know."

"He's intelligent and successful. And a wonderful father."

"The best," Paige agreed. "But there's something about Darren that matters even more than all that. I can't imagine him ever cheating on me. He has too much integrity." She absently glanced at her ring, her expression pensive in the moments before she tipped her head and caught Amy's eye. "There is nothing more important in a marriage than trust. And I trust Darren. I definitely got the better man by marrying him.

"Nick is still gorgeous," she conceded, her voice dropping as if she were admitting something she really shouldn't. "But it's obvious he's not the type who can commit to a woman. Just look at him," she insisted, catching herself from doing just that. "He can't commit to anything. Not even his career. A woman could never count on a man like that."

Amy didn't think it would be a very good idea just then to explain to her sister that she had Nick all wrong. Where his sense of responsibility was concerned, anyway. He was every bit as dedicated to his career as he had always been. And he was totally committed to his family. His uncle was the very reason he was in Cedar Lake. But Nick had warned her that defending him wouldn't set well with her family.

The trouble was, not defending him didn't set well with her.

"He's still an architect, Paige."

Her sister gave her a look that seemed to say, *You're very sweet, child, but a tad slow.* "Drawing plans for a room addition and a wheelchair ramp is not exactly what he trained to do."

"I mean," Amy stressed, trying not to bridle at the implied lack of understanding, "he's still with the firm in New York. He's just helping his uncle through a...business transition," she decided to call it, since she didn't know if he wanted his uncle's plans to retire to be made known just yet. "He'll be going back when he's through here."

The dismissive expression sharpened to interest. "This is only temporary?"

"It would seem so."

"Oh." The word sounded vaguely deflated, like a tire that had just lost the last of its air. Forced to abandon that failing, she focused on those that remained. "That still doesn't change the fact that he's a lousy risk when it comes to everything else that counts. He's obviously attractive, Amy. And you're out here alone with him. The man could charm the habit off a nun if he put his mind to it, so you—"

"Paige." Amy didn't want to be having this conversation. Having set the record straight on Nick's employment without provoking a problem, she glanced pointedly at her watch. "You really should get going. Your company will be arriving, and you won't even be there."

Under any other circumstances, Amy knew she could never have gotten away with such a blatant and obvious interruption. But because of the party her sister had been preparing for during the past couple of weeks, Paige immediately shelved her criticisms of Nick to dart a quick glance at her own watch.

With a moan of disbelief at the hour, the statuesque blonde snapped her attention to her plans for the evening and called the girls over from where they were playing catch with Pete and the birdie. A moment later she gave them both hugs, told them to be good for Aunt Amy, told Amy she'd call her first thing in the morning and breezed past Nick, who straightened from where he'd knelt at the base of the ramp.

Her sister, full steam ahead, was an impressive sight to

behold. Paige didn't slow by so much as a step as she sailed past Nick and slipped into her SUV. All Nick did was glance up as she passed, then head to the truck and drop his tool belt into its bed.

It's obvious he's not the type who can commit to a woman.

He's a lousy risk.

A woman could never count on a man like that.

Amy hadn't needed her sister to point out any of that. She knew what kind of man he was.

Unfortunately, because there were parts of that man that spoke to parts of her, he also wasn't a man she could ignore.

The silver SUV was little more than the fading hum of an engine when Nick turned from his truck. Still wrestling with her sister's very sensible warnings, Amy watched him head back to the ramp. If he was putting tools away, that meant he would be leaving soon.

Trying to ignore the wish that he would stay, she started to turn.

"Amy. Wait."

The demand in his tone stopped her as abruptly as the request itself. Watching his steady strides eat the length of the drive, she had the impression that he'd rather impatiently been waiting for her sister to leave.

He still seemed annoyed. Certain she was about to find out why, she tightened her hug on the nearly deflated beach ball as he stopped in front of her.

From an arm's length away, he looked to where the girls were playing just out of earshot, then settled his glance accusingly on her face.

"Why did you let her do that to you?"

"Do what?"

"Let her steamroll you like that."

Incomprehension had her mirroring his frown. Paige was just being Paige. "What are you talking about?"

"I'm talking about the way you just dropped your plans to accommodate hers. You were looking forward to tonight. You told me so barely two hours ago. But you never said a word to her about what you'd planned to do."

There was no mistaking the reproach in his eyes. It was leashed, but it was definitely there. Confused by his challenge, still not understanding it, she tipped up her chin. "I didn't have to tell her. You did."

"Not until after you'd agreed to do what she wanted," he reminded her, refusing to see what he'd done as a problem. "You didn't even ask if she'd tried to find another baby-sitter. What about your mom?" he suggested. "Did she ask her?"

Amy doubted it. Their parents invariably had some sort of social obligation on Saturday nights. "She asked me," she pointed out ever so reasonably.

"That doesn't mean you couldn't say no." He tried to sound reasonable, too. He just wasn't succeeding quite as well. "Why don't you call your mother? There's no reason you should give up your plans."

"Because she *did* ask me," Amy replied, growing more bewildered with him by the second. "And I said yes. There's no reason to call anyone else."

Nick's glance swept her face, the fragile line of her jaw, the confusion in her warm brown eyes. He couldn't help but notice how she hugged the battered old beach ball, embracing it as if it were some sort of shield. With her hands curled tightly around her biceps, he also noticed the chips in her unpolished nails, little badges of merit from her battle with the cabinets.

He wasn't comparing her to her sister. With him, it had ultimately been the other way around. As he let his glance drift over her slender fingers, he was remembering how she'd once wanted to sculpt—and how she'd abandoned that dream to accommodate her parents' idea of what was best for her. Even with that dream gone, she'd wanted to see the sculptures that had first inspired her. And year after year, she kept abandoning that desire, too, simply to oblige her family.

He wondered if she even realized how long they'd been taking advantage of her inherently generous nature.

"You let them walk all over you. You know that? You do," he insisted before she could try to deny it. "Look at all the times you've canceled your vacation because someone needed you to take care of something for them. Look what you're doing here," he suggested, lifting his hand toward the house. She was giving up her vacation again to do something they all knew they should be helping take care of themselves. "Think about what you just did with your sister."

He shook his head, wanting to reach for her, not trusting why. "I don't understand you, Amy. Why do you think your life is less important than everyone else's in your family?"

"I don't think it is…isn't," she hastily corrected, hating the direction he'd headed. "If I can help, I do. That's all."

"Have they ever dropped their plans for you?"

"There's never been any reason for them to. I've never needed anything."

"Of course you have." He wasn't sure what was pushing him, but it felt very much like frustration. With her. With himself. It also felt a lot like the protectiveness he'd felt before but wouldn't let himself consider. "Everyone needs something."

He had no idea what she needed. Beneath her breastbone, the knot turned to a void. "I'm not doing anything you aren't doing right now for your own family."

"Helping Uncle Mike like this is a one-shot deal."

"I don't believe that for a minute. You'd be right there if they needed you again."

"If I was the only one who could help," he admitted, struck by her certainty. "Of course I would. But the difference is that my family doesn't take advantage of me the way yours does of you. And I know how to say no when I have to."

"You're saying I don't?"

He found it rather telling that she let his other point slip by. "Yeah. I am. With you, it's almost as if you're afraid your family won't love you if you turn any of them down."

The color drained from her face. "That's ridiculous," she insisted, but she stepped back as if he'd slapped her.

He would have reached for her then. Just to keep her from bolting, because he needed to do something to take the sting from his words. But two and a half feet of blue-eyed insistence poked her head between them, and Amy deliberately turned all of her attention to Sarah.

The little girl tipped her curly head back as far as it would go. "We're hungry."

"You are?" Amy's smile was strained, but gentle. "Then let's see what we can fix for supper."

"Amy," Nick began.

"I have to go. The girls need to eat." She had to call JoBeth, too. Mostly, she just needed to get away from the man who seemed intent on systematically knocking holes in the foundation of her admittedly not so well-ordered little world.

With Sarah's small hand clutching hers, she discarded

the colorful ball by the back stairs and hurried inside, Brittany skipping behind in their wake.

Nick watched her go. Torn between going after her and going home, he called himself eight kinds of fool for not having just kept his mouth shut, and decided to head for the truck. He couldn't talk to her with the kids right there. He wasn't even sure what he'd say, anyway. Having known Amy when she was younger, he was beginning to see all too clearly how her family had stifled her. How they used her. But what bothered him most was that she let them.

Pointing that out hadn't exactly been his most sensitive move. Telling her he thought they'd drained the spirit right out of her wouldn't exactly qualify as compassionate, either. But in the past couple of weeks, when it came to her family, the only time he hadn't noticed a sense of strain about her was when it came to her nieces. It was almost as if, with them, she could relax and be herself simply because they accepted her for who she was.

They clearly adored her for being herself, too.

Picking up the last scraps of wood, he tossed them into the back of his truck. She'd make a great mom, he thought, and before he could stop himself he was wondering if she'd be one of those women who had a rough time of being pregnant or the sort who glowed the whole nine months. His cousins ran the gamut, the four of the six who had kids, anyway. It seemed Maureen and Kathleen had lived on soda crackers, while Moira and Kelly had said being pregnant was the greatest feeling in the world. But thinking of Amy pregnant had him thinking about getting her that way. And that had him feeling edgy and restless and like baying at the moon.

He slammed the door on the truck a little harder than was probably necessary.

He wasn't going to do that to himself. He wasn't going to let his thoughts drift around to all the things he'd long ago realized he would never have. A wife. A family. Falling for Amy all those years ago had only proved to him that he was indeed his father's son. And there was no way on God's green earth he was going to repeat that man's mistakes.

Chapter Eight

"Thanks again for bringing the girls home, Amy. And for dropping off the coffeepot. Are you sure you don't mind taking it to the Meiers?"

Hoping she didn't appear as restless as she felt, Amy started the engine of her car and glanced through the open window at her sister. On the seat beside her sat the industrial-sized percolator Paige had borrowed for her dinner party last night.

"Not at all," she replied, anxious to go, even though she had the whole day to kill. "Their house is on the way to the hardware store."

Fidgeting with the band of her watch, Paige gave her a little nod, but she made no attempt to move. She had followed Amy out to the car, leaving the girls playing in the sunroom and Darren buried behind the editorial section of the Sunday newspaper. The fact that she'd rooted herself to the concrete by the driver's side door pretty much indicated to Amy that she wanted something else.

"I was wondering," Paige began, proving Amy's suspicion correct. "I mean, you said you and Nick talk." She hesitated, her brow creasing as she studied the gold links on her wrist. "After I left yesterday...I just wondered if he'd said...anything."

Amy's glance slipped to her lap. He'd had plenty to say. And no matter how hard she tried, she still couldn't understand why he'd felt so compelled to attack the only way she knew to fit into her family.

"He didn't say anything about you...if that's what you mean." Amy's tone was gentle, and filled with more understanding than Paige was likely to hear. "He's never said anything to me about the two of you."

Nothing directly, anyway. He'd said only enough for Amy to assume that there had been something missing in their relationship.

It was all she really cared to know.

"I just wondered if, any of the times you'd talked, if he'd told you who she was. The woman he left me for," she clarified, her tone pensive. "I always wondered what she was like." Paige gave an oddly self-conscious shrug. "That was one of the reasons I took the girls' things to you instead of asking you to come get them. I wanted to see how he looked after all these years," she admitted. "And to ask him about her." She ran her nail along a link. "But I couldn't do it. Ask, I mean."

It wasn't like Paige to seem so hesitant, or to have trouble looking a person in the eye. She always had such a sense of confidence about her. Sometimes Amy envied her the trait. Mostly she admired it. At that moment, she simply noticed it was missing.

"He never married her, Paige."

"I know. He said he'd never married anyone."

"I mean, he never married *her*."

Paige opened her mouth, closed it again. Regarding Amy thoughtfully, she stopped picking at her watchband.

"She couldn't keep him, either," Amy quietly pointed out. "So she must not have meant that much to him, after all." She tipped her head to catch her sister's eye. "That means she couldn't have been all that special. Doesn't it?"

"I hadn't thought about it like that."

"Well, you can think about it that way now."

Looking relieved, or maybe it was absolved, she smiled. "I think you just made my day. Thank you. Really, sis. You can't imagine how I hated that…how I… Never mind," she quickly concluded, giving Amy a look of genuine gratitude as she dismissed it all with a wave of her hand. "It's all in the past. Until he showed up, it had been ages since I'd given any real thought to her. Or him," she confided, sounding as if she really needed Amy to know that.

"I have to agree with Mom, though," she continued, her pensiveness fading to her usual certainty. "It's unconscionable of Grandma to put you in the position of having to deal with him, but it was worth seeing him just to stop wondering about him and that…that woman. It doesn't matter who she was. Like you said, she didn't get him, either."

She brightened, clearly revived by the sisterly support. "That reminds me. Speaking of Mom, I mean. Where do you want to go for dinner on your birthday? I told her I'd make the reservation."

Amy blinked at the abrupt change of subject. She was still busy wondering herself what sort of woman would have drawn Nick's interest from her sister.

Pushing her fingers through her hair, she shook her head as she caught up with Paige.

"My birthday?" Her twenty-eighth birthday wasn't for another three weeks. Her more immediate concern was what to do with today. Specifically, what she could do to avoid the lake house so she wouldn't run into Nick. He tested her loyalties. He awakened yearnings he had no way of satisfying because he wasn't the type who stuck around for the long haul. All he did was make her consider what she'd spent a lifetime battling, then either kiss her sense-less and bolt or pack up his tools and leave. "I like Italian food. How about Petruccio's?"

Paige frowned. "We eat there all the time."

"I don't."

"There's a great new place over in Rockwood Park," Paige suggested, ignoring the fact that Petruccio's truly was a treat for Amy. "Do you want to try there?"

"Is it Italian?"

"It's continental. But it's fabulous. So's that little bistro at the wharf. Or I could do something here." She smiled, mental wheels madly spinning. "Tell you what. I'll take care of everything and surprise you."

Amy managed a passable imitation of her sister's en-thusiasm. With her dinner party over, Paige was ripe for a new project. "Great," she murmured.

"I'll talk to you later in the week, then. Don't forget to drop that off," she admonished, back in big-sister mode as she motioned toward the coffee urn occupying the front seat.

Amy assured her that she wouldn't and slipped her car into gear. The thing was two feet tall, as big around as a dinner plate. It would be pretty hard to overlook.

Paige waved. Amy waved back and eased out of the driveway with Nick's voice echoing in her head.

Why do you let her steamroll you like that?

"Shut up, Nick," she muttered, and turned onto the road that would take her only a mile out of her way to drop off the coffeepot before she headed for the hardware store. It really wasn't an inconvenience. After all, it wasn't as if she had anything else she absolutely had to do.

The Ace Hardware Store behind the Frosty Freeze on Elm Street didn't have the selection of the big home improvement center over on Sycamore. It was also only open between noon and five on Sunday, which meant Amy had time to spare, since it was only eleven-forty when she pulled up in front of it. She had to go to Ace, though. That was where her grandmother had gone to get the red paint for her cabinets mixed, so it was the only place Amy was sure she could get the right color.

In no particular hurry to get to the lake house anyway, she walked around the corner to the Frosty Freeze wondering how long Nick would work that afternoon, and bought a double dip cone. She wasn't sure what she'd do after she bought the paint. She and the girls had stopped at the nursing home to say hi to Grandma Bea on their way to Paige's that morning, but she had an open invitation at Tina Ashworth's, and JoBeth had called telling her to stop by anytime and catch up on what she'd missed last night.

Thinking she might take JoBeth up on her offer, she walked back around the block, licking her cone and checking out the bathing suits and cover-ups in the window of Tammy's Togs, the furniture display in the window of Krause's and the travel posters visible on the walls of a travel agency, the only business that happened to be closed.

She was staring at a poster of a Roman amphitheater in

Nîmes, which hung next to a poster identical to the one she had in her bedroom of an archway at the Louvre, when she became aware of a distinct and profound sense of disappointment.

It would be another year before she got to see the museums.

In the overall scheme of things, the matter was hardly earth-shattering. There was crime in every major city. Children were starving on a planet that was destroying its ozone layer. Those were things that mattered. Those things had significance. The other was just something she wanted to do.

Like have Italian food on her birthday.

She drew a deep breath that smelled of the pink petunias in the barrel planter by the door and exhaust fumes from the traffic on the street behind her and distractedly pushed her fingers through her hair. Her bangs tumbled right back over her forehead, pretty much just as they'd been before.

Rather like her life. She could rearrange bits and pieces of it, but nothing really ever changed.

At the thought, she frowned at her reflection. It had to be the restlessness she'd been feeling lately that made her feel the odd sense of defeat. She hadn't noticed the disquiet so much as she'd worked at her grandmother's house, but it had returned with a vengeance that morning. She wouldn't worry about it, though. She always felt it in this town. Dissatisfied. Discontent.

Once she returned to Eau Claire she'd be fine. School would start, and she would be involved with her students and her friends and she'd be back in her bright and airy little apartment where she'd papered one wall with the lights of Chicago, since she hadn't been able to find a mural of San Francisco.

Nick had once accused her of settling. She preferred to think of it as being happy with what was available.

"Planning a trip?"

The deep tones of Nick's voice jerked her around like a puppet pulled by a string. He was the last person in the entire state of Wisconsin that she wanted to see just then, but what she wanted and what she got were rarely the same thing.

Pulling her sunglasses from where she'd hooked them at the neck of her sleeveless beige blouse, she slipped them on, slipped past him and casually tossed the last of her cone into the green City of Cedar Lake trash receptacle six feet away. When she looked back, she could read nothing in him but a finely honed tension that managed to hum over her nerves like sound waves from a tuning fork.

Hoping to sound as if his presence were of no particular concern, she forced a faint smile. "What are you doing here?"

He held up a butter-yellow spindle that looked very much like one of the turned posts in her grandmother's porch railing. "Getting some paint matched. What about you?"

I'm trying to avoid you, she thought, and obviously not succeeding. "Same thing. I'm just waiting for the hardware store to open."

Seeming conscious of how deliberately she'd moved, he remained where he was, eight feet of concrete and a gum wrapper separating them. "You're heading back to your grandmother's house, then?"

"Not for a while." Wadding her paper napkin into a ball, she tossed it in after the cone. "I have some things I want to do this afternoon."

The honk of a horn melded with the exuberant sound of two young boys chasing each other down the sidewalk. A teenager on a skateboard shot between them, earning glares from an elderly couple sharing a banana split on the bus bench and a young couple leaving the furniture store.

Before anyone else could invade the space separating them, Nick closed the gap. "When do you think you'll be there?"

"I'm sure it won't be until late. At least nine or ten tonight." She grazed what she hoped was an amiable smile past his chin and glanced at her watch. "You know, I really should get going even now. I think I'll just get the paint tomorrow."

She took a step backward and was about to tell him she'd see him later when she heard Nick swear. The sound was low, terse and undoubtedly profane. But she'd barely taken another and started to turn when his hand shot out and he caught her arm.

"Amy, don't." Nick stepped in front of her, hating the way she stiffened as his fingers flexed against her skin. She wasn't acting aloof or indignant or cool, or any of the dozen punishing ways women could act when they'd been offended or hurt somehow. There was no mistaking the way she'd withdrawn from him, but her strained smile had told him she was going to do with him what she did with everyone else and jam down whatever was going on inside her to keep the peace. If keeping the peace meant avoiding him, she would do that, too.

He glanced around them, at the people filling the sidewalk, the cars driving past. "I want to talk to you. Where are you going after you leave here?"

"Nick ..."

"Where?" he insisted.

Amy hesitated. "I hadn't really decided."

His hand slid from her arm, as much to avoid gossip should they be seen by any of the Chapmans' friends as in reaction to her admission. He was right. Avoiding him was exactly how she'd planned to handle the distress he'd seen in her eyes before she'd turned from him yesterday.

He'd tried to tell himself to leave it alone, to just stop thinking about how stricken she'd looked. But trying not to think about Amy was like trying not to breathe. It worked for about twenty seconds, then needs he couldn't consciously control took over and he found himself doing it anyway.

"I shouldn't have said what I did, Amy"

"Forget it. Okay? It doesn't matter."

"It does matter," he countered, his tone absolute. "The way you're acting proves it." His voice dropped. "Look. We're attracting attention. Do you really want to discuss this here?"

She didn't want to discuss it at all. But he was right. They did seem to have an audience. The man and woman from the furniture store and the couple on the bench surreptitiously glanced toward them. The teenagers coming up the sidewalk in a small knot were more obvious. The girls in the group openly stared, then covered their mouths and giggled.

"Come with me," he coaxed, taking advantage of her silence. "I need to run by a job site before I go out to your grandmother's. We can talk in the truck and order the paint when we get back. It's only a couple of minutes from here."

The construction site Nick had referred to was a small medical office half a mile away. The windows bore manufacturer's stickers and concrete had yet to be poured in the frames delineating walkways, but the building looked nearly complete. The parking lot, which was nothing but dirt and piles of construction debris, was in back of the building. Pulling into it, Nick bounced the truck over the ruts left by heavier equipment, eased past a Dumpster and cut the engine.

He'd told her on the way over that he needed to check the work of the drywall subcontractor before his uncle paid for the work. He'd told her, too, that they'd run into a couple of snags with the job that he hoped to resolve soon, because his uncle had just won the bid on a contract to double the space of a county storage facility, and when that job wrapped up in the fall, his uncle would be able to slow down to a couple of jobs a year, if that was what he wanted to do, or retire completely.

Talking about work had glossed over the strain that had filled the cab of the truck for the three minutes it had taken to drive up Pine Street and pull into the deserted and secluded site. But that strain seemed to echo through the cab the moment the rumble of the engine died.

His small collection of keys still swayed from the ignition switch when Nick rested his wrists at the top of the steering wheel. He was staring straight ahead when Amy saw the firm line of his mouth compress. A moment later, he released a long slow breath and glanced toward her.

For a moment, he said nothing. He just sat looking at her as if he were trying to figure out what to do with her now that they had the privacy he'd sought. There wasn't a soul around. Through the truck's open windows she could barely even hear what little traffic there was on the street beyond the building. Mostly what she heard were the birds in the big pines at the back of the lot and an insistent little voice in her conscience that told her she was getting further in over her head by the minute with this man.

"I meant what I said before," he finally began, apology heavy in his tone. "I really shouldn't have said what I did.

The only thing I can say in my defense is that I remember how your family seemed to use your willingness to help years ago. When Paige pulled that on you yesterday, it seemed like things had gotten worse.'' His glance skimmed her face, and the sedate, black-rimmed sunglasses she was hiding behind. ''I just hate to see people take advantage of you.''

There was no longer any apology in his steel-blue eyes. Only concern. It was the concern that disarmed her. But it was the thought that he'd been thinking of her, watching out for her, that made it impossible for her to counter his conclusions.

''They're going to love you no matter what you do, Amy.''

He made it sound as if he believed a person couldn't help but be drawn to her. But she didn't consider that possibility or its implication for a moment. She was sure he was talking about obligation, the responsibility family had to accept one another.

''Spoken like a man who has never doubted his place.''

''I wouldn't say never. There was a time I had no idea where I fit.'' His voice went tight. ''I know some people will push you just as far as you'll let them. But I also know family can be forgiving, even when they don't get their own way.''

He was talking about his mom and his aunt and uncle and their children. That was his family. But he was talking of his father, too. She was sure of it. She'd seen that knee-jerk reaction in Nick before, that quick, banked rancor at the thought of his father. But that betraying reaction was being buried even as they spoke.

She doubted he ever managed to bury it all that deeply. She knew all about denying what she didn't want to think about. And Nick's feelings toward the man who'd abandoned him were too near the surface for her to believe he didn't do a little mental compromising of his own.

"Who pushed you?" she quietly asked.

The carved lines of his face remained impassive as his glance fell to a thread poking up from a seam on the shoulder of her blouse. Leaning back, he reached over and slowly smoothed it down with his index finger.

"We're not talking about me," he reminded her, disappointing her hope of understanding this man whose touch it never occurred to her to question. "We're talking about you. And they do push you, Amy. You know they do."

"What if I told you it doesn't bother me all that much?"

"Then I'd tell you that you were a liar."

He was nothing if not blunt. Amy opened her mouth to tell him that, only to do little more than draw in air when he tipped her chin toward him. Lifting her glasses from her face, he set them on the dashboard.

"Now," he murmured, springs creaking beneath his weight as he rested his arm on the seat back. "Look me in the eye and say that again."

He was close. Close enough for her to see the fatigue in his eyes. Close enough to breathe in the clean scents of soap and spearmint and something that was indefinably Nick.

"I really don't mind that much. Not usually," she qualified, her glance slipping from his before she could stop it. "It's just..."

"Just what?" he coaxed when her voice trailed off.

She'd never put the feeling into words before. She wasn't sure she wanted to now, either. It wasn't as if she were some poor lost soul who had nothing or no one in her life. Her family had hardly cast her aside or done her harm. She had a good family. They just didn't see eye-to-eye about a lot of things. Half the people she knew could sympathize.

"Amy?"

"It's the only way I've ever felt as if I'm really a part of my family," she conceded, trying not to sound defensive, or defeated.

Nick's brow drew down sharply. "Because it makes you feel they need you, you mean?"

"That makes me sound pathetic."

"It makes you sound human."

He didn't play fair. If he were just a little less understanding, she might have been able to ignore the fact that she really did like being with him.

"It's not quite that." Not completely, anyway. "It's more like helping out is my niche. Filling in where I can is sort of like my family job."

She toyed with the hem of her walking shorts, absently drawing the cocoa-colored linen between her fingers before she glanced over at him. "You said you remembered what it was like when you were around before. If you noticed anything about me at all, it had to be that I was the odd man out around there."

With a self-conscious little laugh, she shook her head. "My tastes and interests were so different from my parents' and my sister's. Mom and Dad are both so goal oriented. So is Paige. I would always just go with the flow. If something I wanted didn't work out, I'd go with something else."

"That's not really what I noticed."

The deep timbre of his voice pulled her eyes to his. There was something in his expression she couldn't quite read, a considering look as his glance skimmed her face, but he offered nothing else.

"No," she murmured, drawn simply by the quiet

strength of his presence. "That's not something a person would notice. It wasn't as obvious as what a tomboy I was." She'd been the only one in the house with so much as a passing interest in sports, or spending time with a sketch pad. Her dad was into computers and cars.

"Or how polished Mom and Paige are," she pointed out. "Or how efficient. Mom can do just about anything and do it well. She has awards and commendations from every committee she's ever served on. She knows all the right people. All the right things to say. Paige is just like her. She graduated at the top of her class. She was president of her sorority and she's Junior League president now." She cut herself off, wondering what was wrong with her that the thought of doing what they did bored her silly. "But I guess you would have picked up some of that somewhere along the line."

His fingers trailed over the seam once more. "I did notice a few similarities between the two of them."

She was sure it had been more than a few, but she wasn't going to mention how blond and attractive they both were. Or how, with her dark hair and eyes, she'd spent most of grade school wondering if she were adopted. She had her dad's coloring. His eye color, anyway. "Well, there weren't any between them and me," she conceded lightly, pretty certain that was obvious, too. "I was happiest playing ball with the other kids and couldn't care less about clothes or hair or where the fish fork went on the table. Mom and Dad felt that girls should be little ladies."

Paige had been a natural. Amy had felt like the proverbial square peg.

"I know you know where the fish fork goes." His tone was mild, but faintly chiding. "I saw you set a very impressive table."

"Thanks," she murmured. "But all that means is that

I'm trainable. In some areas, anyway," she qualified, torn between amazement at his memories of her and being scrupulously honest with herself. "I never did learn how to delegate the way they do. I'm always trying to do everything myself and always running behind schedule because of it." Beneath her bangs, her forehead furrowed. "And I still can't seem to keep closets and drawers organized."

She started to shrug off the rest of what she couldn't seem to do anything about. Afraid he would move his hand if she did, she remained still, her focus on her fingers where she was again pleating the hem of her shorts.

Nick watched the slightly agitated motion of her fingers. He couldn't believe what he was hearing. Then again, he could. He remembered the Chapman household as being gracious and hospitable and being run on a timetable that would have put a master sergeant to shame. If cocktails were at six o'clock and dinner at seven, then the first ice cube hit the bottom of the glass the moment the hands were vertical on the clock and people took their seats precisely one hour later. He'd thought at first that it was Mr. Chapman who insisted on that sort of order. As a CPA, he would be drawn to precision. Or so it had seemed. But it hadn't taken long for Nick to figure out that it was Mrs. Chapman who captained their ship, and she ran a household that had been rigidly conventional, correct and with little room for originality or eccentricities.

It was a wonder to him how the decidedly unconventional Bea had ever produced a daughter as traditional in her tastes as Susan Chapman. But he had the feeling now that, deep inside, Amy was far more like her grandmother than her mom.

He had the feeling, too, that with her tendency to run late and lack of personal organization, there was a little subconscious rebellion going on. He couldn't imagine any other reason she'd be driving that screaming yellow Volkswagen.

"So," Amy said, suddenly seeming aware of the silence. "That explains why I do what I do. I'll never be as accomplished as they are, but a person has to go with her strengths in my family." Her smile emerged, soft and accepting. "Mine seems to be taking care of people."

He'd considered before that her potential had somehow been stifled. As he reached over and slipped his fingers under her chin, he couldn't help wonder if it hadn't been smothered entirely.

Hating the thought, he turned her face to him.

"You're very good at taking care of people, Amy. It's you you're not doing such a good job with. No," he murmured, curving his fingers around the side of her neck to keep her from turning away. "Just hear me out."

The guardedness in her dark eyes didn't budge. Yet beneath his hand he felt the tension in her muscles yield to his touch.

"I know you can stand up to your family. I saw you do it with your mother when you sided with your grandma the other day. You just can't seem to stand up for yourself." His thumb slowly grazed upward along her jaw, the pad brushing the delicate lobe of her ear. Her earrings were tiny silver apples. Apples for the teacher.

Thinking the bright shine of them suited her, he rubbed his thumb over the whimsical stud. She was losing so much by not taking care of what she needed to nurture in herself.

"I don't think you have any idea how much you underestimate yourself," he told her, his voice a low rumble in the stillness surrounding them. "And you're not going to find out how much you're capable of until you stop trying to mold yourself into something you're not. You can't get anywhere if you're bound by other people's constraints, Amy. You need to take the brakes off, and just let yourself go."

Amy felt her heart bump her breastbone as his glance slowly swept over her face.

"Do you think you could do that?" he quietly asked.

"I...don't know." The idea of throwing off restraints should have appealed to her. And it did, in some perishing little part of her soul. But it was also frightening. Having spent most of her life denying what she wanted, she wasn't sure she would even know where to start. "I'm not very..." The word *adventurous* came to mind. So did *brave*. "Assertive," she concluded.

"Sure you are. Just remember how strong you are when it comes to your grandmother. And the next time you really want something, don't let anyone talk you out of it."

What if what I want is you?

At the thought, her glance faltered.

"You'll at least think about what I said?" he coaxed, drawing his hand from her neck.

She could still feel his heat on her skin. Wishing he hadn't pulled back, knowing it was probably best that he had, she kept her focus on her hands as she nodded.

"Not good enough," he murmured, tipping her chin up again. "Give me an answer."

"Okay. I'll think about it," she agreed, since just *thinking* couldn't do any harm.

A smile touched his eyes. "Good," he murmured, and because it seemed like the most natural thing in the world to him just then, he leaned forward and touched his lips to hers.

That warm contact stalled her breath.

Caught off guard by what he'd done, Nick edged back far enough to see her face. They were close enough to breathe each other's air, to see the question in each other's eyes.

The beat of his heart felt strangely heavy. "I think we agreed that this isn't a good idea."

"I think we did, too," she murmured, her voice soft and breathy.

"Yeah," he murmured, trailing his thumb along her lower lip. "I'm sure we did."

Amy swallowed past the hammering of her heart in her throat, waiting for him to pull away, praying he wouldn't.

"So." The word was a warm frisson of breath on her face. "I suppose I shouldn't do it again."

For a moment, neither moved. Then the space between them began to shrink as they both ignored what they shouldn't do and his mouth was suddenly covering hers. She opened to him. Warm. Inviting. Craving the feel of her, he curved his hand around her hip, angling her toward him, pulling her closer.

He knew he needed to let her go before he started thinking too much about the unquestioning way she allowed his touch, or how her hands bunched his shirt, gripping it to pull him closer still. But with the honeyed taste of her shooting pure fire through his veins, he just couldn't recall exactly why it was that it had seemed so necessary to pull away a few moments ago. He didn't even try to remember. He just told himself he was sure the reason would come to him eventually as he skimmed his hand over the curve of her ribs and grazed the enticing fullness of her breast.

Amy swallowed a moan as his hand brushed against her. Something warm was gathering low in her belly, something that turned her insides liquid and was threatening to turn her mind to mush.

No, she thought. He'd already done a number on her mind. That had to be why she couldn't seem to summon any real defenses with him. The fact that she so easily exposed the parts of herself that felt the most vulnerable truly defied her understanding. She knew who he was. She knew what he was capable of doing to a woman's heart. But when she was with him, when he touched her, she felt as if she were emerging from a desert and she simply couldn't get enough of the sustenance he offered. With him, she felt hunger. And the hunger she tasted in him, in his slow deep kiss, was plainly, achingly real.

So, eventually, was his restraint.

But that restraint was hard won.

Nick forced his hand from where it had settled on her bare thigh. What he really wanted to do was slip his fingers under the hem of her shorts and slide that hindering fabric away. He wanted more of her. He wanted her naked and lying beneath him. He wanted her breathing his name as he sheathed himself inside her. But those thoughts only added to the torture of how good she felt in his arms. And he didn't think he could torment himself with the feel of her much longer and stay sane.

"Amy." Her name was a deep rasp as he rested his forehead against hers. "You have no idea how hard it is for me to keep my hands off you."

Drawing a deep breath, he raised his head, his tension a tangible thing. "I swear, if you were any other woman, I'd be trying my damnedest to get you into a bed right now." He cared about her far more than he could have imagined. Far more than he had before. "But a relationship with me will only cause problems for you with your family, and you're going to have to deal with them long after I'm gone."

He wasn't even trying to pretend there was any sort of future for them. Amy's chest felt oddly tight at the thought, even though somewhere in the recesses of her slowly clearing brain she knew she should appreciate his candor. No woman in her right mind would want a man to make promises he wouldn't keep. And she was beginning to want those promises with all of her heart and soul.

She eased back, fabric rustling as she smoothed the front of his shirt, and made herself smile.

"I don't suppose being involved with you would be the best way to start asserting myself with my family."

He nudged back her hair, tucking a wisp behind her ear. "Probably not."

Realizing they were still touching each other, she deliberately dropped her faintly trembling hand. He'd barely pulled his back when the sound of a heavy vehicle rolling into the lot had them both jerking around.

Through the long window overlooking the truck bed, Amy watched a dark blue truck similar to the one they sat in lurch to a stop behind them.

"Who's that?" she asked, uneasily watching Nick's handsome features crease in a frown.

"My uncle."

Chapter Nine

The Culhane genes were definitely dominant There was more silver than sable in Michael Culhane's thick hair, and he stood an inch shy of Nick's six feet, but his stockier physique was strong and straight, his eyes the same shocking blue and his weathered features had been carved along the same compelling lines.

He looked enough like Nick that he could have passed for his father.

"What're you doing here?" he called out, his gravelly voice carrying over the slam of truck doors.

Watching through the back window of Nick's truck, Amy saw Nick meet the older man by the back fender. With the side windows down, she could hear their every word.

"I'm checking the drywall," Nick replied, sounding as puzzled as his uncle's craggy face looked. "What about you?"

Mike looked truly confused. "Checkin' the drywall," he echoed with the faint hint of a brogue. "I told you I'd do it."

"You did?"

The older man carried a blue ball cap. Apparently preferring it over sunglasses to cut the glare of the sun, he slapped it on and tugged the brim down to his heavy gray eyebrows. "You don't remember?" he asked, even more puzzled now. "You were at your drafting table last night when I came in to talk to you about the order at the mill. The one for the interior doors they haven't delivered?" he prompted, trying to jog Nick's memory.

The nudge didn't appear to help. For several moments, Nick remained with his hands planted on his lean hips as he silently contemplated the man contemplating him. Then the muscles in his wide shoulders bunched against soft cotton as he lifted his hand and slowly ran it down his face.

"Oh, yeah," he muttered, the words faintly weary. "I remember that. They got us mixed up with some school remodel and the doors they shipped are all wrong. They figure ours went to the school. They're tracking them down now."

"That's what you were saying last night. Right after that was when I told you you looked like the devil himself and needed to get some rest." Admonishment tightened his tone. "You're working too hard, Nicky. You're supposed to be taking the day off."

Nick gave a thoughtful nod. It was coming back to him now. Obviously, as tired as he'd been, parts of their conversation hadn't totally computed. He did, however, have a vague recollection of his uncle telling him to forget about work today. Not that he would. There were advantages to staying busy. Being too tired to think was one of them.

"You're right," he conceded. "You did say you'd check on this."

The creases carved in Mike's tanned cheeks deepened as his mouth thinned. Admonishment gave way to concern. "You're too young to start getting forgetful. Me?" he said, splaying a work-scarred hand over the pocket of his pale gray polo shirt, "I'd forget my own name if someone didn't call me by it once in a while. That's what happens when you get half a dozen decades behind you. But you, you're just entering your prime, lad. And you've always been sharp as a strap-honed razor."

"All I forgot was that you said you'd check this out. It's not that big a deal."

"I still say you need to be getting yourself more sleep."

"I'll get more sleep after I finish drawing the build-outs for that Rhode Island project. I'll have it behind me in another week."

Mike mirrored his nephew's stance, hands on hips, expression determined. "And I've been telling you for the past month that it doesn't make sense for you to be helping me when you've got your own job you need to be doing. I didn't realize you'd have to be bringing work with you to help me here. I can manage if you're needing to go back to New York for a while. Except for the Gardner contract," he amended, thinking of what Nick's sudden absence would entail. "We'd have to put that off until this here project is complete."

"Mike," Nick said, praying for patience, "you know I took a leave of absence. My job is fine. All I'm doing for the firm is tweaking some structural elements for one of my associates and refining designs for another. I don't have to be in New York to do that. And we can't put off the Gardner project. The woman is in a nursing home waiting for us to finish it so she can get out. She wants to go home.''

Mike opened his mouth, only to hesitate when he found himself forced to mentally revise his argument. ''Well, you're right there, I suppose.'' The concession came easily. Mostly because Mike was a man with a compassionate heart and a sentimental streak a mile wide for anything having to do with hearth and home. ''A person needs to be in her own house, if that's what she's wanting. But it's you I'm worried about.''

''I'm fine,'' Nick insisted, and would have asked him to stop worrying if he'd had the chance.

''That's not what your aunt Kate thinks.'' Having evoked the name of the ultimate authority in the Culhane household, Mike crossed his beefy arms. ''Neither one of us can figure out why you're pushing yourself so hard. I'd never have agreed on you coming back to help if I'd known what it was going to take out of you.''

''Mike,'' Nick muttered, wishing he'd drop it.

''Look,'' he muttered right back, having no intention of doing any such thing. ''I know you told me you want to do this because you feel you owe me. And I've told you, you don't. But the way you've been pushing yourself these last couple of weeks is making us both wonder if there's not something botherin' you. You stopped going to your little cousins' ball games and you haven't been out with the fellas to play ball yourself or have yourself a drink. All you do lately is work and sleep. That's not healthy for a man.''

Nick knew it wasn't. And it wasn't the way he'd planned to spend his time there. But he hadn't planned on certain aspects of his life getting complicated on him, either. Until a couple of weeks ago, he'd even been mildly interested in a cute little redhead he'd run into a couple of times at the local Starbucks.

"Mike," he repeated. He loved this man. He really did. He just didn't feel like explaining what those complications were—or considering how Amy seemed to chase the thought of any other woman out of his head. "Not now. Okay?" His voice dropped. "This really isn't a good time."

With a nod, he indicated the cab of his truck. The back window bore the dappled reflection of the truck behind it and clouds billowing in the summer sky. The inside wasn't visible at all. "We're not exactly alone here."

Mike's eyes narrowed on the mirrorlike window. Suddenly curious, he said nothing else as he walked up to the driver's door and glanced inside.

Amy offered him a smile. "Hi," she said, feeling conspicuous and very much as if she were intruding. "I'm Amy." Leaning across the seat, she held out her hand. "You must be Nick's uncle Mike."

A hand rough with calluses engulfed hers.

"That I am," he said, charming her with the way he tried to keep the surprise from his smile. With his free hand he pulled off his hat, his expression unquestionably courteous. "And you'd be a…friend…of Nick's?"

"Amy is Bea Gardner's granddaughter."

"Your company is building her bedroom," she reminded him, aware that Nick had just put a quick end to his uncle's speculation by identifying her as the relative of a client. She wasn't sure how she'd have identified herself, anyway. It was hard to put a label on a relationship when a person wasn't sure exactly what that relationship was. "Nick just finished her wheelchair ramp."

"Ah, yes," he murmured, business taking precedence as Nick had apparently known it would. "We'll be sending over a crew here in about a week. Did he bring you out to check the quality of our work?''

Amy opened her mouth, only to dart a glance over the older man's shoulder. Nick was watching her, his blue eyes guarded. Not sure how to answer, she hoped he would.

Seeing where her attention had gone, Mike pulled back from the window and looked to the taller man looming behind him.

''We ran into each other by the hardware store,'' Nick told him, rather smoothly, she thought. But then, he had survived her mother. It took a lot to shake his control. ''I needed paint for the porch rails, and she's painting cabinets. I had to check the work here…thought I had to check it,'' he corrected with a self-deprecating smile, ''so I brought her with me before we head to her grandmother's.''

''That's where you're going to do your painting?'' Mike asked her.

''Actually, I'm staying at Grandma's house to help her for a while. But yes, that's where I'm painting.''

The lines that lent so much character to Mike's face furrowed with his thoughtful frown. ''And you're working there this afternoon,'' he concluded to Nick, seeming fully aware of the fact that his nephew had carefully avoided saying exactly *why* he'd brought her with him.

''All I have left to do on the ramp is paint it. Then I'll be done with that project. It didn't make sense to me to leave it for later.''

The considering look in Mike's eyes turned to consternation as he slowly shook his head. ''I'm afraid we have a problem here,'' he muttered, looking truly troubled. ''I told you last night you need to take a day off. And this morning I told your aunt that's what you were going to do. She's making you her pot roast. The one she puts the little carrots in. When we came back from church and found you gone, we thought you'd just run to the store or the car wash.'' He turned his thick wrist, glancing at his watch. ''She's planning Sunday dinner at two o'clock. That's only about an hour away.''

Nick closed his eyes and pinched the bridge of his nose. To Amy, his reaction spoke more of fatigue than quandary.

She'd already sensed that he was pushing himself. Considering what she'd overheard his uncle say to him moments ago, she leaned across the seat again.

''I'll paint the rail. I don't have anything else to do this summer but work around there,'' she told Nick, watching his hand fall. ''Just give me the post you were going to use to match the paint and I'll take care of it.''

His blue eyes locked on hers. He looked surprised by her offer. Maybe even touched by it. ''Thanks, but painting was in the bid. I'll do it.''

''So take whatever you charged off the invoice for the bedroom.''

''I said I'd do it.'' If Kate was making him his favorite meal, then he had little choice but to be there. ''I'll just have to do it later.''

''Nick,'' she muttered, wondering if he was only now being thickheaded or if she'd somehow missed the trait before, ''I'm trying to tell you that you don't have to worry about it at all. I don't have anything else I have to do this afternoon. Just take me back to the hardware store so I can get the paint and my car and you go on to dinner.''

Still leaning partway across the seat, she saw his eyes narrow. Less than an hour ago she'd told him she had so many errands to run that she wouldn't be home all day. He'd obviously remembered that. He'd just as obviously remembered that she'd only been trying to avoid him.

For all the good it had done.

With a shrug, she gave him a faint smile.

All he did was shake his head and plow his fingers through his hair as if he fully appreciated how a person's best-laid plans could backfire.

"I'd listen to the lady, Nick," Mike said mildly. Digging a jangling wad of keys from the front pocket of his denims, he moved his assessing glance from her to his nephew. "It sounds to me like she's only thinking of you.

"I've got an idea here," he continued, looking pleased when he found the key that apparently opened one of the unfinished steel doors on the back of the building ahead of them. "Maureen won't be coming to dinner with her family today. So there'll be more than enough food if you'd like to bring Amy along. Being that she doesn't have any plans this afternoon, I mean."

"She just said she wants to paint."

"And I just heard her say she's got all summer to do it."

"Mr. Culhane," Amy murmured.

"It's Mike to you, lass."

"Mike," she corrected, caught totally off guard by his invitation. "Thank you. Very much. But I wouldn't want to impose."

"Impose?" He waved off the word, looking utterly oblivious to her hesitation. "You can't impose when you've been invited. You'd take Kate's mind off the little ones not being around this weekend. Be good for her to have another female in the kitchen to talk to.

"Right, Nick?" he said, slapping his reluctant-looking nephew on the shoulder.

"Right," he muttered, his enthusiasm conspicuously scarce.

"So it's agreed." Pulling a black cell phone from his back pocket, he beamed Amy a smile. "I'll call Kate right now and tell her to set another plate. Do me a favor, though?'' he asked, turning to Nick, who had his brow lowered at Amy. ''She's needing vanilla for the trifle she's making. The clear stuff, she said. Not the brown. Pick some up for her, will you? I'm just going to take a quick walk-through here and I'll be on my way, but you'll likely be getting there before I do.''

If Amy could have figured out a way to decline the invitation, she would have done it. She didn't have to be told to know that Nick wasn't crazy about the idea of taking her to his aunt and uncle's home. But Nick's uncle had known she had no plans, and it would have been unpardonably rude of her to refuse his hospitality.

The moment his uncle, chatting on the phone, had disappeared inside the building and Nick had settled his big frame behind the wheel, she told him that, too.

''Nick, I'm sorry. I couldn't think of a way to get out of it without sounding like I was making excuses.''

''Don't worry about it,'' he muttered, starting the truck. ''Mike wouldn't know how to take no for an answer, anyway.''

''Do you want to just take me back to my car?''

Actually, that was exactly what he wanted to do. It was one thing to see her at the lake house and the nursing home. She belonged in those places. They were…permissible…he supposed was the word he was looking for, because he had legitimate reasons to be in those places with her. But taking her to the place that had been a second home to him, the house that was the only place he thought of as home now that his mom had moved away, wasn't so justifiable. It crossed a line somehow. It didn't matter that it hadn't been his idea. It moved their relationship beyond an area that no one could really question.

It also put her on his turf. And there were things there he'd really rather spare her. And himself. Like his uncle's endless stories about Nick's football feats in high school and Kate's certain speculation over the fact that she was the only woman he'd brought to the house in over ten years.

"It's only for a couple of hours," he finally told her, resigning himself to the idea. "Mike's already told Aunt Kate I'm bringing you, and she'll be disappointed if you don't show up."

"Mike invited her," Nick said to his aunt, who'd met him at the door moments after he'd pulled the truck up in front of the modest old two-story house on the tree-lined street. Mike had pulled up right behind them and snagged Amy to show her where all of his children—and Nick— had pressed their hands into the sidewalk when the cement had been poured a lifetime ago. The man was nothing if not proud of his family. "She's just a friend," he explained, because, in a way, she was. "So don't make a big deal of this. Please?"

"I'm not making a big deal of anything." Soft auburn curls, the gray camouflaged by henna, bounced around Kathleen Culhane's liberally freckled face. Eyes the color of shamrocks sparkled, despite her faintly wounded tone. "I just said it's about time you showed some interest in something other than work." She stretched her neck to peer around his shoulder. "She's cute."

"Yes, she is."

"Rather sweet looking, actually."

"Aunt Kate," he muttered.

"I just made an observation," she said, defending herself. "Did you get my vanilla?"

He held up a sack.

"Is it the clear kind?"

"I'm sure it is. Amy seemed to know what you wanted. She said the kind they had at the first store wasn't right, so we had to go to another one."

Paper crackled as she reached into the little brown bag, read the small box and pronounced it "Perfect. So," she added, lowering her voice. "Who is she? All Mike said on the phone was that you'd be bringing a young lady to dinner."

Nick was spared a response by the sound of footsteps approaching behind him. Stepping back from where his aunt's pleasantly plump frame blocked the front doorway, he watched Amy give him an uncertain smile as she preceded his uncle up the alyssum-lined walkway.

"She said she can't imagine you ever being small enough to make such a handprint," Mike informed him, taking off his hat as he climbed the porch stairs. "I told her you weren't small for long. Soon as you got big enough to get a grip on a football, you started growing like a weed. I remember when he first started playing back in grade school—"

"Now, don't you get started with your stories, Michael," Kate admonished, handing Nick the bag and the box and holding out her hand to Amy. "You'd think the man knows nothing but carpentry and football. He should have had six sons instead of six daughters. I'm Kate," she said, her kind eyes speculative and welcoming. "I'm glad you could join us."

"This is Amy." Nick hesitated ever so briefly. "Amy Chapman."

"Chapman," Kate repeated, releasing her warm grip to usher Amy inside. "Now, that name has a familiar ring to it." The auburn arches of her eyebrows knit thoughtfully.

"Can't place it at the moment, though. Oh, well," she murmured, smiling, "it'll come to me. Come into the kitchen and tell me all about yourself while I finish up the dessert."

"She's a teacher," Nick called from behind them. "First grade."

"Our Maureen's a teacher," Kate said, beaming at Amy as she urged her through rooms that smelled of lemon oil and floor polish and something delicious simmering on the stove. "She teaches fifth grade over at Cedar Lake Elementary."

The mention of that common bond was all it took for Amy to go from feeling slightly overwhelmed to genuinely comfortable with the woman wearing a navy blue apron with her pink shirt and polyester slacks. Kate immediately confided that she had a grandson in the first grade. She also had seven other grandchildren, who were all growing at the speed of light. Or so she claimed as she led her past an upright piano lined with family pictures and into a kitchen that would have made her mother cringe.

Instead of counters neatly lined with accessories that matched and anything that wasn't in use hidden out of sight, the long expanses of yellow Formica held old pink-and-chrome canisters and dog-eared cookbooks. Spices that wouldn't fit in the full spice rack filled the space between a bread machine and a big green bowl that looked as if it collected everything from coupons to car keys. Starched yellow curtains hung on the paned window overlooking a vigorously growing vegetable garden, and the refrigerator, which looked as if it might have been new in 1950, was papered with children's drawings attached by colorful magnets.

It was a room that not only welcomed a person into it, it embraced them with mouthwatering scents from the

Dutch oven atop the old stove and a silent invitation to come in, sit at the green Formica table and make yourself at home.

That was exactly what Amy did. Seeing that the table hadn't been set, she offered to do it while they talked. Kate told her she'd be grateful for the help, only she thought they should eat in the dining room today, it being Sunday, and indicated the maple table visible through a door by the pantry. So, while Kate added the vanilla to the custard she had cooling on the counter and spooned it over cubes of sherry-soaked pound cake and berries, Amy carried plates from the cupboard the older woman indicated and listened while Kate explained that Maureen, their third-born, usually brought her family for dinner on Sunday, but they were in Green Bay that week visiting two of her sisters.

Amy had no idea where Nick had gone. And had Kate not been so charming, she wouldn't have been too pleased with him for abandoning her. But these were people he cared about. The people he loved without drawing boundaries around his heart. Because he cared about them, she wanted to know as much about them as this aunt was willing to share.

"So, how long is it that you've known our Nick?" Kate asked, setting the custard pan in the sink.

"About ten years. I mean, I first met him ten years ago," Amy explained, returning for the napkins Kate had set on the counter. Drawing a hesitant breath, she reached for them. "The reason my last name might be familiar to you is because he was engaged to my sister."

Kate's expression didn't change all that much, though her hand went still on the faucet a moment before she turned it on. "Oh," she murmured, her easy smile quickly resurrecting itself. "Of course. Paige Chapman." She cast

Amy a sideways glance, her still-attractive features more apologetic than assessing. "We only got to meet her a couple of times. With all of us here and all of us tending to talk at once, I think we overwhelmed her a bit. She stayed close to Nick and didn't visit with us much. But I remember her as being quite pretty. How is she?"

"She's just fine. She's married now and has two little girls."

Kate nodded, her expression thoughtful. "I'm glad for her, then. Nick never did say what happened. Why he got cold feet, I mean. He just told us he realized he was making a mistake and said he couldn't go through with it." Sympathy colored her tone. "The girl had to be devastated."

Folding one of the napkins in half, Amy pressed a crease into it. "She was," she murmured. "But she got over it." For the most part. "She adores her husband, and he worships her."

"Then she found the man she was meant to be with. I just wish Nick could find the girl that was meant for him," Kate murmured, sounding as if there was one out there intended for him alone. "But he claims he's content as he is. If that boy's content," she muttered, reaching for the dishcloth to wash out the pot since she was standing there anyway, "then I'm bound for fame as a prima ballerina. Never saw a man more cut out for family than that one, but he hasn't been serious about a girl since your sister. Not that he's ever mentioned, anyway. And I'm sure we'd a' known, since Molly and Moira keep up with him right there in New York."

"Molly and Moira?"

"His cousins. Our two youngest. Molly works in advertising and Moira's studying to be a chef. They've tried fixing him up with their friends, and he keeps turning 'em down. Says if he wants a woman, he'll find one.''

Her cheeks suddenly flushed. "Listen to me go on," Kate muttered, rinsing the pot and reaching for the dish towel. "I'm sure the last thing you want to hear is me carrying on about my nephew. How is it that the two of you stayed friends?''

"It's not that we stayed friends," she replied. "It's more like we met again. He's doing a job for my grandmother. At her house," she explained, folding the rest of the napkins. "I'm staying there to help her this summer and when we started working together, we just…started talking.''

And he'd started listening, she thought. Really… listening.

He didn't always agree with what she said. He especially didn't always agree with what she did. But he listened. So much of the time when she was around her family, she was never heard, her opinion never counted. Maybe that was part of what drew her to him.

Friends, his aunt had called them. And Amy supposed that he was a friend to her. Only a friend wouldn't take advantage of her obvious physical attraction to him. Only a friend would care that there were consequences to a relationship with him that she would have to deal with long after he was gone.

"Well, I'm glad to see there's no bad feeling about him in your family," Kate told her, clearly assuming that Amy's presence and her grandmother's actions meant he had been forgiven. "Nick is like a son to us.''

Seeing no point in distressing the woman by correcting her assumption about the Chapman family's feelings toward Nick, Amy headed past her with the napkins. "He's pretty fond of you, too. I guess growing up around all of his female cousins presented a few challenges," she continued, smiling as she returned for silverware. "But it sounds as if your family was the best thing that ever happened to him. He said after his dad left, he spent a lot of time here."

It relieved Amy to think of him as a little boy in this wonderful house, surrounded by women who'd probably smothered him with affection. "He said he spent summers on jobs with his uncle, too. He really loved that part."

Utensils rattled as Kate pulled open a drawer for her. "He told you that, did he?"

"About working with Mike?"

"About his dad walking out on him and his mom."

Amy glanced up from a row of spoons. "Enough for me to suspect that he doesn't have much use for the man," she said quietly.

Kate must have heard the empathy in her understatement. Or maybe it was the fact that Nick had mentioned his childhood to her that caused the woman to consider her so carefully. But something shifted in the older woman's manner as she turned to the cabinets above the counter. As friendly and open as she already seemed, she now regarded her with a kind of acceptance that hadn't been there moments ago, along with a hint of speculation that hadn't been there, either.

"I'm sorry he's still carrying his hurt," she murmured. "Jack deserves for his son to resent him, but I hate for Nick to carry that kind of feeling inside his heart. I didn't realize he was still feeling it after all this time." Looking thoughtful, she wiped her hands on her apron. "He doesn't mention his father to us, you see."

"Maybe it would help if he did."

"Nothing to be gained by it. It would just bring back

memories that can't be changed. I've never seen a child so devastated as when he learned his dad was divorcing his mom.''

Taking a bowl from the cabinet above her, she lifted it down to set it softly on the counter. Her voice fell right along with it.

''My Michael's a good-looking man, but there was never one more handsome than that younger brother of his,'' she confided. ''When the three of us left Ireland forty years ago, Jack was barely eighteen, but he had girls weeping at the docks when we left to come here. He collected them like flies here in the States, too, but he managed to stay single for...oh, must have been about five years, I suppose it was. Then he fell for my friend Sharon, and they were married. Nicky came along nine months later to the day.

''Sharon was like a sister to me then. She still is,'' Kate admitted, her freckled hands gripping the bowl. ''But she was blind in love with Jack, so when he first started running around on her, she pretended not to see it. It was sort of hard to ignore his philandering, though, when one of his flings got pregnant. He wound up leaving Sharon and the boy for the little harlot.''

Kate slid a glance toward Amy, relaxing her hold on the big porcelain bowl. ''It was hard on the lot of us,'' she candidly admitted, ''Jack being Mike's brother and all. But Mike was just as disgusted with him as the rest of us and tried to be the father Jack wasn't to Nick. He'd always wanted a son, my Michael, and Nick's been just as good as a son to him. When I told Nick the doctor wanted Mike to slow down, it wasn't but a couple of weeks and he had it all arranged to come help him get his business affairs in order. Whatever we gave him, he's given back a hundred-fold.''

Amy quietly lifted the forks from their compartment. "Did he ever see his father after he left?"

"There was some visitation for a couple of years. It was difficult with the other woman being there and a new baby and all. But it got to where the visits were few and far between."

"His mom never remarried?"

"Never did," she confirmed, sounding as if she found the fact decidedly sad. "Lovely woman, too." She smiled at the thought of her friend. "She's having the time of her life down there in Florida, though. Nick has her taking scuba diving lessons, of all things. I suppose he told you she was transferred down there a few years back."

Collecting the rest of the utensils, Amy nodded and said that he had. But just as Kate murmured that it was rather interesting how much Nick had told her, since she'd never known him to talk about himself, a door slammed on the other side of the wall.

The decorative copper plates hanging above the stove had barely bumped back into place when the door by the refrigerator opened.

"Smells like heaven itself in here," Mike announced, rubbing his hands in anticipation as he walked in.

Nick walked in right behind him. His glance hooked Amy's, drawing it to him like the point of a compass to a magnet. He arched his eyebrow, the motion subtle, but the question clear.

Are you doing okay? he seemed to ask.

Her soft smile was more in response to the quick apology in his eyes than assurance that she was holding her own. She liked his aunt. She liked his uncle, too. And despite the fact that Kate had actually raised more questions than she'd answered, right now Amy was simply going to enjoy their company.

Mike didn't appear to be enjoying anything at the moment, however. The anticipation lighting his face had melted to a confused frown.

The dining-room table had his attention. He was looking at it through the doorway on the opposite side of the room, noting the fact that it was barely half-set. "We thought for sure you'd be hollering at us to come in to dinner any time now."

"We've been busy," his wife replied, totally unconcerned with his bewilderment.

Nick's glance bounced from the empty serving dish by the pot simmering on the stove to the vegetables waiting to be prepared for the salad. "Doing what?"

"Talking about you," his aunt said bluntly. "Now, go wash up. The both of you," she said, catching her husband's arm and turning him toward the door they'd come through. "And do it in the utility room. You've been working on something greasy," she accused, frowning at the streaks of black on their hands, "and I don't want grime in my sink. Amy and I will have this on the table in no time."

Chapter Ten

Amy was determined to be sensible about Nick. She knew there was no place for their relationship to go, but that didn't mean she couldn't enjoy his company as long as he was there. She considered what he'd said, too, about how she was holding herself back.

Maybe, in some ways, she was. And maybe she did let her family push her a little. But she also really did enjoy much of what she did for them. If she found herself disappointed once in a while because something didn't go the way she would have liked, she simply focused on the fact that her family meant well. Or at least, they meant no harm. Paige especially.

Her sister had gone all out for her birthday dinner that evening. The luau in her lovely backyard had been truly inspired. Even their mother agreed that Paige had outdone herself. And Amy had been touched by all the work she'd put into the decorations and food. Paige and Darren had even given her a beautiful book of the Hawaiian Islands, inspiration for a trip Paige insisted she really must take someday.

Her parents had given her a beautiful ladies-who-lunch suit that would have looked fabulous on either Paige or her mom. The taupe color was even theirs. But Amy knew that the sincerest gifts were those the recipient would have chosen for herself, so she ignored the fact that she had no idea where she would wear it. For school, she wore jumpers, slacks and skirts. Her personal style, if she had one, was far more casual than theirs the rest of the time, too.

The dress she wore tonight was as fashionable and formal as she ever got. The pale blue sleeveless sheath that skimmed her knees with a row of tiny ruffles was new. She'd bought it on sale at Tammy's Togs last week after her sister, wanting to throw her off her surprise, had told her she'd made reservations at a restaurant for her dinner. On the passenger seat beside her was the hot pink carnation lei she'd worn with it. Wanting the evening to be authentic, her sister had greeted her at the door with the pretty floral necklace and slipped it around her neck.

Her family really had been terribly sweet. And she'd had a lovely time without going to Petruccio's—which was why she felt terrible for feeling so let down as she drove the two miles to her grandmother's house.

It was her birthday, and all she'd really wanted was to see Nick.

It wasn't as if she'd expected him all day and he'd failed to show up. The medical building was finished, but his uncle's company had started the expansion project for the county storage building, and he'd told her yesterday that he probably wouldn't be back until tomorrow. She had no business feeling dispirited.

Still, she hadn't been able to deny how her heart had

lurched every time she'd heard one of his workers' vehicles in the driveway. And how disappointed she'd been every time she'd realized it wasn't him.

It was after ten o'clock when she pulled off the loop road into the drive leading to her grandmother's house. A full moon illuminated the night, making long shadows of the tall, slender pines standing sentinel along the way, and an abstract jumble of the piled construction materials Mike's men were using.

In the past couple of weeks, Mike's men had replaced the foundation under the back porch, closed in the walls, rebuilt the floor and added new windows and doors. Nick was supervising the project, as well as helping on the other job, so he hadn't been doing much of the actual work himself. He'd left most of it to the various crews of framers, electricians and drywallers the company contracted. But he checked the progress of the job and often stayed after the others had gone. Sometimes she fed him dinner while he talked about how Mike planned to take Kate on a cruise next year, or filled her in on how his cousin Maureen's two boys were progressing at T-ball. There had been times, too, when he'd stayed to help her with the kitchen, like the evening he'd helped her rehang the cabinet doors, since the task was easier with two people than one. Or the time he'd helped her add the trim of crimson Bea had asked for to the moldings after the rest of the painting had been finished.

They had fallen into a routine when they were together that felt almost familiar, and would have been quite comfortable had it not been for the awareness that shimmered between them. That awareness was always there, banked like the embers of a fire glowing unseen under ash. Smoldering, waiting for a breath of air to give it life. And because it was always there, and because Nick was being a friend, he denied it the chance to burst into flame by always keeping his hands to himself.

Anticipating the late hour, Amy had left the porch lights on. It wasn't their golden glow that had her attention, however, as she tried to force her thoughts from Nick. It was the glint of her headlights bouncing off the metal bumper ahead of her.

His truck was there.

Pulling up beside it, she cut her engine. A large square draped with a tarp occupied the truck's bed. It had to be something for her grandmother's new bedroom. An air conditioner for the window, perhaps, since it looked as if there was a big box under the dark canvas. She just couldn't imagine why he was bringing it out this time of night.

She couldn't imagine where he was, either.

He wasn't in the truck or on the porch. When she followed the path around to the back of the house, she discovered that he wasn't on the new back porch, either.

It was then that she looked toward the lake and saw his shadowed silhouette near the dock.

The moonlight slanted across the dark water like a swath of white opal on black satin. In that same silvery light, she saw him walking toward her with his hands in his pockets.

"You're earlier than I thought you'd be," he called over the low nighttime croaking of frogs as he came closer.

She moved toward him, her footsteps silent on the dew-kissed grass, her heart happier than it had been all day. "What are you doing here?"

"Waiting for you." His eyes glittered in the pale light as his glance slipped over the filmy fabric skimming her curves. "I was on my way back from my cousin's and was just going to leave your present, but I decided to wait.

"Come on," he said, motioning with his head, his hands

still in the pockets of his khaki slacks. A dark polo shirt, its color impossible to discern with so little light, stretched across his chest. "I need for you to tell me where you want it."

Falling into step beside him, she glanced toward his strong profile as they moved into the glow emanating from the side porch. There was nothing in his expression to make her think he regarded his appearance there as anything extraordinary. Nothing in his casual tone suggested it, either.

"You brought me a present? Nick, you…"

"Didn't have to do that," he concluded with a wry smile. "I know. But it's your birthday, and I wanted to get you something. I wanted to get it here this morning, too," he confessed as they moved down the drive to his truck, " but I couldn't get away from the other job. Then I promised Maureen I'd go to Jason's T-ball game," he explained, speaking of his cousin's youngest son, "so I couldn't come by before you left. By the way, how did it go tonight? Did you have a good time?"

It was the sort of question he often asked. The sort of conversation they often had. Discussing what had gone on during their day had somehow become part of what they did when they were together. So she told him that she'd had a great time, that Paige had gone all out, and how Brittany and Sarah had entertained them all with a hula in little grass skirts.

"I thought you wanted Italian food."

"I've had a really good day, Nick." It was a good day now, anyway. "Don't start. Okay?"

He gave her a level look, his carved features little more than shadows, since the light from the porch barely reached where they'd stopped by his truck. "Only because it's your birthday. Oh, yeah," he muttered, because his statement had reminded him of his purpose for being there, "I couldn't figure out how to get this wrapped."

Pulling his hands from his pockets, he turned to the boxy shape in the truck's bed. "You'll have to forgive the tarp."

Her eyes danced. "Sort of makes it like an unveiling, doesn't it?"

"I think that part comes later. This really isn't much, Amy," he said, leaving her totally puzzled by his comment. "And I really didn't know what to get you, so I went for something I knew you didn't have." His glance skimmed her face, his expression suddenly guarded. "It's up to you to decide if it's impractical or unnecessary, or what you can or can't accomplish with it."

He wasn't sure what she'd think of his gift. It was that kind of uncertainty she saw in his eyes in the moment before he reached over the side of the truck's bedwall and pulled the tarp away. "It's really not much," he repeated. "But it was all I could think of to get you."

It was wrapped in tan plastic, a square block nearly a yard wide and just as tall and she knew without having to tear the plastic away exactly what it was. The material inside would be soft, probably a lovely terra cotta red, and would feel cool beneath her hands until her touch warmed it, gave it life.

He'd brought her modeling clay.

Sitting next to it was a bundle of wire, the sort a sculptor would use to create an armature, or frame, for the clay to cling to so the material wouldn't sag under its own weight.

"I figured you could start with something small, if you wanted. Or jump in and go for life-size."

Amy blinked at the brick of clay, her throat oddly tight. "Or you can turn it into a class project with your students," he murmured, her silence making him question the wisdom of his gift, "if you don't want to use it yourself."

Her profession wasn't the one she would have first chosen for herself. He knew that. But he also didn't doubt for a moment that her students would feel the loss if she wasn't there to share her gifts with them. She nurtured children, helped them to grow, and he couldn't think of anything a person could do that could be more valuable, unless it was saving the lives she molded. But she needed to let herself grow, too. At the very least, he'd hoped she might rediscover the pleasure she'd so obviously once felt with her sculptures.

He could see very little pleasure in the shadowed shape of her profile at the moment, though. She simply stared at his offering and pressed her fingertips to her lips.

"Or I could take it back," he quietly concluded.

She shook her head. "No." Her voice was little more than a whisper. "No," she repeated, and finally glanced up at him.

There was a suspicious brightness in her eyes. Looking into those luminous depths, he took a step closer and felt something like panic squeeze his chest. A single tear slowly slid over the gentle curve of her cheek.

"Hey." Without thinking, he slipped his fingers along the side of her neck and caught the crystalline drop with his thumb. "What's wrong?"

Amy shook her head again, her throat too tight to speak. A forty-pound chunk of clay was hardly the sort of gift that moved a woman to tears, but she felt totally disarmed by what it represented. His belief in her potential. And how very well he knew her.

"Nothing," she finally managed to say. "Absolutely nothing."

Another tear slid after the first. Her skin felt like wet

satin beneath his thumb as he smoothed it away. "It doesn't look like it to me. If I'd known I'd make you cry, I'd have gone with flowers."

Her mouth curved as she tipped her head into his touch. With her eyes shining on his, her soft smile nearly stole his breath.

"I'm not crying."

The fresh scent of her wrapped around him, drew him closer. "Then what do you call this?" he murmured, leaning forward to catch the drop clinging to the corner of her lashes with his lips. "And this?" He caught the one on her cheek, too. And the one that leaked from the corner of her other eye.

Her heart fluttered in her throat. "Allergies."

"I don't think so," he murmured, his lips slick on her skin as he moved toward the corner of her mouth.

The gentleness of his touch beckoned her. Resting her hands on the hard wall of his chest, she edged closer. "Thank you, Nick," she murmured, and felt his mouth close over hers.

Her fingers bunched his shirt, her knees going a little weak in the moments before he slowly lifted his head. "You're welcome," he said, and smoothed her hair back from her face.

He should let her go. He wasn't even sure how she'd come to be in his arms. But it was always that way with her. All he had to do was touch her, and he found himself wondering moments later why he hadn't kept his hands to himself. Which was exactly why he had kept his hands to himself all these weeks.

And why it was so hard to let her go now.

"Nick?"

Her fingers splayed over his chest, the heat of her palms searing through his shirt. She looked so fragile in the moonlight. So innocent. And the thought of her small soft hands moving over his naked chest had him coiled so tight he could barely breathe.

"Yeah?" he murmured, forcing himself to breathe anyway.

Amy tipped her head back, her eyes filling again. "You made today perfect."

"Because I gave you clay?"

"Yes. And because you're here. All I really wanted today was to see you."

The thought that he mattered that much to her stilled his hand at the side of her face. But even as the need to let her go became more pressing, it seemed to become less of an option.

"Amy, don't say things like that."

"Like what?" she asked. "That you're important to me?"

"Yes."

"But you know you are," she murmured, because they'd shared too much for him to think otherwise.

He drew his finger along her cheek, his eyes glittering on her face. "I think you know that I care about you, too, but when it comes to you and me, there are some things we're better off leaving alone."

She knew what he meant. That smoldering coal was a dangerous thing to uncover. "I just wanted you to know how special you've always been to me. How special you are now."

Always. She hadn't meant to say it quite that way, but there was a rightness to her words she couldn't question. He had always been special. He'd become even more so. Infinitely more.

"Amy." His voice was a dark, deep growl as his fingers snaked through her hair. "Why are you doing this?"

She was doing it because at that moment, more than anything in the world, she wanted him to kiss her again. She wanted him to hold her. She simply…wanted. And she was so very tired of being sensible.

"Because you're the one who told me to stop holding myself back."

At her reminder, the glint in his eyes turned fierce. "I think I also told you if you wanted something, you shouldn't let anyone talk you out of it. But I'm not so sure right now that you should listen to me."

Beneath her palm she felt the beat of his heart. It echoed the heavy cadence of her own.

"Then you're telling me I shouldn't go after what I want?"

"Yeah." His hand slipped down her side. "No," he murmured, losing his train of thought when she edged closer so his hand could slide to her back.

"Maybe you should just forget we had that conversation," he suggested. With the taste of her clinging to his lips and his hand moving the silky fabric of her dress over the tantalizing curve of her hip, his voice dropped to a ragged whisper. "Actually, I'm sure of it."

He was saying one thing and doing another as he pressed her closer. He wanted her so badly he ached, but he'd let her go if he had to. Just as he had to give her the chance to back down herself. Because if he kissed her, he wouldn't want to stop there. He could fight himself. He could fight her. But he didn't think he had it in him to fight them both. He'd wanted her far too long.

Amy felt the brush of his heavy thighs against hers, his hard bulge pressed to her stomach. Heat curled through her, lovely and liquid, just the way it had when she used to think of his hands moving over her body. Only, the sensations she'd felt then were a pale imitation of what she felt weakening her limbs with his hands on her now.

"You don't sound very sure," she murmured, amazed by how little reserve she felt with him when he touched her.

"You're not making it easy to let you go," he muttered.

She felt his palm settle at the base of her spine, something electric short-circuiting the nerves there.

Breathless at his provocative touch, she whispered, "I'm not trying to."

She used to wonder what it would feel like to have his hard body touching hers. She'd wondered when she was seventeen. And eighteen, she thought. And sometimes when she'd been with Scott, the only man she'd ever been with. But her last thought vanished like a puff of smoke in the cool night air when Nick went still.

His glance swept her face, his eyes feral in the moments before his head came down and his mouth covered hers. She didn't hesitate. She opened to him, curling her arms around his neck, pulling herself so close she could feel the imprint of iron-hard muscles against her ribs, her breasts.

If he'd been less selfish, more noble, Nick told himself, he would have walked away even now. But he wasn't selfless. He wasn't noble. He was just a man. And knowing she wanted him as badly as he wanted her did something profoundly detrimental to any remaining shred of chivalry he'd possessed.

"Where are your keys?"

He rasped the question against her ear, his breath hot on her cool skin.

Her keys were in her purse in her car. Amy told him that, her voice sounding thready.

Sliding his hand down her arm, he threaded his fingers through hers and turned her around. Moments after she'd retrieved her purse, they were on the porch, he'd unlocked the door and they were moving from the butterscotch glow of the porch light to the shadows of the entryway.

She didn't bother with a light. Neither did Nick. No sooner had he closed the door behind them and she'd heard the heavy click of the lock than he was turning her to him again, his mouth seeking hers.

Her purse hit the floor as she pushed her hands up his chest. Her keys clattered after it as he closed her in his arms.

She was right. The coal burned hot. She'd just had no idea how quickly heat could turn to hunger. Or how hunger compromised everything from common sense to a sense of propriety.

She was in her grandmother's entry with a man who was unzipping her dress while he kissed her senseless. The fact that that man was Nick seemed no more incredible to her than the fact that she was tugging his shirt from his pants as they worked their way across the Aubusson rug.

"Put your arms around my neck," he growled, bending to scoop her into his arms. "Upstairs or down?"

"Up," she told him as he swept her off her feet.

The room she was staying in was through the first door on their right. The narrow twin bed with its eyelet-and-lace comforter sat opposite an antique wall mirror. With the lace curtains open, moonlight streamed into the room, catching itself in the mirror's glass and reflecting back to bathe the space in pale blue shadows.

Nick lowered her to the floor beside the bed, his hands never leaving her body while he nuzzled the skin behind her ear, then traced a path of pure fire to the pulse beating at the base of her throat. That pulse leapt when his hands skimmed up her sides, and he slipped the straps of her dress off her shoulders.

The soft fabric whispered down, puddling at her feet as he cupped her breasts and carried that path of heat to an edge of scalloped lace. Beneath the sheer cloth she felt her nipples tighten. Seconds later, she felt nothing but a hot liquid sensation flowing through her veins when he flicked open the front catch of her bra and his lips closed over one taut bud.

The muscles in his shoulders felt like bands of iron as she gripped them to keep herself upright. His hair felt like silk when she pushed her fingers through it to hold him closer.

Sensation swamped her. He was making her feel things she'd never experienced in her life, melting her bones with each tug of his mouth, each brush of his tongue. He told her she was beautiful, that he couldn't believe how badly he wanted her, how long he'd wanted her.

Weeks, she thought. He was only talking about weeks. She'd wanted him all her life. But all that mattered to her at that moment was that he wanted her now.

He told her that, too. And he told her how he wanted her. Naked and under him. He whispered the provocative words against her skin, his breath as hot as the look in his eyes in the moments before he pulled off his shirt and eased her hands to his belt.

His chest and arms looked like hammered bronze in the shadowy light. Perfectly sculpted. Beautifully masculine. Her hands were trembling as she undid his buckle. The dull clink of it preceded the soft rasp of his zipper and the sharp sound of his deeply drawn breath when she skimmed her hands over those warm, corded muscles.

She'd imagined this. Years ago, she'd yearned for it. Yet her imagination hadn't prepared her for the reality of feeling his warm, supple flesh beneath her hands. She couldn't believe she was actually touching him, that the look in his eyes was turning fierce at the feel of her hands moving over him.

She couldn't believe, either, how bold she was with him, how little she hesitated, when always before she'd tended to be so reserved when it came to men. There was just such a feeling of rightness about being with Nick when they were touching each other that she didn't question what she did now. Touching him felt necessary. And he made her feel as necessary to him as his next breath when they skimmed their remaining clothes from each other and he claimed her mouth once more.

There was hunger in his kiss, soul deep and demanding as he eased her onto the bed. The honed angles and planes of his body felt as hard as granite against her yielding, feminine curves. She sucked in a breath at the brush of his chest hair against her sensitized breasts, glorying in the feel of his rougher body as his legs tangled with hers and his big hands shaped, explored, stroked. He mastered her senses, commanded them, coaxed responses that filled her with a sharp, deep ache so exquisite it nearly bordered on pain.

She wanted him to feel the same consuming need that was swamping her. She wanted him to want her with the same reckless desperation. The need she felt for him shimmered through her. Radiant, like a sun coming from behind a cloud to spread its rays through her body.

Passion.

The word whispered through the sensual fog filling her mind. Her grandmother had spoken of it so simply, as if it were as elemental to a woman as the air she breathed. She'd said a woman needed a man who made her melt when he touched her, who was so essential to her existence that her life would not be the same without him. Amy hadn't truly understood what she was talking about.

She did now. With Nick she now knew desire so strong, so driving that it eclipsed the bounds she'd imposed on herself. But she also knew that the passion was there only because of everything else she felt with him. A sense of protection, of connectedness. He knew her, understood her, encouraged her to simply let herself go.

The way he was doing just then as he rolled to his back, drawing her with him, encouraging her to explore all she wanted—until the feel of her hands and lips had him clenching his jaw and catching her wrists.

In a voice thick with need, he told her she was driving him out of his mind and groped for his pants so he could get the little foil packet in his wallet. Seconds later, he'd rolled the condom over himself and tucked her back beneath him, his eyes glittering like diamonds on her face.

The pale light illuminated his beautifully tortured features. Raw tension radiated from his big body. But it was possessiveness she felt in him when his hand swept down her thigh and he drew her leg over his. That same need to claim was in his touch when he pushed her hair from her forehead. And in the sound of his voice when he asked her to tell him what she wanted.

"You," she whispered. "Just you."

There was something else she understood now. Something that explained why it was only with him that she felt the passion.

She was completely, hopelessly in love with him.

Nick watched the exquisite play of emotions move over her fragile features in the moments before her lashes fell. Her hands rode up his back, urging him closer. She was beautiful in her desire for him, everything he could ever have imagined and far more than he had dreamed possible. He wanted her with a fierceness that stole his breath, and he ached to bury himself in her heat.

But there was something he wanted more.

"Amy," he murmured, his voice ragged. "Open your eyes."

With every nerve in his body screaming for release, he watched her dark lashes drift back up. Only then did he nestle himself completely between her long, slender legs. Only then, with his eyes locked on the need in hers, did he slowly ease inside the welcoming folds of her body.

Sensations ripped through him, catching his breath, gripping him in a fist of need so intense it took every ounce of willpower he possessed to take it slowly.

And he wanted to go slowly with her. He wanted to see her eyes while he filled her body again and again. He didn't know why it was, but with Amy he wanted more than just the release. He wanted to bond her to him, to burn his image into her brain while she clung to him, moved with him.

He eased forward.

She lifted to meet him.

He drew back, unable to imagine how he'd gone so long without her.

"Nick." The sound of his name on her lips echoed the plea in her eyes.

"Say it again," he murmured, going deeper, stronger. "My name."

"Nick," she whispered, urging him closer, her eyes still locked on his. "Please."

He murmured her name back to her, felt her fingers digging into his heated flesh. Then her eyes closed, and she was shattering, taking him with her as he gritted his teeth against the explosion that tore through him, burning so hot, he swore it fused their souls.

Chapter Eleven

Nick stood in the kitchen doorway, watching Amy fill the coffeepot at the sink. On either side of her, the cherry-red cabinets gleamed against the freshly painted, stark white walls. The stained glass birds she'd rehung along the top of the window shot rays of sapphire, topaz and emerald into the room. What had his attention, however, was the elegant line of her neck at the nape of her short, shining hair, and the robe she wore. The short white garment hit her midthigh and was tied at the waist. Unless she'd put something on under it while he'd been dressing, she was completely naked beneath that soft, concealing fabric.

The temptation to slip his arms around her and taste the silky skin of her neck was strong. All he would have to do was untie that narrow belt and he could slip his hands under that thin terry cloth. He could fill his palms with her breasts, stroke the tantalizing skin of her belly, make her moan for him the way he had when they'd awakened wanting each other near midnight. And at dawn.

And in the shower twenty minutes ago.

He'd never felt such hunger for a woman. Or such a sense of peace when he held her. But he was on unfamiliar turf now, and he needed to be careful. He rarely spent the entire night with a woman. Something about waking up together seemed to complicate a relationship, and he always made it clear from the outset that once a relationship started to involve expectations, he was history. But this was Amy, and it wouldn't have mattered if he'd stayed or gone. Their relationship had become complicated long before he'd carried her up the stairs.

Her back was still to him as she poured the water into the coffeemaker. Walking up behind her, he settled his hands at her waist and heard the carafe slide into place with a quiet click.

"Smells good," he murmured, caving in and kissing the tempting spot behind her ear. She smelled like soap and shampoo, and her hair was still damp from their shower.

"It'll be ready in a minute," she told him, thinking he meant the coffee.

"I'm talking about your skin." Giving her earlobe a tug with his lips, he whispered, "But if I start thinking about that, I'll forget about breakfast. We need food."

Amy felt a shiver of pure anticipation as she turned in his arms. Nick had already dressed in his black polo shirt and khakis and he'd combed his damp hair back from his handsome face. She'd been feeling anxious, nervous, but what he'd just done and the smile in his blue eyes went a long way to alleviate the worst of that anxiety.

As long as they'd been touching each other, she'd been fine. She'd experienced no doubts at all each time she'd wakened in his arms, each time they'd reached for each other. It had only been in the few minutes since she'd left him while he was shaving with the disposable razor she'd loaned him that she'd acknowledged how totally their relationship had changed in the past ten hours.

She just had no idea where he would let them go from there.

She took it as a good sign that he didn't appear anywhere near ready to bolt.

"Food, huh?" She mirrored his smile, toying with one of the black buttons on his placket. He was a true paradox to her—a man of enormous restraint, and enormous appetites. "That probably means you want something more than half a cantaloupe."

"Probably," he muttered.

"Yogurt?"

Giving her a look that told her he never touched the stuff, he threaded his fingers through hers and led her to the refrigerator.

He was eyeing the eggs in the carton on the second shelf and the cheese beside it when Amy heard the low hum of a vehicle engine and glanced toward the window over the sink. "It sounds like one of your workers is here."

Instead of reaching for the eggs, Nick closed the refrigerator door. "No one's scheduled to come out here today. It's Saturday."

It was also eight-thirty. An hour and a half past the time workers normally arrived. But Amy hadn't been thinking about the time or what day it was. When Nick had backed her into the shower, telling her on the way that there wasn't anyplace he needed to be before noon, she'd promptly forgotten everything but what he was doing to her.

The sound of the engine grew closer, its low purr refined and ominously familiar. By the time Amy made it to the sink and caught sight of the silver Mercedes SUV that had pulled to a stop behind her car, the engine had been cut, her sister was checking out Nick's truck and a knot the size of a fist had lodged in her empty stomach.

She felt the warm weight of Nick's hand on her shoulder. A scant second later, he pulled it back, as if he'd just realized he really shouldn't touch her when anyone else was around.

"I'm going to go move that clay from the back of my truck. Where do you want it?"

He hesitated as she turned, his glance skimming the apprehension shadowing her face. "It's okay," he murmured, tugging her away from the window so they couldn't be seen. He hated that. The idea that he needed to hide what he was doing with her. "As far as she knows, I just got here."

That was true, Amy supposed, resenting the feeling that she'd done something wrong. It wasn't just the quick slam of apprehension at the sight of her sister disturbing her, though. It was the guardedness in Nick's expression. And the knowledge that their fragile peace had been compromised.

She wished desperately that they'd had more time before the reality of their situation intruded. What was happening between them was too new to withstand any tests. "Would it be in the way if you put it on the new porch?"

He told her it wouldn't, that he'd set it in the middle of the new space where it wouldn't interfere with the workers, and headed out through the new construction as Paige and the girls clamored up the front steps.

Amy met them at the door. Letting them in, she kept her attention on the bubbly and blond little girls who threw themselves at her knees for a hug, then, chattering about going swimming, headed straight for the pantry.

Grandma Bea had always kept animal crackers in there for them. Amy had maintained her tradition.

"Only two apiece," Paige called after them, absently noting Amy's damp hair, robe and bare feet. Her glance caught on the purse and keys in the middle of the Aubusson rug. "Is that Nick's truck out there?"

"Yes," Amy replied, keys jingling as she swiped them up and carried her purse into the kitchen. "Do you want some coffee?"

"No. Thanks," she said distractedly. "We just had breakfast." Puzzlement filled her tone. "I didn't realize they were working here on the weekends, too."

"They're not."

"They why is he here?"

"He brought me a present." Opening one of the newly painted red cupboard doors, Amy studiously ignored the way the knot in her stomach was jumping, took down two cups and reached for the coffeepot. "What are you doing here so early?"

"The girls are taking swim lessons again this year. We're on our way to the club now, but their swim goggles are in the utility bag in our boat." Smoothing the front of the aqua blouse she wore with her crisp linen shorts, she frowned at the coffee cups. "I said no, thanks, Amy. On the coffee," she explained when Amy glanced up. Still frowning, she asked, "What kind of a present?"

The other cup was for Nick. Rather than mentioning that, since her sister was already curious enough, Amy headed to the refrigerator for milk. She wasn't going to lie about Nick. But she wasn't going to explain any more at the moment than she had to, either.

"Clay," she said, smiling at the way Sarah and Brittany stood at the table in the breakfast nook trying to decide which animal shapes they wanted, since they could pick only two.

"Clay?"

"Modeling clay. Can the girls have milk, or is it too close to their lesson?"

"Too close. They probably shouldn't be having the cookies, either." Her brow pinched. "Why would he get you something like that?"

"Because he..." Listens to me, she thought. "Thought I could use it," she said. "What time do the girls' lessons start?"

"Nine o'clock. And stop changing the subject."

"I'm not."

"You are, too." Paige's glance sharpened, her eyes narrowing as she looked from Amy's drying hair and her robe to the purse Amy had picked up from the entry floor and set on the counter. From there, her glance darted to the doorway they'd just come through. The one that led to the entry and the stairs that led to the bedrooms. "Where is he?"

Amy was lousy at deceit, but she thought she could handle omission as long as she didn't have to look anyone in the eye. "Outside." She set the carton of milk next to the cups. "He's putting my present on the back porch."

For a moment, Paige said nothing. But Amy could feel her watching her as her own glance slipped toward the window and the dark-haired man hefting the block of tan plastic from the back of his truck.

"He didn't just get here, did he?"

It was the conclusion in Paige's flat tone as much as the question itself that caused Amy to hesitate.

The fact that she hesitated at all seemed to give Paige all the answer she needed.

"Oh, Amy." Disappointment, accusation and bewilderment melded in those two sighed words. "How could you?"

It was simple, Amy thought. I fell in love with him. But there was really nothing simple about anything at the moment. Not with her relationship with Nick. And, at that moment, not her relationship with her sister.

She wasn't accustomed to fighting for what she wanted for herself.

"Do you still have feelings for Nick?" Amy asked, her voice quiet in deference to the children debating whether there was more cookie in a giraffe or a bear.

Paige looked stunned. "Feelings? You mean, do I still love him?"

That was exactly what she meant.

"Of course not," Paige muttered, sounding as if the thought were absurd.

"Then don't judge what I'm doing," Amy said. "And don't be angry with me."

"Don't be angry because of who he is? Or don't be angry because you're being stupid?" Paige stepped closer when the girls' heads popped up, her sky-blue eyes incredulous, her voice dropping to nearly a whisper. "You know what he's like, Amy. And it's not like you to be so reckless. Is it just an affair you want?"

"No," Amy shot back, too quickly to think about the ammunition she'd just handed her sister.

"Well, that's all you're going to get from him before he moves on," she informed her flatly. "And he will move on. He's obviously been doing it for years. In the meantime, it's not like you can bring him home for holidays. Mom and Dad would have a cow."

"Grandma has a cow?"

"No, Sarah," Amy and Paige replied in unison.

"It's just an expression," Amy expanded, feeling the knot in her stomach clone itself.

"You girls need to put the cookies back in the pantry now," their mom told them. "We need to leave as soon as I finish talking to Aunt Amy."

Amy's arms snaked around her middle. "Don't forget their goggles. And thanks again for last night. Everything was wonderful."

She meant that. She sincerely did. She was also putting an end to their conversation before Paige could pick it up again. The fact that she was being so blunt in her dismissal wasn't lost on her sister, either.

Paige's eyes narrowed. "Amy—"

"I'm not discussing him, Paige." Nick had told her she needed to stand up for herself, to go after what she wanted. Since he felt as essential to her as her heartbeat, she couldn't do anything else. "There's nothing I can say that will make you change the way you feel about him. And there's nothing you can say that will change how I feel. Okay?"

There was no arguing that particular point. Paige didn't even try. Suddenly looking more worried than confounded by her little sister's behavior, she made one last attempt to make Amy see the light.

"Have you even considered what Mom and Dad will think of this?"

Of course she had. She'd been considering her family for as long as she could remember. But she just gave her sister a look that made it clear she meant what she said and wondered how long it would be after Paige left before her mother called.

The clatter of Nick's tailgate slamming into place finally had Paige giving up. But Amy could have sworn she saw something like sympathy move through her sister's expression before Paige told her she was going to get the goggles, then told the girls to give their aunt a hug and wait for her in the SUV.

Nick knew from the way Paige muttered, ''Snake'' when she swept past him on her way to the boathouse that the woman hadn't bought the idea that he'd shown up only that morning. Since he sincerely doubted that Amy would have volunteered the information, he could only assume that some sort of female radar had been involved. That, and the fact that Amy was really lousy at evasion.

Wanting to give Amy a little time, wanting a little time himself, he took the wire to the back porch, too, then spent a minute listening to Sarah and Brittany, who'd run down the ramp opposite the French doors, tell him about going swimming at a pool somewhere. The girls were climbing into their mom's vehicle when he saw Paige aiming for it herself.

Thinking he'd spare them both another encounter, he headed for the French doors himself. He had let himself in and was passing the dining-room table when he heard Paige's driver's side door close. The engine had started when he found Amy leaning against the counter by the coffeepot. With her head bent, she was slowly massaging her forehead with her fingertips. Her other arm was banded at her waist.

Having heard him come in, she lifted her head.

His first instinct was to reach for her. Following it, since he could hear her sister backing out the drive, he curved his hand at the side of her neck. ''Are you all right?''

He could tell she was upset. Her skin was pale and her dark eyes troubled. But, amazingly, she smiled.

''Sure,'' she murmured, touching the button on his shirt she'd been playing with before. ''How about you?''

"I wasn't the one who had to deal with your sister. What happened?"

"She came to get the girls' swim goggles and saw your truck." Beneath his hand her shoulder rose in a faint shrug. "She asked why you were here, and I told her you brought me a present. She kept asking questions and I kept answering and before long, she…"

"Figured out that we'd slept together."

"Pretty much," she agreed.

"So, what did she say to you?"

She had reminded her about how upset her parents would be to know she was involved with him, Amy thought. And about how he would eventually move on. But she didn't want to tell him that. She didn't want to dwell on negatives or doubts at all just then. She wanted to believe there was hope for her and this man. She wanted to believe the concern in his eyes meant he would give them a chance to see what it was that had grown between them. They shared a bond. She could feel it. She just prayed that he could feel it, too.

"It doesn't matter," she murmured.

With the tip of his finger he tipped up her chin. "It does matter, Amy." His glance swept her face, concern now hidden behind certainty. "I've been telling you all along that I don't want to cause trouble for you with your family."

Before Paige had shown up, he'd thought that maybe he and Amy would be okay for a while. That they could protect whatever relationship they had at least until one of them had to leave Cedar Lake. They wouldn't have been able to go anywhere together. But even as much as he hated the thought of having to sneak around to be with her, he would have done it to keep her from getting any grief from her sister or her parents.

That was what had mattered to him. Protecting her. But they'd been lovers less than a day, and their secret was out. She was even already trying to hide her sister's displeasure from him.

"I can choose my own relationships," she gamely replied.

"Then choose one that won't hurt you," he urged, and felt her body go still.

Her arms slipped back around her middle, her voice suddenly losing its strength. "What do you mean?"

Caution suddenly clouded her lovely features. Feeling a fair amount of it himself, he pulled his hand away and slowly pushed it into his pocket. Even as he did, he could feel the need to reach for her again tearing at his insides.

"I never wanted to put you in the position you're in now," he told her, because, all along, he honestly had been thinking of her. "That's why I never intended for us to get this involved."

The muscle in his jaw jerked as he tried to find a way to phrase the rest of what he needed to say. He truly didn't know what it was he felt for her. He'd never wanted to examine it. All he did understand was that the incredible physical need he felt for her was getting all tied up in that need he'd felt to protect her, and that what he needed to protect her from most was himself.

"I want you, Amy. But I can't give you anything in return that's worth the distress you'll face because of me. I'm not a guy who wants a home and kids. You know that. And I'm definitely not a guy who's going to fit into your family."

Amy felt numb. Not that long ago, she'd been in his arms, knowing with utter certainty that in his arms was exactly where she was meant to be. She loved him. It was entirely possible that she'd been in love with him since she was seventeen. But now he was echoing exactly what her sister had said and telling her that what they'd shared should never have happened.

"I don't recall saying that I wanted any of that," she told him, the knot turning into an ache.

"You're saying you don't?"

She couldn't look him in the eye and answer that. Instead, dying inside, she grazed a glance past his chin. "Maybe you're just an act of rebellion."

He shook his head, his eyes too knowing. "You wouldn't start with something like that."

He knew her far too well.

"Amy," he began when she swallowed hard.

"It's okay, Nick. Really." The numbness wasn't so bad. It actually made her feel almost calm. Unnaturally so. But it allowed her to tip her chin up and meet his veiled eyes. "I knew all along that you don't do commitment. I'd be a fool to think you'd make an exception for me, wouldn't I?"

It was hurt talking. Nick knew he'd have to be as insensitive as a rock not to realize that. But knowing he'd caused that hurt made him feel like the snake her sister had called him, and that put him on the defensive.

"This isn't about making an exception, Amy. I don't 'do commitment' because I don't know that I can."

His voice was rough with self-recrimination, his expression dark with it as he stepped back to pace. "My father certainly couldn't do it," he muttered tightly. "I don't even know which wife he's running around on now. Last I heard, it was number four. Or maybe he was just living with that one. Hell," he muttered, "I don't even care. What I do care about is making sure I never leave a woman to raise a child alone, or subject a child of mine to a string of stepmoms and visitation battles. I swore I'd never be like that man, and the easiest way to make sure of that is to avoid commitments in the first place.''

From behind Amy came the click of the coffeepot as the warmer went off. She barely noticed the sound. All she could think about as the tension in Nick's body radiated toward her from six feet away was that she now understood why his resentment for his father sat so close to the surface. The man's influence still affected every day of his life.

''You're amazing, you know that?'' Watching him frown as he thrust his fingers through his hair, she stepped closer. ''You've been encouraging me to look beyond the limits you think I've placed on myself, yet you're denying yourself a wife and children because you had a jerk for a father.''

''It's not the same thing.''

''Of course it is,'' she shot back, unable to believe he couldn't see it. ''It's exactly the same thing. Did it ever occur to you that maybe you're nothing like that man? That maybe you're more like your uncle? He's the one who raised you, Nick. And he's been married to the same woman for forty years.''

It wasn't as if infidelity came from a defective gene. She thought about pointing that out, too, but his silence made her all too aware of what it sounded as if she was doing, and the last thing she wanted was for him to think she was trying to change his mind about her.

It was one thing to go after what she wanted.

It was another entirely to beg.

''I'm sorry,'' she murmured, defenses she didn't realize she possessed locking into place. ''I don't want to argue with you.''

The man didn't want her. There was nothing to argue about.

"I don't want to argue with you, either." The admission came quietly, and with a hint of defeat. "This isn't getting us anywhere."

"No," she murmured. "It's not. Maybe you should just go. Okay?"

"Amy—"

"Now, Nick." Swallowing hard, she backed up. "Please."

Chapter Twelve

"Darren and I will be there with the girls in about half an hour. Did Mom and Dad get there yet with Grandma?"

Amy held her grandmother's remote telephone to her ear with her shoulder as she removed a ceramic pot of baked beans from the oven and set it atop the stove. Trying to keep the reserve from her voice, aware of it in her sister's, she tossed the hot pads onto the counter and closed the oven door.

"About an hour ago," she replied, afraid that reticence was there, anyway. She and Paige had spoken only a couple of times all week. And both times they'd studiously avoided any mention of the man they avoided mentioning now. "Grandma wanted to check her flower beds, so Mom's pushing her around outside. Dad's been checking out the new construction. I think he's under the back porch."

"Figures," Paige muttered over Brittany's "Ow." From

the occasional yelps and whining, it sounded as if she was combing her daughter's hair. "Well, like I said, we'll be there soon."

"Listen, Paige." Amy spoke hurriedly, sensing that her sister was about to hang up. There would be little privacy with everyone around later and there was something she really needed to say. "I need to thank you for not saying anything to Mom. About Nick," she explained, because her sister didn't always seem to hear what she was saying.

Whether or not Paige had been paying attention before, Amy knew she had her attention now. The silence on the other end of the line became pronounced, then grew deafening.

"Paige?"

"I'm not really sure why I haven't," her sister finally admitted.

"Well, I appreciate it, anyway."

Paige ignored her gratitude. "Maybe it's because I can't figure out how I feel about you being involved with him. Or maybe," she said, her voice growing quiet, "it's because the more I think about it, the more I realize he'd have to be pretty serious about you to risk a relationship." It sounded as if she drew a deep breath. A faint rush of air filtered through the line. "I just really hope you know what you're doing, Amy."

A bruised sensation pressed around Amy's heart. "I'm not doing anything," she said as the irony of her sister's words sank in. Unless she was seriously mistaken, Paige was actually coming around to the idea of her and Nick together. But the understanding Amy would have hoped for wasn't necessary. Nick was running true to form. All she had to do now was get over him. Which she was sure she would. In about a hundred years. "You were right about him,'' she had to admit, then let the matter go. ''I'll see you in a while.''

From Paige's momentary silence, Amy was sure her admission had caught her sister completely off guard. But she'd already confused her sister's concept of her by getting involved with Nick in the first place.

''Right,'' Paige replied, throwing Amy a little off guard herself when she didn't say *I told you so.* ''We'll be there soon.''

She paused, seeming to weigh whether or not to ask what had happened. Apparently, as Amy had, she decided that where Nick was concerned there were some things best left unshared. ''Are you sure you don't want me to bring anything other than dessert and potato salad?''

''You might want to get a bag of ice.'' Amy latched on to the subject, grateful that her sister hadn't pressed. The ache wasn't so sharp when she was thinking about something else. It was just sort of there, a dull, constant sense of loss that sometimes made it hard to breathe, but was otherwise hardly noticeable at all. ''There are a couple of trays here, but if Dad and Darren are going to be working, they're going to get thirsty.''

''A bag of ice. No problem. Oh, one more thing. Darren wants to know if everything's finished in Grandma's new room.''

''Just about. Someone's supposed to be out today to put in the light fixtures and the screens. So tell him he's not getting out of this. He and Dad can still move the furniture down from her bedroom.''

''He still thinks we should hire someone to do it.''

''Talk to Dad. He's the one who said no one will do the job for less than an hour's wage. It didn't make any sense to him to pay a couple of other guys that much to do what he and your husband can do in half an hour for nothing.''

Amy heard Darren grumble something in the background when her sister repeated her message. But the grumbling was good-natured, because the big, bald orthodontist was a good-natured guy.

A few moments later, Amy had slipped the phone back on its base and glanced toward the kitchen doorway. Between the gathering clouds, sunlight poured through the row of tall, narrow windows lining the new hallway that led past her grandmother's new bedroom and onto the new porch.

Her grandmother loved her new space. Bea hadn't been home from the nursing home for five minutes before she'd pronounced everything about her house perfect. She'd given an approving nod to the ramp as her son-in-law had pushed her up it, then sat in her wheelchair with her wrinkled and beringed fingers folded in the lap of her multicolored caftan and beamed at the transformation in her cheerful kitchen.

I adore it, she'd told Amy, then edged herself toward her new hallway while her very conventional daughter dubiously eyed the unorthodox color of the cabinets, shrugged as if to say there was no accounting for taste and caught up with her mom.

Bea had been equally pleased with her spacious new room and new porch. The only time her smile had faded was when she'd asked Amy what she thought of the job Nick had done.

Amy's glance had immediately faltered. On whom? was her first thought.

''He's very good at what he does'' was all she'd actually said. But her grandmother's eyebrow had arched in that quietly observant way she had. And Amy, feeling far too transparent where the older woman was concerned, had immediately sought to avoid her scrutiny by asking the same question of her mother.

There was no doubt in Amy's mind that both of her parents were more impressed with the new addition than they wanted to let on. Her father, tall, graying and thin as a switchblade, had rubbed his chin as he'd walked around the room, his patrician features schooled in an analytical mask while he'd assessed quality and design. He'd nodded a lot, which he did a lot anyway, and allowed that he'd seen worse, which was as close to a compliment as he was likely to get for the man who'd once seriously elevated his blood pressure.

Her mother, however, being her mother, did remind them all that Nick had said he'd have the project finished today. Which he didn't, she also felt compelled to mention, since the light fixtures and screens were still missing.

The light fixtures for the bedroom and hall had been back ordered, which was why the electrician hadn't installed them. Nick had left Amy a note yesterday saying they were in and, as Amy had mentioned to Paige, someone was supposed to remedy that minor situation soon.

Since she and Nick had been avoiding each other most of the week, it didn't occur to her that that someone might be Nick—until she considered that it was Saturday. He made a point of not working his men on weekends whenever possible so his uncle wouldn't have to pay overtime. The only other person he could send would be Mike, and the whole point of Nick being around was to take some of the work burden off the man's shoulders.

The suspicion that Nick would soon be there made her more than a little uneasy as she watched her mom wheel her grandma along the path by the hydrangea hedge. That unease shrank to a knot of anxiety with the sound of a truck pulling into the drive.

She didn't have to see who was behind the wheel to know who was there when the vehicle pulled to a stop. Her mom and Bea had both looked up at the vehicle's deep rumble. Seconds later, her mom's mouth had pinched. The expression was mirrored in her father's face when she saw him emerge from the side of the house to walk over to her mother and jam his hands on his hips.

Nick had hoped that Amy would be alone. He'd hoped she wouldn't have made herself scarce, either, the way she had all week by leaving just before quitting time so he couldn't hang around to talk to her. That was why he hadn't mentioned that he would be there himself that morning when he'd left her a note yesterday. There were things he wanted her to know before he disappeared completely from her life. And after he'd finished the job today, that was exactly what he was going to do. In the morning he'd be leaving for New York for a few days. He'd figured it would be easier on both of them if he said what he needed to say now rather than drag things out for another week. He'd have no reason then to see her when he returned.

His hopes, however, had faded within seconds of turning into Mrs. Gardner's drive. Amy's bright yellow car was there, but so was a beige Oldsmobile sedan. Not too far from the vehicles, a little knot of people was gathered by the hedge.

He recognized the couple behind Bea in the time it took his heart to sink.

Had he been made of less stubborn stuff, he might have pretended he'd made a wrong turn and backed right out. But even if the trio hadn't already spotted him, he wasn't in the habit of running from a little adversity. As far as he was concerned, the only choice he had was to take a deep breath, get the encounter over with and go do the rest of what he'd come to do.

He had told Susan Chapman that the job for Mrs. Gardner would be finished today. He'd made a point of it, in fact, and he had every intention of keeping his word. It was a matter of pride. Of honor. And contrary to what she and the distinguished-looking man glaring at him from behind her right shoulder undoubtedly thought of him, he did possess a strong sense of both.

Birds scattered with the muffled slam of his door. Pocketing his keys, wondering if this was how Daniel had felt as he'd entered the den, he drew a resigned breath and headed toward the hedge.

At least Bea wasn't frowning.

The two women were a true study in contrasts. Susan Chapman, in a nautical striped shirt and navy culottes, her pale hair smoothed back and anchored at her nape, looked ready for a day on a yacht. The flowing garment of bright geometrical shapes Bea wore made the lady with the intricate silver braid look as if she should be dancing circles around a Gypsy's fire.

He nodded to them both, then looked to the man in the navy polo shirt and tan walking shorts. Paul Chapman's expression was easily as rigid as his wife's.

"Culhane," Paul muttered in a tone that made the word anything but a greeting.

"Sir," Nick returned evenly, and immediately sought the friendlier face of the elderly lady in the wheelchair. The warm, humid air felt decidedly oppressive under the weight of the Chapmans' scrutiny. "I'm glad to see you're home, Mrs. Gardner. I hope everything is the way you want it."

"Thank you, Nick. And it seems to be." She paused significantly. "With the house, anyway."

At that particular moment, the house was all he was concerned about. "Good," he murmured, relieved by that. "If you'll excuse me, then, I'll get the truck unloaded so I can finish up, and you and I can do the walk-through. Check over everything to make sure there are no problems," he explained, in case she wasn't familiar with the term.

"You can do it with Amy," Bea informed him, watching him closely herself. "She's inside now."

Nick started to glance toward the windows at the side of the house. Instead, catching himself, he pushed his hands into the pockets of his jeans. He wanted to talk to Amy, but not with anyone else around. Especially not her parents.

"I'd rather do it with you."

"You've been working with Amy all along."

"It's your name on the contract."

He doubted Amy would believe it, but he was hurting, too. And, hurting, he grew defensive. With his ruthless control firmly in place, all he let Bea see was what looked like determination.

The woman's neatly penciled eyebrow slowly arched. "Finish what you have to do," she told him calmly. "Then we'll see."

Considering himself dismissed, feeling more as if he'd been freed, Nick acknowledged Susan and Paul because it was the civil thing to do and headed for the truck.

He had it almost unloaded and was on his way around from the far side of the house where he'd carried the last of the screens when he noticed Sarah and Brittany racing toward the picnic table in the middle of the backyard. The kids being there didn't bother him at all. But it was all he

could do not to groan when he saw Paige walking toward
the back stairs with a big bowl in her hands. Right behind
her, carrying the same kind of flat plastic thing his aunt
used for cakes, was a big, bald guy with a rim of wheat-
brown hair and shoulders like a linebacker.

It was Brittany who blithely informed him that the linebacker was her daddy and that after he and Grandpa moved
Grandma's bed, they would get to go out in the boat. Sarah
simply ran over when she saw him and, apparently remembering how he'd sympathized with her scrapes, wrapped
her arms around one of his knees. Her cherubic little face
beamed up at him while she informed him that Mom said
Pete had to stay home today.

It appeared to Nick as if the whole family was there.

The uncomfortable realization had no sooner hit than he
saw Paige stop at the top of the stairs. He didn't hear what
her husband had said to her, but an instant later, her glance
swung to where her youngest daughter was still hanging
on his knee.

Even from where he stood thirty feet away, he could
see Paige say, "That's Nick."

"Sarah. Brittany," the man called in a voice that
sounded like gravel rolling in a can. "Come help Mom."

Paige's husband was staking his claims. All of them. He
looked straight at Nick, but his expression didn't challenge, the way Paul Chapman's had. He just held Nick's
glance while he opened the door for his wife, making it
clear that he knew who Nick was and what he'd done, and
that he would protect what now belonged to him.

As unpleasant situations went, the one unfolding around
him held nightmare potential. But the only thing Nick felt
he could do was head for the truck for his tools and keep
his focus on finishing the job. He wouldn't think about
anything beyond that.

It was with that conviction in mind that he set to work, doing his best to stay out of everyone's way. To escape the worst of the tension that snaked through the atmosphere because of his presence, he hung the window screens on the far side of the house and around the new porch first, because that kept him outside while the men carried Bea's dresser and nightstands and bed into her room. He couldn't blame the men for being cool toward him. To the big orthodontist, he was the man his wife had almost married. To Mr. Chapman, he was the man who'd done a number on his oldest daughter. If they knew he'd hurt Amy, too, Nick figured they'd want to tack his hide to the nearest tree.

Not that he'd blame them. He hated what he'd done himself. More than anything, he hated that he might have caused trouble for Amy with her family.

Over the next half hour he saw her only twice. The first time, she was on her way down the stairs with a pitcher. He'd barely run a glance over her white T-shirt and khaki shorts when she glanced over to find him watching her. They'd barely made eye contact before she looked away, set the pitcher on the table and disappeared back inside the house. A few minutes later, she reappeared with a stack of paper plates and cups and sent Brittany over to ask him if he was thirsty.

With a warm breeze blowing and the summer clouds adding to the humidity coming off the lake, something cold and wet sounded like pure heaven to him. So he told Brittany he was and, with Bea watching from her wheelchair by the table, Amy sent the little girl back with a large glass of iced tea a few moments later.

From everyone else, the silence toward him seemed punishing.

From her, it felt more like the need to protect herself.

Because his presence clearly made her uncomfortable, he figured the best thing he could do for her was to hurry up and go. There wasn't anything he could say that would change the way things were meant to be. And all he cared about now was not hurting her more.

Knowing it would take him less than an hour to install the two wall sconces and the overhead fixtures in the bedroom and hall, he moved inside as soon as the women had carried the food to the picnic table and called everyone to eat.

Half an hour later, he had the two brass sconces installed on either side of Bea's cherrywood dresser when he slipped out the French doors to get his ladder and noticed Mr. and Mrs. Chapman on the dock, getting into the boat with the girls. Minutes later, he'd gone back out to bring in the two large boxes with the overhead fixtures when it started to sprinkle again and he saw Amy pushing her grandmother toward the house.

Thirty more minutes, he told himself, and was back inside on the ladder, screwing the foot plate to the ceiling fixture in Bea's room, when he heard Amy and her grandmother in the kitchen. He couldn't hear what they said. He didn't even try to listen. He just focused on what he had to do and ignored the way the muscles in his gut tightened when he saw Amy slip past the door, and he heard the back screen door close.

Through the window near the big brass bed he saw her walking to where her sister stood on the dock. From the way her hair whipped around her head, it looked as if the wind was coming up.

"I want to know why you and my granddaughter aren't speaking."

Feeling caught, or maybe it was trapped, he looked down to see that Bea had pushed herself into the hall.

Framed by the window behind her, a single shaft of sunlight piercing the thickening clouds, she maneuvered herself around to face him.

He recognized the determined expression in her creased and regal features. He'd seen it before. The night she'd picked him up out on the highway a couple of hours after he'd broken up with Paige.

It was with a gathering sense of certainty that he climbed down and walked to where she regarded him with her hands folded primly in her lap.

"What are you trying to do, Mrs. Gardner?"

"I'm trying to find out what the problem is between you and Amy," she said, sounding as if she thought she'd made herself clear enough the first time.

"That's not what I mean, and you know it." His voice dropped, his glance moving behind her as if to make sure they were alone, even though he knew full well that they were. "I don't intend any disrespect, ma'am, but I'd like to know what you're hoping for here. You're the only one who knows why I walked away from Paige, and you've been pushing Amy and me together for over a month."

Behind her silver-rimmed glasses, her sharp hazel eyes moved from his jeans and gray T-shirt to settle easily on his face. As she tipped her head, her meticulously braided hair gleamed like threads of platinum.

"You know, Nick," she said, completely ignoring his accusation, "I've always been rather proud of you for having done the right thing all those years ago. A lesser man might have stayed and caused far more heartbreak than you did."

She waited a moment, seeming to have expected his sudden silence as her unexpected admission sunk in.

"I'll admit I was always fond of you. We all were," she felt compelled to tell him. "Until you broke up with

Paige, of course. But, as you said, no one knew why you had done that but me. No one could know," she insisted, "because of what it would do to the girls' relationship. It would be very difficult for a woman to discover that the man she loved preferred her younger sister."

With one coral-tipped finger she traced a triangle of chartreuse on the fabric covering her lap. "That was a long time ago, though. And much has changed. I'd also wondered if, perhaps, much hadn't."

"Ma'am?"

"With you and Amy," she clarified, looking up. "I thought nothing of it when I learned you were back working for your uncle, until my friend mentioned that you'd never married. You were building her grandson a medical office," she explained, when his eyebrows merged. "Anyway, I thought that was rather curious. Don't you?"

"What was?"

"That you never married."

A muscle in his jaw twitched. "There's a reason for that."

"Which is?"

Had this woman been anyone else, he'd have been sorely tempted to politely mention that it was none of her business. But it was her business because of what she'd badgered out of him ten years ago, after he'd dulled his defenses with a few too many tequila shooters.

"It was because of what I learned before I broke up with Paige," he told her, tension flowing through his veins as he faced the need to admit to her what he hadn't quite been able to admit to Amy. It had hardly been Amy's fault that she'd been the catalyst in his little discovery.

"I doubt that my father was faithful to any woman a day in his life, Mrs. Gardner. I told Amy that. I also told her that I didn't want to be anything like him." Nerves knotted at the thought of how he refused to subject a child to the turmoil of being abandoned the way he had. And of how he couldn't stand the thought of a woman being as devastated as his mother had been. As devastated as Paige had looked when he'd broken up with her.

"What I didn't tell her was that it was because of her that I discovered I was just like him after all."

Genuine confusion registered in Bea's eyes. "I'm afraid I don't understand."

"I was engaged to Paige," he pointed out, biting back the edge in his voice as he tried to make himself as clear as he could, "but I was already being unfaithful to her because I couldn't get her sister out of my mind. I wasn't even married and when she'd kiss me, it was Amy I was thinking about. The things I was feeling toward Amy taught me right there that I had no business committing to anyone."

"I see." She spoke thoughtfully, seeming far less disquieted by the discussion than he was. "Then you've been in other relationships and had other women come along who disturbed you just as much?"

Not as much as Amy had, he thought, unable to believe he was discussing his sex life with this woman. Never as much as Amy.

"No," he replied, thinking of all the times he'd been with someone and an image of her had flashed in his mind. Even years after he'd last seen her, the remembered warmth of her spirit had left him dissatisfied with whoever he was with.

His brow furrowed at the thought, even as the glint of compassion entered Bea's eyes.

"I rather had the feeling that you and Amy were becoming friends."

"We were."

"Then you know, Nick," she said quietly, "you might want to think about what you just said. And for what it's worth, I don't think Amy has come across anyone who's disturbed her as much as you did all those years ago, either. That could very well be why she picks men she can't fall in love with." She shook her head, reaching for the metal ring on the wheel to back herself up. "I know for a fact that she adored you."

For a moment, Nick said nothing. He just stared at the elderly woman quietly turning away from him, vaguely aware of the tree branches visible behind her whipping about in the wind. He'd had no idea how Amy had felt about him back then. But even had he known, it wouldn't have changed a thing. The circumstances would have been the same. As for the rest of what Bea had just said, he had no time to consider it before he saw a different kind of concern knit the woman's face.

"What on earth...? Nick," she called, her tone urgent as she focused on something beyond the windows. "There's something wrong at the dock. Come see what's the matter."

"I'm trying, Paige. It just won't start."

Darren planted his feet wider in the rocking ski boat, the wind snatching his words as he rewound the rope on the outboard motor's starter flywheel. Behind him, the engine's big blue cover slid to the leeward side of the deck.

Waves buffeted the shining white fiberglass hull. They splashed against pilings of the little pier, spraying Amy's legs, soaking her sandals. On the dock next to her, Paige bounced on the balls of her feet with her fingers pressed to her mouth.

"But they're drifting farther out!"

"I know that!"

Amy stepped back. "I'm getting Nick."

Trying not to panic herself, she turned on her heel. She wasn't going to wait for her sister or brother-in-law to tell her his help wasn't necessary. She didn't care that most of her family regarded Nick as a pariah. At that moment, she didn't even care that his presence had put her on edge and kept her there the entire time he'd been working on the house. All she wanted was to get her parents and her nieces on dry land before the whitecaps swamped the little boat drifting farther and farther from shore.

She and Paige and Darren had watched for the past five minutes while the wind grew stronger and their dad tried to row back in. With every stroke he'd taken, the boat had bobbed like a cork and turned wherever the waves had decided to take it.

The fact that the waves were higher than the low sides of the boat meant it could well be taking on water, too. Her parents and her nieces were all wearing life jackets. But people, especially small children, could easily drown being tossed about in such waves should the boat go down.

Amy hurried across the lawn, glancing behind her once to see the dinghy becoming more distant. Darren still worked furiously on his boat.

With her heart pounding in her throat, she turned back to the house, shouting Nick's name. She doubted he could hear. The wind grabbed her voice, carrying it back toward the lake and churning the water higher. Yet his name had no sooner left her mouth than she saw his strong and solid body fill the back door. The wind caught the new aluminum screen when he pushed it open, slamming it against its frame as he took the steps and hit the ground at a jog. It had been showering in fits and starts, but the fat drops hitting her face were coming faster now and the wind was coming in gusts that had all of the plates and most of the dishes from the table flying across the lawn.

It wasn't as if the wind had come from nowhere. It had been breezy all day. It was just that in the past several minutes the gusts had grown increasingly stiffer, until what had seemed like a harmless bit of summer weather had turned into something far more sinister. Summer showers were as common as the flowers they nourished. But strong winds turned them into a summer squall and that wasn't anything a person wanted to be caught in on a lake.

"They can't get back," she called out to him, the rain pelting harder as she pointed behind her. "Dad's been trying to row them in, but the water's too choppy. I can't tell for sure, but I think he's lost an oar."

"Can't you get them in the other boat?"

"Darren can't get the engine started."

Amy saw the quick slam of Nick's dark eyebrows, then felt the heat of his hand as he grabbed hers to run with her back to the dock. "The girls are wearing life jackets, aren't they?"

She wasn't surprised at all that his first concern was the children. She wasn't even surprised by his lack of hesitation to help. She was just grateful he was there as Paige watched them hit the wet boards of the pier and Amy glanced out to where the little blue dingy had been bobbing around only seconds before.

The rain was coming in earnest now, slanting sideways with the wind and turning the vista a misty silver. The gray of the sky merged with the gray of the water and the second Amy realized she could see nothing but whitecaps, Paige apparently realized it, too.

"Darren! Oh, my God," her sister cried, her words a panicked prayer. "Darren, the boat! I can't see the boat!"

Darren swung around, frustration washing from his even

features as alarm set in. With another pitch of the deck, his face registered the same fear that had Paige running to the end of the dock. The moment she got there, she ran right back, shaking her hands as if to rid them of water, helpless to know what to do.

Apparently fearing she'd jump in and go after them if she had to, Darren started to climb out after her, then abruptly glanced back to the ominously silent engine.

Nick was off the dock and in Darren's ski boat in one long stride.

He raised his voice against the wind and slap of waves. "Is it flooded?" he called over his shoulder, and was wrapping the rope around the flywheel before the big guy in the Minnesota Vikings T-shirt could decide which way he should turn.

Worry slashed Darren's expression as he focused on the middle of the lake and shoved his palm over his bald head. At that moment, it didn't matter that the man taking over for him was the one they'd all tried to pretend wasn't there. "Yeah," he promptly called back. "I had the throttle wide open and kept cranking on it, but the battery ran down."

Nick whipped the last few feet of rope into place. "How long have you been pulling on this thing?"

"A few minutes." Panicked, trying not to be, he dropped his hand to rub the sore muscles in his arm and stepped forward. "Five or six maybe."

Nick figured the man's arm had to feel like jelly. The lettering on the motor bonnet on the deck indicated that the engine was a hundred horsepower. He'd seen men collapse in a sweat working to start an engine that size with the battery dead. It took a lot of strength to accelerate the wheel fast enough to create an electrical charge. "I'll pull. You rewind."

Moving back far enough to get leverage, Nick planted

his feet. Muscles bunched beneath dampening gray cotton as he ripped back on the rope.

Mirroring the grim set of Nick's jaw, Darren reeled in the rope, winding it around the flywheel as he did, and let go for Nick to jerk it back again.

The engine sputtered.

Without wasting a beat, the rope went back around the wheel.

"Oh, Darren! Hurry!"

"Paige, we're working on it!" her husband snapped back.

"Amy," Nick called, muscles bunching again. "You and Paige keep your eyes on the water. See if you can spot anyone out there."

Amy knew it was fear that had made Darren snap at his wife. He was doing all he could. He and Nick both were. She knew her sister would eventually realize it, too. But Amy also knew that Paige was actually in a worse position than her husband because there was nothing she could physically do to help. That was why she grabbed her by the wrist as Nick whipped back the rope again and tugged her a few feet back from the boat. They both needed to watch the water, she told her. With two sets of eyes, they should be able to spot something.

Shaking inside, suspecting that her sister was shaking harder, she peered hard at the forbidding lake, willing the dinghy into view. She couldn't see anything, but she didn't know if it was because the rain was blurring the shallow blue boat or because the boat was no longer there.

Over the rushing beat of rain on the water, Amy heard the engine sputter again.

A few moments later, it sputtered and caught with a deafening roar.

Spinning around with her sister, she saw Darren jump in front of the motor, adjusting controls. Nick was already at the tie lines, unlashing the stern rope from the cleat on the dock even as Amy reached for the one at the bow and bent to get in.

Paige was already trying to get in down by Darren. But her husband had pushed the end of the boat from the dock so she couldn't and was yelling over the engine noise that there was no way she was going out there with him.

Nick seemed just as adamant to Amy when he gripped her arm to keep her on the dock. Rain pelted his face, his expression as dark as the sky. "What do you think you're doing?"

"I want to help."

"Then stay here and take care of your sister. There's only one life jacket." Pushing her back, he grabbed the green life vest from where he'd spotted it on a bench and tossed it toward Darren. "I don't want to have to worry about you out there."

"But you need a jacket, too."

"Don't worry about me. Did you see anything?" he demanded.

"Nothing. And you need a jacket, Nick," she insisted, worrying anyway. "Nick!"

She had no idea if he even heard her over the cacophony of the engine, the wind and the rain. He'd done what the other man had and pushed the boat out so neither she nor Paige could get in. It was already drifting away.

Then it wasn't drifting at all. Darren hit the throttle. An instant later, the sleek boat shot forward and a white rooster tail was flying behind the stern as they cut an arc and bounced toward the three tiny orange dots suddenly visible in the rising and falling waves.

Amy grabbed Paige and pointed to what she saw, frantically searching the whitecaps for whoever was missing.

It was Paige who spotted the fourth.

* * *

"We started taking on water, and there just wasn't anything I could do." Paul Chapman had just emerged from the downstairs bathroom, barefoot and wrapped in a blue blanket Amy had pulled off her grandmother's bed. Lowering himself to a chair beside his wife at the kitchen table, he glanced across the bowl of fruit in its center to where Paige sat cuddling her youngest daughter. "We could see the three of you on the dock and kept calling and waiting for Darren to come get us."

With Sarah wrapped in a thick towel in her lap, Paige cuddled her shivering little girl closer. Beside her, Bea dried Sarah's feet with one of the bath towels Amy was passing out. "He couldn't get the boat started, Dad."

"Oh." He pronounced the word flatly. "He didn't say anything about that."

Amy knew there really hadn't been much of a chance for anyone to say anything. Once the men had plucked her family out of the water, she didn't imagine anyone had been interested in anything other than finding out if everyone was all right and speeding them back to shore. There'd been no time for discussion in the few minutes since they'd hit the dock, either. Everyone had been busy peeling off wet clothes and checking over the children, who were cold and shaken, but otherwise unscathed.

Since Paige and Amy had stayed on the dock until the men had returned, they were nearly as wet as everyone else. So were Darren and Nick. But only Darren was in the house. He was on the back porch stripping down Brittany. Nick had jogged back down to the dock as soon as he and Darren had carried the girls to the back porch.

Amy had heard him tell Darren to stay with his family and that he'd take care of putting the cover back on the engine. She'd been too busy being relieved that everyone was okay to catch whatever else he'd said.

After slipping off her wet shoes so she wouldn't keep adding to the drips and tracks on the floor, Amy handed her mother a towel so she could dry her hair.

"I tried bailing with my hands," Susan told them. Her voice shook a little less than it had a couple of minutes ago, but there was still a tremor in her hands as she reached for what Amy offered and gave her a grateful smile. "But there was just no keeping up. Then waves just pulled the oars right out of Paul's hands and we didn't know what to do. He was already so tired from rowing," she murmured, still pale at the thought of all that could have happened, and at what had. "I was so afraid for the girls."

"I was scared, Mommy." Shivering, Sarah curled tighter into her mom's arms.

Paige smoothed the sodden and stringy hair back from her daughter's face, touching her as if she couldn't bear the thought of letting her go.

"I'm sure you were, sweetheart. We were scared, too."

"Daddy saved us."

"Your daddy couldn't have done it without help." Darren appeared in the new hall's doorway with Brittany perched high in his arms. He looked years younger than he had just a short while ago, but still rather solemn. "I never could have started that engine without Culhane."

Gently he stroked his oldest daughter's skinny little shoulder. Like her sister, the little girl was wrapped in a towel. Her soggy pigtails hung limply from their sodden pink bows.

"There's no way I could have gotten you in the boat without him at the rudder, either. We were blowing all over the place." He wasn't speaking only to Sarah, even though it was her claim he addressed. He was telling them all that he couldn't take all the credit for their being safely where they were now. It had been a team effort. "He was pretty insistent about which one of us got the life jacket, too."

From the quick way her parents glanced at each other, it was fairly clear to Amy that they had noticed some of what their son-in-law was pointing out, but it was only now that the significance of Nick's actions was beginning to register. A faintly troubled look passed over her father's expression. Something like surrender entered her mother's. But whatever either had been about to say was cut off by the sound of the screen door opening behind Darren.

Nick crossed the porch and stopped at the open door leading to the hallway he'd designed himself less than six weeks ago. He was wet and miserable and he wanted nothing more than to head for his aunt and uncle's house, take a hot shower and forget that the day had ever happened. But he had one lousy fixture to hang, which he decided on the spot would just have to stay unhung until he could send someone out Monday morning, because his pride wasn't that damned important. He also had one message to deliver.

From where he stopped at the threshold, he could see Darren's broad back and Brittany's skinny one and not much else. "I put your boat in the boathouse," he called to him, wiping rain from his face. "The starter rope is stowed in the floor-well."

"Culhane. Nick," Darren amended, turning with his daughter in his arms. "Wait."

"Come in, Nick," he heard Bea call.

Through the space that had opened up when Paige's husband had stepped back, he saw the elderly woman glance around her kitchen as if she were daring anyone in the room to question her invitation. Since he had the feeling that everyone he wanted to avoid was in that room, it was the last place on earth he wanted to go.

"I'll send someone out to hang the last fixture, Mrs. Gardner. I don't want to drip on your new carpet."

Susan Chapman stepped into view behind her mother. "Please," she said, looking bedraggled and pale. Her glance moved hesitantly over him. "You're as wet as we are."

The fact that he was soaked to the skin was totally irrelevant as far as Nick was concerned. The significance of her observation was not. He could practically hear a hefty chunk of ice falling from her attitude toward him.

"Amy," her mother murmured, "get him a towel."

"I'll do it."

It was Paige who spoke. Rising, she handed Sarah to her grandma Bea. But it was Amy Nick watched as he cautiously joined his rescue partner in the doorway. She stood by the doorway to the dining room, back from everyone else. He didn't doubt for an instant that she was the one responsible for the blankets and towels everyone huddled in, and the teapot heating on the stove. She'd been doing what she did best. Taking care of the people she cared about.

All he cared about was that her eyes were the only ones that didn't meet his when she handed Paige the towel her sister carried over to him.

With her usually perfect hair plastered to her head, Paige held out the folded blue terry cloth.

"Thank you, Nick," she said, and wrapped her arms around his neck to give him a hug. "Break her heart and you die," she whispered, and pulled back to give him a genuinely grateful smile before she slipped under her husband's arm.

Bea's smile was grateful, too. And there was no mistaking the sincerity in Paul Chapman's handshake when the man walked up to him a moment later and, doing the best he could on short notice, told him he was glad he was there that day after all. The only person who didn't say something to him was Amy.

She'd left the room.

Nick knew her grandmother had seen her go. So had Paige. They were both darting looks from each other to him. He had the feeling Susan was beginning to see some significance to her daughter's disappearance, too, when her glance bounced between the three of them and, shaking her head, she sank back into her chair without a word.

"She's going upstairs," Bea said, and turned her attention to drying her great-granddaughter's curls.

Nick found her at the top of the landing. She stood just outside her open bedroom door, her hand on the door frame and her shirt so wet he could see her bra through the back.

Refusing to let his mind wander in that direction, he focused on the rain-soaked tendrils of hair clinging to her neck. Even though it was easily seventy-five degrees inside the house, a layer of goose bumps sprang up on her smooth skin. Since she wasn't turning at the sound of his cautious footfall on the carpet, he was more inclined to think the phenomenon was due to a flight-or-fight reaction than a chill.

Not wanting to fight, he came up behind her and settled the towel over her shoulders. Because her whole body stiffened at the contact, he immediately pulled his hands away—and prayed that she wouldn't bolt. He'd barely realized why he'd never been able to get her out of his head, and the thought that he might lose her now shot pure fear through his heart.

"Are you all right?" she asked, her back still to him.

"Yeah," he murmured, wishing she'd turn around. "I'm fine. A little wet. How about you?"

"A little wet," she echoed.

Beneath the rectangle of royal blue terry cloth, Amy's shoulders rose with her deeply drawn breath. She clutched the ends in her fists, trying hard to get past the anxiety she'd felt while he'd been out there without a life vest. Most of her family had been bobbing around in the lake, but underlying every other fear going through her mind was the prayer that he'd be all right. It hadn't even mattered that their relationship had met a dead end. She'd just needed him to be safe.

"I don't know that I can ever thank you enough for what you did, Nick. For my family."

She heard him step closer, an old plank squeaking beneath his weight. "I'm just glad I was around." There was hesitation in his deep voice, subtle but definitely there. "Your dad even said he was okay with the idea. That I was here," he clarified, sounding a little amazed by the admission. "They all seem to have thawed a little. Except Paige just threatened me with bodily harm."

He wasn't going to touch her again. Amy could feel his restraint as surely as she could the wariness that kept her from facing him. But she could feel him waiting, too.

Sensing that he wouldn't leave until she faced him, she turned her back to the eyelet-covered bed visible through the door and met his hooded blue eyes. He stood an arm's length in front of her, his gray shirt clinging to the solid muscles of his chest and shoulders, his dark hair glistening.

"Bodily harm?"

"Yeah. She threatened to end my life as I know it if I don't straighten this out."

His glance skimmed the sudden confusion in her face as he stepped toward her. She promptly backed up, which put her in her room. Stepping in himself, he reached behind him and closed the door with a quiet click.

Surrounded by walls of deep lavender, he watched her stop in the middle of the room's dark purple rug. "I have to admit, she's the last person I ever thought I'd have on my side, but I really need another chance here, Amy. If that's possible."

Amy swallowed, her heart suddenly feeling tight in her chest.

"I don't understand why you'd want that." He'd told her before that she needed to go after what she wanted. And she wanted him. But he couldn't give her what she needed. And what she needed was his heart. As hard as it had been to lose him after such a short time, she couldn't begin to imagine how she'd survive losing him again. "You don't do commitment, remember?"

Caution settled in his chiseled features as he slowly lifted his hand toward her face. Looking as if he couldn't bear to have her pull from his touch again, he curled his fingers at his side. "I didn't think I did."

He really hadn't. He hadn't thought he was capable of it—until the words of an amazingly insightful old woman had sunk in as he was trying to keep Amy out of the boat. It made no sense that the realization should have hit then. Not with everything else that had been going on. He'd always felt a sense of protection for her, but at that moment, his need to keep her out of harm's way had collided with the stark concern she'd felt for him, and everything Bea had said hit home.

"I just realized I've actually been committed to one

woman all along. I think you're right about me," he told her, watching disbelief join the confusion in her fragile features. "I am more like my uncle than my father." He'd fought the thought that she'd planted. Just as he'd fought the idea that he'd limited himself the same way she had by the influence of certain members of her family. "I've been in love with one woman all my life."

Until that moment he hadn't put a name to what he'd felt for her all those years ago. But there was no doubt in his mind now that he'd fallen in love with her then. "You see, Amy," he said, "the woman who stole me from your sister was you."

Amy felt her entire body go still. "Me?"

"I couldn't stop thinking about you. I still can't." He looked guarded, a little uncertain. "Rumor has it that you once felt that way about me. I'm just hoping I can get you to feel that way again." The telltale muscle in his jaw bunched as he lifted his hand. Letting it hover long enough to see that she wasn't going to back away, he nudged back the wet hair clinging to her forehead. "That's why we need another chance."

We.

The word shimmered in her mind, along with wonder, disbelief and utter amazement. "Only Bea knew how I felt about you."

"She was the only one who knew what had happened with me, too. But I need to know how you feel about me now, Amy. I love you. And I want to live in a loft if that's what you want and go to all those museums with you, and when we're ready to buy a house, we'll have the kids and the dog. I don't even care what order we do it all in." He cupped her face, skimming back her hair, drawing her closer. "I just want to do it all with you."

She'd wanted to ask him how her grandmother could

possibly have known why he'd done what he had all those years ago. But the question had fled—along with her ability to speak. The tightness in her chest had bloomed to a bubble of pure joy, and her throat was suddenly as tight as the hold she had on his shirt. He'd never cheated on anyone. Everything he'd done, he'd done because of her.

With that knowledge filling her heart to near bursting, all she could manage was a strangled "Oh, Nick."

"What does that mean?" he murmured. His glance glittered over her face. Then his eyes narrowed, his thumbs sweeping her cheeks. "You're not going to cry, are you?"

She shook her head.

"Oh, honey. I didn't mean to make you do that."

She swallowed, remembering the last time he'd made her cry. The night he'd brought her clay.

The constriction in her voice made her words a whisper. "I love you, Nick."

Nothing beyond that seemed to matter to him. Relief swept his handsome face in the instant before the light in his eyes turned possessive and his mouth came down hard on hers. She gave as good as she got. Locking her arms around his neck, she pulled herself as close as she could get and met him in a kiss that answered a lifetime of longing for them both.

That kiss filled her senses, her mind, her heart, and ran soul deep.

He loved her. She'd loved him since she was seventeen. As he drew her more tightly in his embrace, she remembered how they'd once talked about timing. And about how some things were never meant to be. But there was no question in her mind about what they'd finally found in each other. Their best friend. Their lover. Their soul mate. And this time, the timing was absolutely right.

*   *   *   *   *

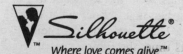

where love comes alive—online...

your romantic escapes

—Indulgences—
♥ Monthly guides to indulging yourself, such as:
  ★ Tub Time: A guide for bathing beauties
  ★ Magic Massages: A treat for tired feet

—Horoscopes—
♥ Find your daily Passionscope, weekly Lovescopes and Erotiscopes

♥ Try our compatibility game

—Reel Love—
♥ Read all the latest romantic movie reviews

—Royal Romance—
♥ Get the latest scoop on your favorite royal romances

—Romantic Travel—
♥ For the most romantic destinations, hotels and travel activities

If you enjoyed what you just read,
then we've got an offer you can't resist!

Take 2 bestselling love stories FREE!
Plus get a FREE surprise gift!

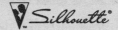

Don't miss the reprisal of Silhouette Romance's popular miniseries

When King Michael of Edenbourg goes missing,

Royally Wed
The Stanbury Crown

his devoted family and loyal subjects make it their mission to bring him home safely!

Their search begins March 2001 and continues through June 2001.

On sale March 2001: **THE EXPECTANT PRINCESS**
by bestselling author **Stella Bagwell** (SR #1504)

On sale April 2001: **THE BLACKSHEEP PRINCE'S BRIDE**
by rising star **Martha Shields** (SR #1510)

On sale May 2001: **CODE NAME: PRINCE**
by popular author **Valerie Parv** (SR #1516)

On sale June 2001: **AN OFFICER AND A PRINCESS**
by award-winning author **Carla Cassidy** (SR #1522)

Available at your favorite retail outlet.

Silhouette®
Where love comes alive™

COMING NEXT MONTH

#1381 HER UNFORGETTABLE FIANCÉ—Allison Leigh
Stockwells of Texas
To locate her missing mother, Kate Stockwell teamed up
with private investigator Brett Larson to masquerade as a married
couple. Together they discovered that desire still burned between
them. But when former fiancé Brett asked Kate to be his wife for
real, she feared that she could never provide all that he wanted...

#1382 A LOVE BEYOND WORDS—Sherryl Woods
Firefighter Enrique Wilder saved Allie Matthews from the rubble
of her home and forever changed her silent world. A shared
house and an undeniable chemistry caused passion to run high.
But would Allie be able to love a man who lived so close to
danger?

#1383 WIFE IN DISGUISE—Susan Mallery
Lone Star Canyon
Josie Scott decided it was time to resolve the past and showed
up at her ex-husband's door a changed woman. Friendship and
closure were all that Josie was after, until she looked into
Del Scott's eyes. Finally, with a chance to explore their
daunting past, would the two discover that love was still alive?

#1384 STANDING BEAR'S SURRENDER—Peggy Webb
Forlorn former Blue Angel pilot Jim Standing Bear had lost his
ambition...until he found gentle beauty Sarah Sloan. She
reminded Jim that he was all man. But Sarah—committed to
caring for another—would have to choose between loyalty and
true love....

#1385 SEPARATE BEDROOMS...?—Carole Halston
All Cara LaCroix wanted was to fulfill her grandmother's final
wish—to see her granddaughter marry a good man. So when
childhood friend Neil Griffen offered his help, Cara accepted.
Could their brief marriage of convenience turn into an everlasting
covenant of love?

#1386 HOME AT LAST—Laurie Campbell
Desperate for a detective's help, Kirsten Laurence called old
flame J. D. Ryder. She didn't have romance on her mind, but they
soon found themselves in each other's arms. Would their embrace
withstand the shocking revelation of Kirsten's long-kept secret?